征服指考

王靖賢

學歷：國立臺灣師範大學英語學系碩士

經歷：臺北市立建國高級中學英文教師

張秋雲

學歷：國立成功大學外國語文學系碩士

經歷：國立桃園高級中學英文教師

三民書局

© 英文歷屆指考超絕剖析&模擬實戰

編 著 者	王靖賢　張秋雲
責任編輯	淩　翔
美術設計	郭雅萍
封面設計	郭雅萍
內頁設計	郭雅萍
發 行 人	劉振強
著作財產權人	三民書局股份有限公司
發 行 所	三民書局股份有限公司
	地址　臺北市復興北路386號
	電話　(02)25006600
	郵撥帳號　0009998-5
門 市 部	(復北店) 臺北市復興北路386號
	(重南店) 臺北市重慶南路一段61號
出版日期	初版一刷　2018年1月
編　　號	S 804680

行政院新聞局登記證局版臺業字第〇二〇〇號

4712780658314

http://www.sanmin.com.tw　三民網路書店

編輯大意

一、本書彙集各學年度大學入學學科能力測驗之英文科試題，讀者可藉此了解歷屆考題命題重點，模擬考試情境，並掌握未來準備方向。

二、本書編排採年份由近到遠，讓讀者一開始即能掌握最新考試趨勢，再逐一複習歷屆試題。每學年度的試題皆附解答與詳盡解析，包括題型分析、命題重點提示、解題技巧、文章與題目翻譯以及相關補充，讓讀者深入研讀試題核心，檢視不足之處，突破得分障礙。

三、本書提供四回學測英文模擬實戰，每回皆附解答與詳盡解析，讓讀者透過模擬實戰，更加熟悉相關考試題型，並藉此增進字彙片語、文法句型與英文作文寫作的練習。務求讓讀者能充分了解命題趨勢，紮實練習考題，確實學會答題技巧。

四、本書編纂力求詳盡完備，然疏漏之處在所難免，如有未盡善之處，請不吝指教。

Contents

106 學年度　指考英文試題

◆ 第壹部分：單選題 (占 72 分)

一、詞彙題 (占 10 分)

說明：第 1 題至第 10 題，每題有 4 個選項，其中只有一個是正確或最適當的選項，請畫記在答案卡之「選擇題答案區」。各題答對者，得 1 分；答錯、未作答或畫記多於一個選項者，該題以零分計算。

1. Martha has been trying to ________ her roommate since their quarrel last week, as she doesn't want to continue the argument.
(A) overgrow　(B) bother　(C) pursue　(D) avoid

2. As David finished the last drop of the delicious chicken soup, he licked his lips and gave out sounds of ________.
(A) contentment　(B) dominance　(C) explosion　(D) affection

3. After several rounds of intense fighting, the boxer punched his ________ right in the face, knocked him out, and won the match.
(A) performer　(B) attendant　(C) opponent　(D) messenger

4. Watch out! The bench has just been painted. You can fan the wet paint if you want to ________ its drying.
(A) fasten　(B) hasten　(C) lengthen　(D) strengthen

5. Warm milk ________ sleepiness. So if you have trouble falling asleep, try drinking some warm milk before going to bed.
(A) conceals　(B) recruits　(C) absorbs　(D) induces

6. Having worked five years as a data processor in a small town, Alice is tired of the routine of her job and the ________ of her life.
(A) disturbance　(B) salvation　(C) remainder　(D) monotony

7. Peter has never been on time to meetings or appointments. It would be interesting to look into reasons why he is ________ late.
(A) chronically　(B) hysterically　(C) simultaneously　(D) resistantly

8. The film *Life of Pi* won Ang Lee an Oscar in 2013 for Best Director—one of the most ________ awards in the movie industry.
(A) populated　(B) surpassed　(C) coveted　(D) rotated

9. According to environmental scientists, the earth is likely to experience significant ________ changes within the next century.
(A) provincial　(B) ecological　(C) authentic　(D) redundant

10. Traditional Chinese medical practices include ________ remedies, which use plants, plant parts, or a mixture of these to prevent or cure diseases.

(A) herbal (B) frantic (C) magnetic (D) descriptive

二、綜合測驗 (占 10 分)

說明：第 11 題至第 20 題，每題一個空格，請依文意選出最適當的一個選項，請畫記在答案卡之「選擇題答案區」。各題答對者，得 1 分；答錯、未作答或畫記多於一個選項者，該題以零分計算。

第 11 至 15 題為題組

France, home to such major fashion houses as Chanel, Dior, and Yves Saint Laurent, has joined Italy, Spain, and Israel in adopting laws against super-skinny models on catwalks or in ads.

The French government has passed a bill that will __11__ the use of excessively skinny models. Modeling agencies violating the law can receive a fine of up to US$81,000, with up to six months in jail for staff involved. According to French officials, the measure aims to __12__ the glorification of dangerously thin models.

Under the approved legislation, models will have to present a medical __13__ that proves they are healthy before being allowed to work in the fashion industry. Moreover, they will be __14__ regular weight checks. Modeling agencies will have to produce a medical report showing that their models have maintained a __15__ body mass-to-height ratio. This bill is expected to change young women's view on the ideal female form.

11. (A) forecast (B) represent (C) criminalize (D) distinguish
12. (A) put up with (B) crack down on (C) give in to (D) look out for
13. (A) coverage (B) certificate (C) operation (D) prescription
14. (A) subject to (B) accustomed to (C) blessed with (D) familiar with
15. (A) healthy (B) pleasant (C) frequent (D) distinctive

第 16 至 20 題為題組

One factor that separates a living thing from an inanimate object is the organism's ability to carry out chemical reactions that are crucial for its survival. Imagine the infinite amount of reactions that a large organism such as human carries out every single day. __16__ of these reactions are possible without enzymes.

Enzymes consist of various types of proteins that work to drive the chemical reactions __17__ for certain types of nutrients to take effect. Enzymes can either launch a reaction or speed it up. In the absence of enzymes, reactants may take hundreds of years to convert into a usable product, if they are able to do so __18__. This is why enzymes are crucial in the sustenance of life on earth.

Enzymes, __19__, do not always function perfectly. In 1902 Sir Archibald Garrod was the first to attribute a __20__ to an enzyme defect, which he later referred to as an "inborn error of metabolism." Today, newborns are routinely screened for certain enzyme defects such as PKU (phenylketonuria) and galactosemia, an error in the handling of the sugar galactose.

16. (A) Any	(B) Al	(C) None	(D) More
17. (A) requires	(B) required	(C) requiring	(D) to require
18. (A) at all	(B) at hand	(C) at first	(D) at ease
19. (A) hereafter	(B) instead	(C) likewise	(D) however
20. (A) disease	(B) balance	(C) measure	(D) statement

三、文意選填 (占 10 分)

說明：第21題至第30題，每題一個空格，請依文意在文章後所提供的(A)到(L)選項中分別選出最適當者，並將其英文字母代號畫記在答案卡之「選擇題答案區」。各題答對者，得1分；答錯、未作答或畫記多於一個選項者，該題以零分計算。

第21至30題為題組

Hundreds of years ago, a savory idea—called the century egg—was hatched in rural China. As the story goes, a farmer found naturally preserved duck eggs in a muddy pool of water and slaked lime. After surviving a tasting, he set out to replicate them manually, resulting in a __21__ that would endure for centuries as a comfort food in Hong Kong, China and parts of Southeast Asia.

Though details of the century egg's discovery are undocumented, scientists estimate that it __22__ more than 500 years to the Ming Dynasty. And aside from some techniques used for large-scale production today, the egg preservation process has remained relatively __23__.

To make the eggs, a vat is typically filled with a combination of strong black tea, lime, salt and freshly burned wood ashes, and left to cool overnight. The next day, duck, quail, or chicken eggs are added to the __24__. Then they soak anywhere from seven weeks to five months—not for a century as the name __25__.

The century egg also __26__ many other names, such as hundred-year egg, thousand-year egg, or millennium egg. But no matter what it's called, this common snack has a rather uncommon taste and is often grouped by travelers with other __27__ Asian foods such as chicken feet or snake soup. Getting beyond the egg's appearance is the first __28__. Instead of being white with a bright orange yolk, the jelly-like egg takes on a less __29__ dark brown and swampy green hue. There's also a pungent ammonia-like odor to contend with, which has earned the snack yet another nickname: the "horse urine egg."

While the century egg draws a following from older generations and curious travelers, it is falling out of __30__ with the younger set, who are weary of China's preserved and fermented foods. The future of the humble snack is uncertain, but chefs in Chinese restaurants are still trying to preserve this nostalgic bite of culinary heritage.

(A) provokes	(B) exotic	(C) delicacy	(D) dates back
(E) refreshed	(F) implies	(G) appetizing	(H) mixture
(I) goes by	(J) unchanged	(K) challenge	(L) favor

四、篇章結構 (占 10 分)

說明：第 31 題至第 35 題，每題一個空格。請依文意在文章後所提供的(A)到(F)選項中分別選出最適當者，填入空格中，使篇章結構清晰有條理，並將其英文字母代號畫記在答案卡之「選擇題答案區」。各題答對者，得 2 分；答錯、未作答或畫記多於一個選項者，該題以零分計算。

第 31 至 35 題為題組

One of the most difficult things for a human to face is the loss of a limb. If a person loses an arm or a leg, he/she must be fitted with an artificial limb.

The situation is very different for a starfish. If a starfish loses an arm, it can grow a new one. __31__ Snails can even regrow their heads—imagine what the world would be like if humans could do that. But we can't. Nor can we grow new limbs or even fingers. That's why scientists are studying animals that can regrow body parts, that is, regenerate. __32__

Many different kinds of animals show some form of regeneration. Most of them are, however, limited to the sort a lizard is capable of, like regrowing a lost tail. A cockroach can grow back a missing limb, but the limb itself can't generate a new cockroach. __33__ Bidirectional regeneration, on the other hand, refers to a situation in which splitting of an animal will result in separate fully functional animals. __34__ Cut a hydra in half, and you'll get two hydras. Cut it into four pieces, and you'll get four.

__35__ A single one can be cut into hundreds of pieces and each will grow back into a whole in a week or so. Because of this remarkable ability, one planarian can be created over and over, giving it a sort of immortality. Whether this phenomenon can be achieved in humans will likely require years of research.

(A) Scientists call this unidirectional regeneration.
(B) Humans aren't completely without regenerative talents.
(C) The same thing happens for lobsters, salamanders, and many other animals.
(D) When it comes to regeneration, few animals can equal the magic of the planarian.
(E) This type of regeneration is demonstrated in a few animals, such as hydras and sea stars.
(F) They hope that this line of research will make regeneration possible in humans someday.

五、閱讀測驗 (占 32 分)

說明：第 36 題至第 51 題，每題請分別根據各篇文章之文意選出最適當的一個選項，請畫記在答案卡之「選擇題答案區」。各題答對者，得 2 分；答錯、未作答或畫記多於一個選項者，該題以零分計算。

第 36 至 39 題為題組

Often named as the most prominent contemporary female architect, Zaha Hadid, an Iraqi-born British woman, is significant for her intellectual toughness and her refusal to compromise on her artistic ideas. For many years, her designs filled the pages of architecture journals but were dismissed as impractical or too radical. Also, being female in a male-dominated field didn't help her succeed.

Despite these setbacks, **her star began to rise** when her design for Cincinnati's new Center for Contemporary Art was selected and built, earning her worldwide acclaim. The New York Times described the building as "the most important new building in America since the Cold War." Once her talent was recognized, commissions started coming in to design a variety of projects, including public transportation, libraries, and opera houses. In 2004, Hadid became the first woman to win the prestigious Pritzker Prize. She also won the Stirling Prize in 2010 and 2011.

Hadid's interest in architecture had roots in a trip her family took to the ancient Sumer region in southern Iraq, the site of one of the world's oldest civilizations, when she was a teenager. She recalled: "The beauty of the landscape—where sand, water, reeds, birds, buildings, and people all somehow flowed together—has never left me. I'm trying to discover—invent, I suppose—an architecture, and forms of urban planning, that do something of the same thing in a contemporary way."

Nature's forms appear as a recurrent source of inspiration for Hadid's architecture. Her designs are daring and visionary experiments with space and with the relationships of buildings to their urban surroundings. She consistently pushes the boundaries of architecture and urban design in the pursuit of a visionary aesthetic that expresses her ideals.

36. According to the passage, what is a major factor in Hadid's success?
(A) Her family support.
(B) Her ethnic origin.
(C) Her gender and education.
(D) Her vision and talent.

37. What does the author mean by "**. . . her star began to rise . . .**" in the second paragraph?
(A) She started to make a fortune.
(B) She became more recognized.
(C) Her designs became classical.
(D) Her ideas started to take shape.

38. What is the third paragraph mainly about?
(A) The cultural background of Hadid's family.
(B) The beautiful landscape of Hadid's hometown.
(C) A vivid recollection of Hadid's life as a teenager.
(D) A fundamental source of Hadid's architectural philosophy.

39. According to the passage, which of the following is true about Hadid's career in architecture?
(A) She built the first Center for Contemporary Art in New York.
(B) Her architecture projects mainly involve museums in urban areas.
(C) Her works can be characterized as boldly contemporary and innovative.
(D) Her early designs were often rejected because of her political background.

第 40 至 43 題為題組

Todd Bol, a retired businessman, could never have expected that a wooden container he built on his deck one day in 2009 would have the global impact it does today.

Bol built a dollhouse-size structure that looked like a schoolhouse on a post, and he put it on his lawn as a free community library to commemorate his mother, who was a book lover and school teacher. Bol's **prototype** gave birth to Little Free Library (LFL), a nonprofit organization that seeks to place small, accessible book exchange boxes in neighborhoods around the world. The concept is simple: Neighbors are invited to share a book, leave a book, or both. Today, there are over 50,000 of these libraries registered in 70 countries.

Almost everyone can register with LFL and start a library as long as the person keeps it in good shape and makes sure that book materials are appropriate for his/her neighborhood. Library owners can create their own library boxes; therefore, the libraries are usually unique in appearance, and there seems to be no limit to the possibilities. One library in California was built out of a used wine crate; another in Texas had tiny stairs and bright colored walls. Once registered, libraries are assigned a number at LFL's website. The LFL Index lists the locations of all libraries with GPS coordinates and other information. Owners receive a sign that reads "Little Free Library."

People say they have been more inclined to pick up a book when walking by a Little Free Library, out of curiosity and because it's convenient. Some sidewalk librarians say they have met more neighbors since having a little library in their front yard. Bol is also most proud of the way Little Free Library is bringing communities together. "It's started a neighborhood exchange. It gets people talking and more comfortable with their neighbors," he says. "This leads to them helping each other."

40. Which of the following statements is **NOT** mentioned about Todd Bol?

(A) His mother used to be a school teacher. (B) He was engaged in trade and commerce.

(C) He provided a great service to his neighborhood. (D) He built a schoolhouse to pay tribute to his mother.

41. What does "**prototype**" refer to in the second paragraph?

(A) A community center. (B) A book exchange box.

(C) A dollhouse on a post. (D) A nonprofit organization.

42. Which of the following is true about the operation of a Little Free Library?

(A) The library can come in any shape and color.

(B) There is no limit to the selection of its materials.

(C) The owner must first be assigned a number from the LFL website.

(D) The librarian is in charge of checking the books in and out of the library.

43. What is a contribution of Little Free Library?

(A) The LFL Index can improve GPS functions.

(B) It promotes reading and literacy in a simple way.

(C) It helps to strengthen library associations around the world.

(D) Its location satisfies people's curiosity about their neighbors.

第 44 至 47 題為題組

The term "forensic linguistics," in its broadest sense, covers all areas of study where language and law intersect. A famous example of its application is the case of Chris Coleman, who was suspected of killing his family in 2009. Robert Leonard, the head of the forensic linguistics program at Hofstra University, presented some important linguistic evidence in the trial against Coleman. Relying heavily on word choice and spelling, Leonard suggested that the same person had written the threatening e-mails and sprayed the graffiti, and that those samples bore similarities to Coleman's writing style. Coleman was later found guilty of the murder.

Robert Leonard was not the first one who resorted to linguistic evidence in criminal investigation. The field of forensic linguistics was brought to prominence by his colleague James Fitzgerald in 1996 with his work in the case of the Unabomber, who had sent a series of letter bombs to college professors over several years, causing serious casualties. Working for the FBI, Fitzgerald urged the publication of the Unabomber's letter—a lengthy declaration of the criminal's philosophy.

After the letter was published, many people called the FBI to say they recognized the writing style. By analyzing sentence structure, word choice, and other linguistic patterns, Fitzgerald narrowed down the range of possible authors and finally linked the letter to the writings of Ted Kaczynski, a solitary former mathematician. For instance, Kaczynski tended to use extensive parallel phrases, which were frequently found in the bomber's letter. Both Kaczynski and the bomber also showed a preference for dozens of unusual words, such as "chimerical" and "anomic." The bomber's use of the terms "broad" for women and "negro" for African Americans also enabled Fitzgerald to roughly calculate the suspect's age. The linguistic evidence was strong enough for the judge to search Kaczynski's isolated cabin in Montana; what was found there put him in prison for life.

On some level, finding hidden meanings from linguistic evidence is what we all do intuitively in our daily language interaction. This is exactly the same work forensic professionals do. As one forensic-linguistics firm, *Testipro*, puts it in its online promotional ad, the field can be regarded as "the basis of the entire legal system."

44. What is the main idea of the passage?

(A) Robert Leonard has provided linguistic evidence in court cases.

(B) The FBI relies mainly on language experts to solve its crime cases.

(C) Studying texts can provide critical evidence in criminal investigations.

(D) Finding hidden meanings in language use is important for daily interactions.

45. Which of the following is true about the Unabomber?

(A) He didn't like to be called negro.

(B) He was good at analyzing the use of language.

(C) He declared his philosophy in a written statement.

(D) He was a professor of mathematics living on Hofstra campus.

46. What type of language feature is **NOT** mentioned in the passage?

(A) Sound pattern. (B) Spelling of words. (C) Selection of words. (D) Grammatical pattern.

47. What can be inferred from the passage?

(A) Meaning can be distorted in the process of writing.

(B) Some features in language use are shared by everyone.

(C) Crimes are usually committed by people who are highly educated.

(D) People tend to stick to certain habitual patterns in their use of language.

第 48 至 51 題為題組

During the past three hundred years, when a country gains its freedom or independence, one of the first things established is a national anthem. National anthems are generally played and sung at formal state occasions and other events which celebrate or support the country's national identity.

Holland's 16th-century hymn "Het Wilhelmus" is widely considered the world's oldest national anthem, followed by the U.K.'s "God Save the King/Queen"—also a hymn, popularized in the 1740s. As nationalism spread throughout Europe in the 18th and 19th centuries, so did anthems. Many countries, such as the independent states that are today part of Germany, took "God Save the King/Queen" as a model and adopted hymns (songs of prayer typically addressed to a deity or VIP). Others, notably Spain and France, chose marches (songs with a strong, regular rhythm often performed by military bands)—which expressed a martial rather than monarchic spirit. With imperialism, Europeans spread their musical taste. Even when former colonies gained independence, they often imitated the traditions of their former rulers. The result is that most anthems are either hymns or marches, played on European instruments.

Japan's anthem makes for a good case study of European influence. In the 1860s a British bandmaster living in Japan, John William Fenton, noted that the country did not have a national anthem. A local military officer, Ōyama Iwao, selected the lyrics from a Heian era poem and Fenton wrote the melody. About a decade later, a Japanese committee chose a replacement melody by a court musician—one that had been composed for traditional Japanese instruments, but in a mixed style influenced by Fenton's arrangement. The version in use today was also altered by German Franz Eckert to fit a Western scale.

In addition to hymns and marches, British composer Michael Bristow identifies a couple of more minor categories. National anthems in South and Central America are often operatic, with long, elaborate orchestral introductions. These were influenced by 19th-century Italian opera. Burma and Sri Lanka are both in a folk group, as they rely more on indigenous instruments.

48. Which of the following is **NOT** mentioned as a basis to compose national anthems?
 (A) Prayer songs. (B) Marching songs. (C) Italian opera music. (D) Movie theme music.

49. What is the second paragraph mainly about?
 (A) The function of national anthems. (B) The world's oldest national anthem.
 (C) The origin and spread of national anthems. (D) Reasons why many countries have national anthems.

50. Which of the following is true regarding Japan's national anthem?
 (A) It was not written until the 20th century.
 (B) The lyrics was written by a Japanese officer.
 (C) The melody was first composed by a British musician.
 (D) The current version is barely influenced by western music.

51. What can be inferred about the influence of European imperialism on national anthems?
 (A) Human rights are a common theme in national anthems.
 (B) National anthems of some countries share similar musical features.
 (C) Many national anthems were chosen by ruling European countries.
 (D) Local traditions were excluded in the composition of national anthems.

◆ 第貳部分：非選擇題 (占 28 分)

說明：本部分共有二題，請依各題指示作答，答案必須寫在「答案卷」上，並標明大題號 (一、二)。作答務必使用筆尖較粗之黑色墨水的筆書寫，且不得使用鉛筆。

一、中譯英 (占 8 分)

說明：1. 請將以下中文句子譯成正確、通順、達意的英文，並將答案寫在「答案卷」上。
 2. 請依序作答，並標明子題號 (1、2)。每題 4 分，共 8 分。

1. 世界大學運動會 (The Universiade) 是一項國際體育與文化盛事，每兩年一次由不同城市舉辦。
2. 在比賽中，來自全球大學的學生運動員建立友誼，並學習運動家精神的真諦。

二、英文作文 (占 20 分)

說明：1. 依提示在「答案卷」上寫一篇英文作文。
 2. 文長至少 120 個單詞 (words)。

提示：每個人從小到大都有覺得寂寞的時刻，也都各自有排解寂寞的經驗和方法。當你感到寂寞時，有什麼人、事或物可以陪伴你，為你排遣寂寞呢？請以此為主題，寫一篇英文作文，文長至少 120 個單詞。文分兩段，第一段說明你會因為什麼原因或在何種情境下感到寂寞，第二段描述某個人、事或物如何伴你度過寂寞時光。

Notes

105 學年度　指考英文試題

◆ 第壹部分：單選題 (占 72 分)

一、詞彙題 (占 10 分)

說明：第 1 題至第 10 題，每題有 4 個選項，其中只有一個是正確或最適當的選項，請畫記在答案卡之「選擇題答案區」。各題答對者，得 1 分；答錯、未作答或畫記多於一個選項者，該題以零分計算。

1. Microscopes are used in medical research labs for studying bacteria or ________ that are too small to be visible to the naked eye.
(A) agencies　(B) codes　(C) germs　(D) indexes

2. Lisa hopped on her bicycle and ________ as fast as she could through the dark narrow backstreets to get home after working the night shift.
(A) bounced　(B) commuted　(C) tumbled　(D) pedaled

3. Rated as one of the top restaurants of the city, this steak house is highly ________ to visitors by the tourism bureau.
(A) encountered　(B) recommended　(C) outnumbered　(D) speculated

4. The manager ________ agreed to rent his apartment to me. Even though the agreement was not put in writing, I am sure he will keep his word.
(A) barely　(B) stably　(C) verbally　(D) massively

5. For Jerry, practicing yoga three times a week is a relaxing ________ from his tight work schedule.
(A) diversion　(B) medication　(C) nuisance　(D) fulfillment

6. Parents could be charged with neglect or abandonment if they leave their young children home alone without adult ________.
(A) intuition　(B) supervision　(C) compassion　(D) obligation

7. Walking at a ________ pace for a shorter amount of time burns more calories than walking at a slow pace for a longer period of time.
(A) joyous　(B) superb　(C) brisk　(D) decent

8. Plants and animals in some deserts must cope with a climate of ________—freezing winters and very hot summers.
(A) extremes　(B) forecasts　(C) atmospheres　(D) homelands

9. The success of J.K. Rowling is ________, with her Harry Potter series making her a multi-millionaire in just a few years.
(A) eligible　(B) marginal　(C) confidential　(D) legendary

10. The high-tech company's ________ earnings surely made its shareholders happy since they were getting a good return on their investment.
(A) robust　(B) solitary　(C) imperative　(D) terminal

二、綜合測驗(占 10 分)

說明：第 11 題至第 20 題，每題一個空格，請依文意選出最適當的一個選項，請畫記在答案卡之「選擇題答案區」。各題答對者，得 1 分；答錯、未作答或畫記多於一個選項者，該題以零分計算。

第 11 至 15 題為題組

Have you been irritated by someone standing too close in line, talking too loud or making eye contact for too long? Or, they may have ___11___ you with the loud music from their earphones, or by taking up more than one seat on a crowded subway car. You feel unhappy because your personal space has been violated.

According to scientists, personal space involves certain invisible forces imposed on you through all the ___12___. For example, people may feel their space is being invaded when they experience an unwelcome sound, smell, or stare.

In certain situations such as in crowded subway cars or elevators, it is not always possible for people to keep their ___13___ distance from others. They learn coping strategies to deal with their discomfort. For instance, people often avoid eye contact with someone standing ___14___ them, or they pretend that these people are lifeless objects in their personal space. Given the opportunity, they may ___15___ to a corner, putting distance between themselves and strangers. Or, they may sit or stand equidistant from one another like birds on a wire.

11. (A) offended (B) controlled (C) acquired (D) supplied
12. (A) angles (B) events (C) senses (D) regions
13. (A) prefer (B) preferring (C) preferred (D) being preferred
14. (A) long before (B) close to (C) aside from (D) soon after
15. (A) retreat (B) explore (C) dispense (D) connect

第 16 至 20 題為題組

Alan Turing was one of the leading scientific geniuses of the 20th century. Many scholars consider him the father of modern computer science. He was also the man who cracked the ___16___ uncrackable Enigma code used by Nazi Germany. His code-breaking turned the tide of World War II and helped save two million lives. Nevertheless, ___17___ people have even heard his name.

Turing displayed signs of high intelligence in math and science at a young age. By the time he was 23, he had already come up with the idea of what ___18___ the modern computer—the Turing machine. Today, Turing machines are still used in theoretical computation. He also proposed the now famous Turing test, used to determine whether a computer exhibits intelligent behavior equivalent to that of a human.

The postwar era, however, was a disaster for Turing. He was gay, which was then a crime in Britain. ___19___ being hailed as one of the crucial figures in defeating the Nazis, Turing was convicted of "gross indecency." This __20__ drove him to commit suicide in 1954, at the age of 41. Nearly 60 years after his death, Queen Elizabeth II granted Turing a formal pardon for his conviction, upon an online petition signed by prominent scientists and technology leaders around the world.

16. (A) eventually (B) precisely (C) concernedly (D) supposedly
17. (A) many (B) some (C) any (D) few
18. (A) would become (B) should become (C) could have become (D) had become
19. (A) Because of (B) Instead of (C) In addition to (D) With respect to
20. (A) compromise (B) procession (C) humiliation (D) supplement

三、文意選填（占 10 分）

說明：第 21 題至第 30 題，每題一個空格，請依文意在文章後所提供的(A)到(L)選項中分別選出最適當者，並將其英文字母代號畫記在答案卡之「選擇題答案區」。各題答對者，得 1 分；答錯、未作答或畫記多於一個選項者，該題以零分計算。

第 21 至 30 題為題組

The Great Sphinx in the Giza desert is a mythological creature with the body of a lion and the head of a human being. This monumental __21__ is often regarded as a national symbol of Egypt, having guarded the famous Egyptian pyramids for 4,000 years. Nevertheless, the stone creature does not look like it did 4,000 years ago; wind, water, pollution, and human contact have slowly __22__ the rock. Scientists are now trying to restore it. They not only want it to look like it did when it was first built but also are looking for ways to keep it from __23__ more than it has.

Fixing the Sphinx, however, is not an easy job. It takes several years of __24__ before the work begins. Each stone in the Sphinx is carefully __25__. Scientists use computers to help figure out the size and shape of each stone. Each old stone is given a number. Then, one by one, replacement stones are carved by hand, just like people did long ago, in the __26__ sizes and shapes as the ones they are replacing. When the new stones are ready, they are __27__ and the worn ones removed.

Scientists are also worried about how to keep the Sphinx from falling apart again. They have talked about __28__ a wall around the Sphinx to protect it from the wind and sand, or perhaps covering it completely with a glass pyramid. Some think that burying part of it in the sand would serve the purpose. One scientist has even suggested building a __29__ shelter to protect it at night and during bad weather. The walls of the shelter could be retracted into the ground during the day so that visitors could see the Sphinx.

There are no easy solutions to the __30__, not to mention solutions that are agreeable to all parties. The one thing that is agreed upon is that something needs to be done to protect this ancient sculpture.

(A) movable (B) installed (C) diversified (D) problem
(E) aged (F) planning (G) measured (H) constructing
(I) exact (J) deteriorating (K) statue (L) religious

四、篇章結構 (占 10 分)

說明：第 31 題至第 35 題，每題一個空格。請依文意在文章後所提供的(A)到(F)選項中分別選出最適當者，填入空格中，使篇章結構清晰有條理，並將其英文字母代號畫記在答案卡之「選擇題答案區」。各題答對者，得 2 分；答錯、未作答或畫記多於一個選項者，該題以零分計算。

第 31 至 35 題為題組

Starting a business on one's own can be quite challenging and costly. To reduce the risks involved in starting a business from scratch, many people buy a franchise instead. __31__ Under the license, the individual acquires the right to use the big company's brand name and agrees to sell its products.

The concept of the franchise dates back to the 19th century in the U.S. __32__ Then, in the 1930s, Howard Johnson restaurants skyrocketed in popularity, paving the way for restaurant chains and the subsequent franchises that would define the unprecedented rise of the American fast-food industry.

There are many advantages to investing in a franchise. One of the benefits is the ready-made business operation. __33__ Depending on the franchise, the franchisor company may offer support in training and financial planning. Some even provide assistance with approved suppliers. To new business owners, the most recognized advantage of a franchise is perhaps the well-established brand name of the franchisor such as that of McDonald's. __34__

Disadvantages include heavy start-up costs as well as ongoing royalty costs on the part of the franchisee. To take the McDonald's example further, the estimated minimum cost for a franchisee to start a McDonald's is US$500,000. And it has to pay an annual fee equivalent to 12% of its sales to McDonald's. __35__ Other disadvantages include lack of territory control or creativity with one's own business.

(A) Whether a franchise is profitable or not depends largely on the nature of the business.

(B) Research has shown that customers tend to choose a brand they recognize over one they don't.

(C) A franchise comes with a built-in business formula including products, services, and even employee uniforms.

(D) Moreover, the franchisee is given no right to renew or extend the franchise after the term of the contract.

(E) The most famous example was Isaac Singer, who created franchises to distribute his sewing machines to larger areas.

(F) A franchise is a license issued by a large, usually well-known, company to an individual or a small business owner.

五、閱讀測驗 (占 32 分)

說明：第 36 題至第 51 題，每題請分別根據各篇文章之文意選出最適當的一個選項，請畫記在答案卡之「選擇題答案區」。各題答對者，得 2 分；答錯、未作答或畫記多於一個選項者，該題以零分計算。

第 36 至 39 題為題組

Some people call it a traveling museum. Others refer to it as a living or open-air museum. Built in Brazil to celebrate the quincentennial of Columbus' first voyage to the New World, the *Nina*, a Columbus-era replica ship, provides visitors with an accurate visual of the size and sailing implements of Columbus' favorite ship from over 500 years ago.

I joined the crew of the *Nina* in Gulf Shores, Alabama, in February 2013. As part of a research project sponsored by my university, my goal was to document my days aboard the ship in a blog. I quickly realized that I gained the most valuable insights when I observed or gave tours to school-age children. The field-trip tour of the *Nina* is hands-on learning at its best. In this setting, students could touch the line, pass around a ballast stone, and move the extremely large tiller that steered the ships in Columbus' day. They soon came to understand the labor involved in sailing the ship back in his time. I was pleased to see the students become active participants in their learning process.

The *Nina* is not the only traveling museum that provides such field trips. A visit to Jamestown Settlement, for example, allows visitors to board three re-creations of the ships that brought the first settlers from England to Virginia in the early 1600s. Historical interpreters, dressed in period garb, give tours to the *Susan Constant*, *Godspeed*, and *Discovery*. These interpreters often portray a character that would have lived and worked during that time period. Students touring these ships are encouraged to interact with the interpreters in order to better understand the daily life in the past.

My experience on the *Nina* helps substantiate my long-held belief that students stay interested, ask better questions, and engage in higher-order thinking tasks when they are actively engaged in the learning process. The students who boarded the *Nina* came as passive learners. They left as bold explorers.

36. What line of business is the author engaged in?

(A) Shipping. (B) Education.

(C) Ecological tourism. (D) Museum administration.

37. Which of the following is true about the *Nina* introduced in the passage?

(A) She is a replica of a ship that Columbus built in Brazil.

(B) She is always crowded with foreign tourists during holidays.

(C) She is the boat Columbus sailed in his voyage to the New World.

(D) She displays a replica of the navigational equipment used in Columbus' time.

38. What is the third paragraph mainly about?

(A) Guidelines for visitors on the ships.

(B) Life of the first settlers in Jamestown Settlement.

(C) Duties of the interpreters in the British museums.

(D) Introduction to some open-air museums similar to the *Nina*.

39. What does the author mean by the last two sentences of the passage?
(A) The students are interested in becoming tour guides.
(B) The experience has changed the students' learning attitude.
(C) The students become brave and are ready to sail the seas on their own.
(D) The museums are successful in teaching the students survival skills at sea.

第 40 至 43 題為題組

An ancient skull unearthed recently indicates that big cats originated in central Asia—not Africa as widely thought, paleontologists reported on Wednesday.

Dated at between 4.1 and 5.95 million years old, the fossil is the oldest remains ever found of a pantherine felid, as big cats are called. The previous felid record holder—tooth fragments found in Tanzania—is estimated to be around 3.8 million years old.

The evolution of big cats has been hotly discussed, and the issue is complicated by a lack of fossil evidence to settle the debate.

"This find suggests that big cats have a deeper evolutionary origin than previously suspected," said Jack Tseng, a paleontologist of the University of Southern California who led the probe.

Tseng and his team made the find in 2010 in a remote border region in Tibet. The fossil was found stuck among more than 100 bones that were probably deposited by a river that exited a cliff. After three years of careful comparisons with other fossils, using DNA data to build a family tree, the team is convinced the creature was a pantherine felid.

The weight of evidence suggests that central or northern Asia is where big cats originated some 16 million years ago. They may have lived in a vast mountain refuge, formed by the uplifting Himalayas, feeding on equally remarkable species such as the Tibetan blue sheep. They then dispersed into Southeast Asia, evolving into the clouded leopard, tiger and snow leopard lineages, and later movements across continents saw them evolve into jaguars and lions.

The newly discovered field has been called Panthera Blytheae, after Blythe Haaga, daughter of a couple who support a museum in Los Angeles, the university said in a news release.

40. According to the passage, why is the origin of big cats a hot issue?
(A) Because not many fossils have been found.
(B) Because they moved across continents.
(C) Because no equipment was available for accurate analysis.
(D) Because they have evolved into many different species of felid.

41. Where was the new felid fossil found?
(A) In Tanzania. (B) In Tibet. (C) In California. (D) In Southeast Asia.

42. According to the passage, which of the following statements is true regarding big cats?
(A) Some big cats evolved into jaguars 16 million years ago.
(B) The oldest fossil of big cats ever discovered is 3.8 million years old.
(C) Big cats are descendants of snow leopards living in high mountains.
(D) Tibetan blue sheep was a main food source for big cats in the Himalayas.

43. What is the purpose of this passage?
(A) To promote wildlife conservation.
(B) To report on a new finding in paleontology.
(C) To introduce a new animal species.
(D) To compare the family trees of pantherine felids.

第 44 至 47 題為題組

American cooking programs have taught audiences, changed audiences, and changed with audiences from generation to generation. In October 1926, the U.S. Department of Agriculture created this genre's first official representative, a fictional radio host named Aunt Sammy. Over the airwaves, she educated homemakers on home economics and doled out advice on all kinds of matters, but it was mostly the cooking recipes that got listeners' attention. The show provided a channel for transmitting culinary advice and brought about a national exchange of recipes.

Cooking shows transitioned to television in the 1940s, and in the 1950s were often presented by a cook systematically explaining instructions on how to prepare dishes from start to finish. These programs were broadcast during the day and aimed at middle-class women whose mindset leaned toward convenient foods for busy families. Poppy Cannon, for example, was a popular writer of *The Can-Opener Cookbook*. She appeared on various television shows, using canned foods to demonstrate how to cook quickly and easily.

Throughout the sixties and seventies, a few chef-oriented shows redefined the genre as an exhibition of **haute** European cuisine by celebrity gourmet experts. This elite cultural aura then gave way to various cooking styles from around the world. An example of such change can be seen in Martin Yan's 1982 "Yan Can Cook" series, which demonstrated Chinese cuisine cooking with the catchphrase, "If Yan can cook, you can too!" By the 1990s, these cooking shows ranged from high-culture to health-conscious cuisine, with chefs' personalities and entertainment value being two keys to successful productions.

At the beginning of the 21st century, new cooking shows emerged to satisfy celeb-hungry, reality-crazed audiences. In this new millennium of out-of-studio shows and chef competition reality shows, chefs have become celebrities whose fame rivals that of rock stars. Audiences of these shows tend to be people who are interested in food and enjoy watching people cook rather than those who want to do the cooking themselves, leaving the age-old emphasis on following recipes outmoded.

44. Which of the following is closest in meaning to "**haute**" in the third paragraph?

(A) Coarse. (B) Civilian. (C) Various. (D) High-class.

45. Which of the following is true about audiences of American cooking shows?

(A) Those in the '30s preferred advice on home economics to cooking instructions.

(B) Those in the '40s and '50s were interested in food preparation for busy families.

(C) Those in the '60s and '70s were eager to exchange recipes with each other.

(D) Those in the '80s enjoyed genuine American-style gourmet cooking.

46. According to the passage, which of the following is true about the most recent cooking programs?

(A) They are often hosted by rock stars.

(B) They are often not filmed in the studios.

(C) They attract many celebrity viewers.

(D) They invite hungry audience members to be judges.

47. Which of the following would most likely be a hit cooking show in the '90s?

(A) A show dedicated to European cuisine and gourmet food.

(B) A show sponsored by food companies advertising new products.

(C) A show hosted by a humorous chef presenting low-calorie dishes.

(D) A show with a professional cook demonstrating systematic ways of cooking.

第 48 至 51 題為題組

Screaming is one of the primal responses humans share with other animals. Conventional thinking suggests that what sets a scream apart from other sounds is its loudness or high pitch. However, many sounds that are loud and high-pitched do not raise goose bumps like screams can. To find out what makes human screams unique, neuroscientist Luc Arnal and his team examined a bank of sounds containing sentences spoken or screamed by 19 adults. The result shows screams and screamed sentences had a quality called "roughness," which refers to how fast a sound changes in loudness. While normal speech sounds only have slight differences in loudness—between 4 and 5 Hz, screams can switch very fast, varying between 30 and 150 Hz, thus perceived as being rough and unpleasant.

Arnal's team asked 20 subjects to judge screams as neutral or fearful, and found that the scariest almost always corresponded with roughness. The team then studied how the human brain responds to roughness using fMRI brain scanners. As expected, after hearing a scream, activity increased in the brain's auditory centers where sound coming into the ears is processed. But the scans also lit up in the amygdala, the brain's fear center.

The amygdala is the area that regulates our emotional and physiological response to danger. When a threat is detected, our adrenaline rises, and our body prepares to react to danger. The study discovered that screams have a similar influence on our body. It also found that roughness isn't heard when we speak naturally, regardless of the language we use, but **it** is prevalent in artificial sounds. The most aggravating alarm clocks, car horns, and fire alarms possess high degrees of roughness.

One potential application for this research might be to add roughness to alarm sounds to make them more effective, the same way a bad smell is added to natural gas to make it easily detectable. Warning sounds could also be added to electric cars, which are particularly silent, so they can be efficiently detected by pedestrians.

48. What is the first paragraph mainly about?
(A) Different types of screams. (B) Human sounds and animal cries.
(C) Specific features of screams. (D) Sound changes and goose bumps.

49. According to the passage, which of the following is **NOT** a finding by Arnal's team?
(A) Changes in volume make screams different from other sounds.
(B) Only humans can produce sounds with great loudness variation.
(C) Normal human speech sounds vary between 4 to 5 Hz in loudness.
(D) Drastic volume variation in speech can effectively activate the amygdala.

50. What does "**it**" in the third paragraph refer to?
(A) The study. (B) Language. (C) Roughness. (D) The amygdala.

51. Which of the following devices may be improved with the researchers' findings?
(A) Smoke detectors. (B) Security cameras. (C) Electric bug killers. (D) Fire extinguishers.

◆ 第貳部分：非選擇題 (占 28 分)

說明：本部分共有二題，請依各題指示作答，答案必須寫在「答案卷」上，並標明大題號 (一、二)。作答務必使用筆尖較粗之黑色墨水的筆書寫，且不得使用鉛筆。

一、中譯英 (占 8 分)

說明：1. 請將以下中文句子譯成正確、通順、達意的英文，並將答案寫在「答案卷」上。
2. 請依序作答，並標明子題號 (1、2)。每題 4 分，共 8 分。

1. 蚊子一旦叮咬過某些傳染病的患者，就可能將病毒傳給其他人。
2. 它們在人類中快速散播疾病，造成的死亡遠超乎我們所能想像。

二、英文作文 (占 20 分)

說明：1. 依提示在「答案卷」上寫一篇英文作文。
2. 文長至少 120 個單詞 (words)。

提示：最近有一則新聞報導，標題為「碩士清潔隊員 (waste collectors with a master's degree) 滿街跑」，提及某縣市招考清潔隊員，出現 50 位碩士畢業生報考，引起各界關注。請就這個主題，寫一篇英文作文，文長至少 120 個單詞。文分兩段，第一段依據你的觀察說明這個現象的成因，第二段則就你如何因應上述現象，具體 (舉例) 說明你對大學生涯的學習規劃。

Notes

104 學年度　指考英文試題

◆ 第壹部分：單選題 (占 72 分)

一、詞彙題 (占 10 分)

說明：第 1 題至第 10 題，每題有 4 個選項，其中只有一個是正確或最適當的選項，請畫記在答案卡之「選擇題答案區」。各題答對者，得 1 分；答錯、未作答或畫記多於一個選項者，該題以零分計算。

1. John is very close to his family. Whenever he feels depressed, he returns to the warm, ________, and comfortable atmosphere of his home.
   (A) crucial　(B) sloppy　(C) secure　(D) cautious

2. Tom ________ something before he left the room, but I couldn't figure out exactly what he said.
   (A) mumbled　(B) perceived　(C) summoned　(D) trampled

3. The content of the book is very much technical and specialized; it is too difficult for a ________ to understand.
   (A) patriot　(B) hacker　(C) layman　(D) tenant

4. Food shortages are one of the main causes of ________ nutrition among children in developing countries.
   (A) distinctive　(B) vigorous　(C) inadequate　(D) abundant

5. Good writers do not always write ________; on the contrary, they often express what they really mean in an indirect way.
   (A) explicitly　(B) ironically　(C) persistently　(D) selectively

6. According to the weather report, some light rain or ________ is expected today. You may need to take an umbrella with you when you go out.
   (A) hail　(B) breeze　(C) tornado　(D) drizzle

7. The movie was so popular that many people came to the ________ conclusion that it must be good; however, many professional critics thought otherwise.
   (A) acute　(B) naive　(C) confidential　(D) skeptical

8. In ancient times, people used large shells to ________ voices in open-air ceremonies so that their tribal members near and far could hear what was said.
   (A) amplify　(B) mobilize　(C) penetrate　(D) undermine

9. The audience held their breath and sat motionless in the theater as they watched the tragic historical event ________ in front of their eyes.
   (A) ascending　(B) elaborating　(C) illustrating　(D) unfolding

10. According to government regulations, if employees are unable to work because of a serious illness, they are ________ to take an extended sick leave.
   (A) adapted　(B) entitled　(C) oriented　(D) intimidated

二、綜合測驗 (占 10 分)

說明：第 11 題至第 20 題，每題一個空格，請依文意選出最適當的一個選項，請畫記在答案卡之「選擇題答案區」。各題答對者，得 1 分；答錯、未作答或畫記多於一個選項者，該題以零分計算。

第 11 至 15 題為題組

Ernest Hemingway (1899–1961) was an American author and journalist. His writing style, characterized by simplicity and understatement, influenced modern fiction, as ___11___ his life of adventure.

Hemingway started his career as a journalist at 17. In the 1920s, he was sent to Europe as a newspaper correspondent to ___12___ such events as the Greek Revolution. During this period, he produced his early important works, including *The Sun Also Rises*. Among his later works, the most outstanding is *The Old Man and the Sea* (1952), which became perhaps his most famous book, finally winning him the Pulitzer Prize he had long been ___13___.

Hemingway liked to portray soldiers, hunters, bullfighters—tough, at times primitive people whose courage and honesty are set against the brutal ways of modern society, and who in this ___14___ lose hope and faith. His straightforward prose is particularly effective in his short stories, some of ___15___ are collected in *Men Without Women* (1927). In 1954, Hemingway was awarded the Nobel Prize in Literature. He died in Idaho in 1961.

11. (A) was (B) being (C) did (D) doing
12. (A) cover (B) approve (C) predict (D) escape
13. (A) planned (B) achieved (C) examined (D) denied
14. (A) limitation (B) classification (C) confrontation (D) modification
15. (A) what (B) which (C) them (D) these

第 16 至 20 題為題組

Road running is one of the most popular and accessible athletic activities in the world. It refers to the sport of running on paved roads or established paths as opposed to track and field, or cross country running. The three most common ___16___ for road running events are 10K runs, half marathons (21.1K), and marathons (42.2K).

Road running is unique among athletic events because it ___17___ all ages and abilities. In many cases first time amateurs are welcome to participate in the same event as running club members and even current world-class ___18___. Sometimes it may also include wheelchair entrants.

Road running often offers those ___19___ a range of challenges such as dealing with hills, sharp bends, rough weather, and so on. Runners are advised to train prior to participating in a race. Another important factor contributing to success is a suitable pair of running shoes.

Road running is often a community-wide event that highlights or raises money for an issue or project. ___20___, Race for the Cure is held throughout the U.S. to raise breast cancer awareness. This race is also run in Germany, Italy, and Puerto Rico.

16. (A) journeys	(B) distances	(C) destinations	(D) measurements
17. (A) caters to	(B) depends on	(C) goes after	(D) identifies with
18. (A) matches	(B) civilians	(C) associations	(D) champions
19. (A) involving	(B) involved	(C) to involve	(D) are involved
20. (A) Above all	(B) For example	(C) As it appears	(D) To some extent

三、文意選填 (占 10 分)

說明：第 21 題至第 30 題，每題一個空格，請依文意在文章後所提供的(A)到(L)選項中分別選出最適當者，並將其英文字母代號畫記在答案卡之「選擇題答案區」。各題答對者，得 1 分；答錯、未作答或畫記多於一個選項者，該題以零分計算。

第 21 至 30 題為題組

The 1918 influenza epidemic, which occurred during World War I, was one of the most devastating health crises of the 20th century. Between September 1918 and June 1919, more than 600,000 Americans died of influenza and pneumonia, making the epidemic far more ___21___ than the war itself. The influenza hit Americans in two waves. The first wave attacked the army camps and was less fatal than the second. The second wave arrived in the port city of Boston in September 1918 with war ___22___ of machinery and supplies. Other wartime events enabled the disease to ___23___ the country quickly. As men across the nation were joining the ___24___ to serve the country, they brought the virus with them everywhere they went. In October 1918 alone, the virus killed almost 200,000. In the following month, the end of World War I resulted in an even ___25___ spread of the disease. The celebration of the end of the war with parades and parties was a complete disaster from the standpoint of public health. This ___26___ the spread of the disease in some cities. The flu that winter was destructive beyond imagination as millions were ___27___ and thousands died. In fact, it caused many more deaths than any of the other epidemics which had ___28___ it.

Medical scientists ___29___ that another epidemic will attack people at some point in the future. Today's worldwide transportation makes it even ___30___ to control an epidemic. Therefore, doctors advise that we continue to get our annual flu shots in order to stay healthy.

(A) military	(B) crisis	(C) harder	(D) wider
(E) deadly	(F) come across	(G) shipments	(H) infected
(I) preceded	(J) warn	(K) accelerated	(L) sweep through

四、篇章結構 (占 10 分)

說明：第 31 題至第 35 題，每題一個空格。請依文意在文章後所提供的(A)到(F)選項中分別選出最適當者，填入空格中，使篇章結構清晰有條理，並將其英文字母代號畫記在答案卡之「選擇題答案區」。各題答對者，得 2 分；答錯、未作答或畫記多於一個選項者，該題以零分計算。

第 31 至 35 題為題組

Since the early 1990s, the lithium-ion battery has been the most suitable battery for portable electronic equipment. Today, they're commonly used for cellphones, computers, tablets, digital cameras, and other devices.

Lithium-ion batteries have nearly twice the energy density of traditional nickel cadmium batteries. __31__ This feature has important implications for cellphones and computers, because it makes these items more portable for consumers. It also makes power tools easier to use and allows workers to use them for longer periods of time.

__32__ Lithium-ion batteries retain no "memory" of their power capacity from previous charging cycles. Thus they require no scheduled cycling and can be fully re-fueled to their maximum capacity during each charging cycle. Other rechargeable battery types, in contrast, retain information from previous charging cycles, which wastes valuable storage space. Over time, this makes these rechargeable batteries hold less of a charge.

__33__ It is fragile and requires a protection circuit to maintain safe operation. A high load could overheat the pack and safety might be jeopardized. __34__ After 2–3 years of use, the pack often becomes unserviceable due to a large voltage drop caused by high internal resistance.

It should be noted, however, that manufacturers are constantly making improvements on lithium-ion batteries. __35__ With such rapid progress, the use of lithium-ion batteries will certainly expand further.

(A) The lithium-ion battery is also a low maintenance battery.
(B) Despite its overall advantages, the lithium-ion battery has its drawbacks.
(C) New and enhanced chemical combinations are introduced every six months or so.
(D) Attempts to develop rechargeable lithium-ion batteries failed due to memory problems.
(E) That is, they carry more power in a smaller unit, helping to reduce overall weight and size.
(F) Another downside is the increase of the internal resistance that occurs with cycling and aging.

五、閱讀測驗 (占 32 分)

說明：第 36 題至第 51 題，每題請分別根據各篇文章之文意選出最適當的一個選項，請畫記在答案卡之「選擇題答案區」。各題答對者，得 2 分；答錯、未作答或畫記多於一個選項者，該題以零分計算。

第 36 至 39 題為題組

Fabergé eggs are jeweled eggs that were made by the famous Russian jeweler, the House of Fabergé, from 1885 to 1917. The eggs were made of valuable metals or stones coated with beautiful colors and decorated with precious jewels.

The first Fabergé egg was crafted for Tsar Alexander III, who gave his wife, the Empress Maria Fedorovna, an Easter egg to celebrate their 20th wedding anniversary. He placed an order with a young jeweler, Peter Carl Fabergé, whose beautiful creations had caught Maria's eye earlier. On Easter morning of 1885, what appeared to be a simple enameled egg was delivered to the palace. But to the delight of the Empress, the egg opened to a golden yolk; within the yolk was a golden hen; and concealed within the hen was a diamond miniature of the royal crown and a tiny ruby egg. Unfortunately, the last two surprises are now lost to history.

Empress Maria was so delighted by this gift that Alexander appointed Fabergé a "goldsmith by special appointment to the Imperial Crown." The Tsar also asked Fabergé to make an Easter egg every year. The requirements were straightforward: Each egg must be unique, and each must contain a pleasant surprise. With excellent craftsmanship and an inventive spirit, **Peter Fabergé and his successors repeatedly met the challenge**. The House of Fabergé made approximately 50 Imperial Easter Eggs for Tsar Alexander III and his son Nicholas II until 1917, when the Russian revolution broke out.

Today, the term "Fabergé eggs" has become a synonym of luxury and the eggs are regarded as masterpieces of the jeweler's art. More significantly, perhaps, they serve as reminders of the last Russian imperial family.

36. Why did Tsar Alexander III choose Peter Fabergé to make the first Easter egg?
   (A) Peter Fabergé was the goldsmith for the royal family.
   (B) Empress Maria was impressed by Peter Fabergé's work.
   (C) Tsar Alexander III received an order from Empress Maria.
   (D) Peter Fabergé owned the most famous Russian jewelry house.

37. What went missing from the first Fabergé egg?
   (A) A golden hen and a ruby egg.
   (B) A golden hen and a golden yolk.
   (C) A ruby egg and a diamond crown.
   (D) A golden yolk and a diamond crown.

38. What does it mean by "**Peter Fabergé and his successors repeatedly met the challenge**" in the third paragraph?
   (A) They repeated their designs over and over.
   (B) They fulfilled the Tsar's requirements each time.
   (C) They challenged the Tsar's expectations every year.
   (D) They were faced with unexpected difficulties time and again.

39. Which of the following statements about the Fabergé eggs is true, according to the passage?
 (A) They were all genuine creations of the jeweler, Peter Fabergé.
 (B) They were created to represent Russian emperors and their dynasty.
 (C) They were made for annual Easter parties in the Russian imperial court.
 (D) They were connected to the last two Russian emperors and their families.

第 40 至 43 題為題組

Six Sigma is a highly disciplined process that helps companies focus on developing and delivering near-perfect products and services. The word "sigma" is a statistical term that measures how far a given process falls short of perfection. The central idea behind Six Sigma is that if a company can measure how many "defects" they have in a commercial production process, they can systematically figure out how to eliminate the problems and get as close to "zero defects" as possible.

Training and teamwork are essential elements of the Six Sigma methodology. In other words, companies need to have their team leaders and team members trained to implement the Six Sigma processes. They must learn to use the measurement and improvement tools. They also need to learn communication skills necessary for them to involve customers and suppliers and to serve their needs.

Six Sigma was developed in 1986 by Motorola, an American telecommunications company. Engineers in Motorola used it as an informal name for a plan to reduce faults in production processes. A few years later, Motorola extended the name "Six Sigma" to mean a general performance improvement method, beyond purely "defect reduction" in the production process. In 1995, Jack Welch, CEO of General Electrics (GE), decided to implement Six Sigma in GE; and by 1998 GE claimed that Six Sigma had generated over three-quarters of a billion dollars of cost savings.

By 2000, Six Sigma was effectively established as an industry in its own right, involving the training, consultancy and implementation of Six Sigma methodology in all sorts of organizations around the world. Organizations as diverse as local governments, prisons, hospitals, the armed forces, banks, and multi-national corporations have been adopting Six Sigma for quality and process improvement.

40. According to the passage, what is "Six Sigma"?
 (A) A digital device to speed up production processes.
 (B) A near-perfect process in business communication.
 (C) A statistical term that measures a company's budgets and profits.
 (D) A quality measure that detects problems to improve products and services.

41. For Six Sigma to be applied successfully, which of the following are the most crucial factors?
 (A) Customers and suppliers' needs.
 (B) Tools in statistics and marketing.
 (C) Strong teamwork and proper training.
 (D) Good leadership and sufficient budget.

42. How are the author's ideas developed in the last two paragraphs?

(A) By definition. (B) By comparison. (C) In time order. (D) In space order.

43. According to the passage, which of the following is true regarding Six Sigma?

(A) It helped Motorola and General Motors to promote sales.

(B) It requires multi-national efforts to generate satisfactory results.

(C) It has gained popularity mostly among large telecommunications companies.

(D) It has become a business model which provides services to organizations worldwide.

第 44 至 47 題為題組

Imagine two bottlenose dolphins swimming in the Gulf of Mexico. You hear a series of clicks, whistles, and whines coming from each, much like a conversation. We can't be sure what they are discussing, but scientists do believe dolphins call each other by "name."

A recent study suggests the marine mammals not only produce their own unique "signature whistles," but they also recognize and mimic whistles of other dolphins they are close to and want to see again. It seems that dolphins can call those they know by mimicking their distinct whistles. "They're abstract names," said Randall Wells, one of the authors of the study.

To conduct the study, the researchers listened to recordings of about 250 wild bottlenose dolphins made around Florida's Sarasota Bay from 1984 to 2009, and four captive dolphins at a nearby aquarium.

Some wild dolphins were briefly captured and held in separate nets by the research team, allowing them to hear but not see each other. Researchers found that dolphins familiar with each other would mimic the whistle of another in that group when they were separated. Most of **this** took place among mothers and calves, or among males who were close associates, suggesting it was affiliative and not aggressive—somewhat like calling out the name of a missing child or friend. Whistle copying of this sort was not found in dolphins that happened to cross paths in the wild.

This use of vocal copying is similar to its use in human language, where the maintenance of social bonds appears to be more important than the immediate defense of resources. This helps differentiate dolphins' vocal learning from that of birds, which tend to address one another in a more "aggressive context."

If confirmed, this would be a level of communication rarely found in nature. If dolphins can identify themselves and address friends with just a few squeaks, it's easy to imagine what else they're saying. However, as the authors of the study point out, all we can do right now is still imagine.

44. What is the main idea of the passage?

(A) Bottlenose dolphins show strong ties to their family members.

(B) Bottlenose dolphins recognize their friends' voices in the wild.

(C) Bottlenose dolphins produce whistles that distinguish themselves.

(D) Bottlenose dolphins demonstrate a unique type of animal communication.

45. Which of the following statements is true about Wells's research team?
(A) Their data were collected over two decades.
(B) They recorded the calls of dolphins and birds.
(C) Their major research base was in Mexico.
(D) They trained 250 wild dolphins for observation.

46. What does "**this**" in the third paragraph refer to?
(A) Recording messages. (B) Conducting research. (C) Behavior learning. (D) Whistle copying.

47. Which of the following can be inferred from the passage?
(A) Birds may use their calls to claim territory.
(B) Male dolphins whistle when fighting for mates.
(C) Dolphins make harsh squeaks when hunting for food.
(D) Both dolphins and birds tend to mimic their enemies' whistles.

第 48 至 51 題為題組

With soaring rock formations, uniquely-rippled landscapes, and mysterious underground cities, the Goreme National Park is an incredible tourist attraction in central Turkey.

Thousands of years ago a group of ancient volcanoes spewed out layer upon layer of thick ash and lava which formed the Cappadocia region, where the Goreme National Park is now located. Over the centuries the wind and rain worked their magic on this land, carving out spectacular gorges and leaving behind the dramatic towering formations of rock pillars that reach heights of 40 meters. These amazing structures are usually called "fairy chimneys." They come in an extraordinary range of shapes and sizes, but most are tall and resemble king trumpet mushrooms with a cap on top. The top stone is the hardest part of each formation and protects the softer rock underneath from erosion. Eventually, however, these caps fall off, whereupon the wind and rain start to cut away the cone until it, too, collapses. The unique landforms of the Goreme valley have created its lunar-like landscape, also known as a moonscape.

But the Goreme National Park has always been much more than its dramatic scenery. Humans, too, have left their unique mark on the region. The Byzantine Christians inhabited the area in the fourth century. They carved thousands of cave churches, chapels, and monasteries out of rock. Many of these churches were decorated with beautiful wall paintings whose colors still retain all their original freshness. The Byzantine Christians even carved out entire underground villages in an effort to hide from the Romans and later, the Muslims. To this day, many of these villages are still inhabited and many of the rock-cut storerooms are still stuffed with grapes, lemons, potatoes and flat bread waiting for the winter.

48. How is the landscape of the Goreme National Park formed?
(A) It is the effect of erosions of volcanic rocks by wind and water.
(B) It is the outcome of cumulative ash and lava from volcanoes.
(C) It is the creation of some mysterious forces from the moon.
(D) It is the result of rock cutting by the Byzantine Christians.

49. Which of the following descriptions of the "fairy chimneys" is true?

(A) They are almost identical in size and shape.

(B) They have mushrooms growing on the top.

(C) They are formed by rocks of different hardness.

(D) They have strong bottoms to support their 40-meter height.

50. Which of the following has **NOT** been a function served by the carved rocks in the Goreme National Park?

(A) Refuge. (B) Gallery. (C) Residence. (D) Place of worship.

51. Which of the following sentences best states the main idea of the passage?

(A) Goreme is a wonder where nature meets man.

(B) Goreme is a representation of ancient Turkish life.

(C) Goreme is a living example of the power of nature.

(D) Goreme is an attraction that mixes the new and the old.

◆ 第貳部分：非選擇題 (占 28 分)

說明：本部分共有二題，請依各題指示作答，答案必須寫在「答案卷」上，並標明大題號 (一、二)。作答務必使用筆尖較粗之黑色墨水的筆書寫，且不得使用鉛筆。

一、中譯英 (占 8 分)

說明：1. 請將以下中文句子譯成正確、通順、達意的英文，並將答案寫在「答案卷」上。
2. 請依序作答，並標明子題號 (1、2)。每題 4 分，共 8 分。

1. 台灣便利商店的密集度是全世界最高的，平均每兩千人就有一家。
2. 除了購買生活必需品，顧客也可以在這些商店繳費，甚至領取網路訂購之物品。

二、英文作文 (占 20 分)

說明：1. 依提示在「答案卷」上寫一篇英文作文。
2. 文長至少 120 個單詞 (words)。

提示：指導別人學習讓他學會一件事物，或是得到別人的指導而自己學會一件事物，都是很好的經驗。請根據你過去幫助別人學習，或得到別人的指導而學會某件事的經驗，寫一篇至少 120 個單詞的英文作文。文分兩段，第一段說明該次經驗的緣由、內容和過程，第二段說明你對該次經驗的感想。

Notes

103 學年度　指考英文試題

◆ 第壹部分：單選題 (占 72 分)

一、詞彙題 (占 10 分)

說明：第 1 題至第 10 題，每題有 4 個選項，其中只有一個是正確或最適當的選項，請畫記在答案卡之「選擇題答案區」。各題答對者，得 1 分；答錯、未作答或畫記多於一個選項者，該題以零分計算。

1. When dining at a restaurant, we need to be ________ of other customers and keep our conversations at an appropriate noise level.
(A) peculiar (B) defensive (C) noticeable (D) considerate

2. John shows ________ towards his classmates. He doesn't take part in any of the class activities and doesn't even bother talking to other students in his class.
(A) indifference (B) sympathy (C) ambiguity (D) desperation

3. To meet the unique needs of the elderly, the company designed a cell phone ________ for seniors, which has big buttons and large color displays.
(A) necessarily (B) relatively (C) specifically (D) voluntarily

4. A well-constructed building has a better chance of ________ natural disasters such as typhoons, tornadoes, and earthquakes.
(A) undertaking (B) conceiving (C) executing (D) withstanding

5. Our family doctor has repeatedly warned me that spicy food may ________ my stomach, so I'd better stay away from it.
(A) irritate (B) liberate (C) kidnap (D) override

6. Because the new principal is young and inexperienced, the teachers are ________ about whether he can run the school well.
(A) passionate (B) impressive (C) arrogant (D) skeptical

7. Many universities offer a large number of scholarships as an ________ to attract outstanding students to enroll in their schools.
(A) ornament (B) incentive (C) emphasis (D) application

8. Since Diana is such an ________ speaker, she has won several medals for her school in national speech contests.
(A) authentic (B) imperative (C) eloquent (D) optional

9. The candidate made energy ________ the central theme of his campaign, calling for a greater reduction in oil consumption.
(A) evolution (B) conservation (C) donation (D) opposition

10. Concerned about mudslides, the local government quickly ________ the villagers from their homes before the typhoon hit the mountain area.

(A) evacuated　(B) suffocated　(C) humiliated　(D) accommodated

二、綜合測驗 (占 10 分)

說明：第 11 題至第 20 題，每題一個空格，請依文意選出最適當的一個選項，請畫記在答案卡之「選擇題答案區」。各題答對者，得 1 分；答錯、未作答或畫記多於一個選項者，該題以零分計算。

第 11 至 15 題為題組

Brushing your teeth regularly will help you maintain a healthy smile. But that smile won't last long if you don't take proper care of your toothbrush and switch to a new one often. According to the American Dental Association (ADA), toothbrushes can harbor bacteria. These germs come from the mouth and can __11__ in toothbrushes over time.

Many Americans replace their toothbrushes only once or twice a year. The ADA, however, recommends __12__ a new toothbrush every three to four months. Children's toothbrushes may need to be changed more __13__.

During those three to four months of use, there are several ways to keep a toothbrush clean. __14__, rinse your toothbrush thoroughly with tap water after use, making sure to remove any toothpaste and debris. Store your toothbrush in an upright position, and let __15__ air dry. Most importantly, do not share toothbrushes.

11. (A) accumulate　(B) crumble　(C) establish　(D) radiate

12. (A) use　(B) to use　(C) using　(D) used

13. (A) essentially　(B) frequently　(C) typically　(D) objectively

14. (A) In short　(B) Otherwise　(C) Nevertheless　(D) For example

15. (A) it　(B) one　(C) the　(D) which

第 16 至 20 題為題組

Hiding herself among the trees near a chimpanzee habitat, Elizabeth Lonsdorf is using her camera to explore mysteries of learning. The chimpanzee she records picks up a thin flat piece of grass and then digs out tiny insects from a hole. Dinner is __16__! But how did the chimp develop this ingenious skill with tools? Do the chimp babies copy their parents in using tools? Do the mothers most skilled with tools have offspring who are also good at using tools? Here in Africa, Lonsdorf is conducting one of the world's longest wildlife studies, trying to discover how learning is transferred __17__ generations.

Lonsdorf has always been interested in animal learning and tool use, __18__ the way young animals grow up and learn their way in the world. Her chimpanzee study shows a clear link between humans and the rest of the animal kingdom. The chimps make and use tools and have mother-child relationships very ___19___ to those of humans. Through observing chimpanzees' learning process, researchers hope to gain insight into what the development of our earliest ancestors ___20___ like.

Lonsdorf hopes that by understanding the complexity of animal behavior, we can better appreciate and protect the diversity of life on this planet.

16. (A) proposed (B) ordered (C) digested (D) served
17. (A) across (B) beside (C) upon (D) within
18. (A) especially (B) originally (C) consequently (D) fortunately
19. (A) casual (B) similar (C) direct (D) grateful
20. (A) is to be (B) was to be (C) might have been (D) will have been

三、文意選填 (占 10 分)

說明：第 21 題至第 30 題，每題一個空格，請依文意在文章後所提供的(A)到(L)選項中分別選出最適當者，並將其英文字母代號畫記在答案卡之「選擇題答案區」。各題答對者，得 1 分；答錯、未作答或畫記多於一個選項者，該題以零分計算。

第 21 至 30 題為題組

The practice of burning paper money or paper model offerings at funerals in Chinese society can be traced back to the Tang dynasty (618–907 AD). Chinese people believe that when someone passes away, there is a death of the body, but the ___21___ continues to live in the next world. This "next world" is a mirror of the human world, where the "residents" need places to live, money to spend, daily necessities, and entertainment just like when they were ___22___. Some of these necessities are buried with the deceased, while most others are "shipped" to them by burning paper models. As the ashes fly high, the offerings are ___23___ by the residents in the next world.

Relatives of the deceased want to see their beloved family members live comfortably in the next world, so the paper houses are big and the cars are very ___24___, mostly Mercedes-Benzes. A complete package of paper offerings may include a couple of servants, cash, and credit cards so that the deceased will have all their ___25___ satisfied.

These traditional paper offerings were sold only at specialty stores in the past. The style and variety of the products were ___26___. For example, "houses" looked all the same and were built by pasting paper around a bamboo frame, with ___27___ of a door, windows, and a roof printed on it. There were no trendy, modern supplies to choose from. Now, the ___28___ can be made on the Internet. And with the incorporation of new materials and designs, paper offerings come in many more varieties. The old one-style-fits-all houses have been ___29___ by buildings that are fully equipped with decorations, furniture, and household appliances. Digital cameras, iPhones, and even skin care products are also ___30___. It seems that, with the help of a simple click, this old Chinese tradition has been given a face-lift.

(A) replaced	(B) mortal	(C) spirit	(D) available
(E) journey	(F) luxurious	(G) collected	(H) purchase
(I) alive	(J) needs	(K) limited	(L) images

四、篇章結構 (占 10 分)

說明：第 31 題至第 35 題，每題一個空格。請依文意在文章後所提供的(A)到(F)選項中分別選出最適當者，填入空格中，使篇章結構清晰有條理，並將其英文字母代號畫記在答案卡之「選擇題答案區」。各題答對者，得 2 分；答錯、未作答或畫記多於一個選項者，該題以零分計算。

第 31 至 35 題為題組

Eccentrics are people who have an unusual or odd personality, set of beliefs, or behavior pattern. They may or may not comprehend the standards for normal behavior in their culture. They simply don't care about the society's disapproval of their habits or beliefs.

Once considered socially unacceptable, eccentric people have been found to possess some positive characteristics. __31__ They often have more curiosity about the world and, in many cases, are contentedly obsessed by hobbies and interests. __32__ They live in a world of their own and do not worry about what others think of them. So they are usually less restricted and therefore more carefree in forming new ideas.

__33__ Statistics show they visit their doctors less—about once in eight to nine years, which is 20 times less than the average person. This could be partly due to their innate traits such as humor and happiness. __34__ This may explain why eccentrics are, on the whole, healthier.

Psychologists therefore suggest that we pay attention to those who do not conform. It could be our aunt who has been raising pet lizards. __35__ Their crazy hobby or strange sense of humor is what keeps them going. Eccentric people may seem odd, but they will likely live a happier and healthier life because they enjoy what they are doing. In fact, many of history's most brilliant minds have displayed some unusual behaviors and habits.

(A) Eccentrics are also found to be healthier.

(B) According to a recent study in England, eccentrics are more creative.

(C) Or it could be our best friend's brother who wears shorts to a formal dance.

(D) People may have eccentric taste in clothes, or have eccentric hobbies.

(E) Psychologists also find that eccentric people do not follow conventions.

(F) Such personal traits are found to play an important role in boosting the body's immune system.

五、閱讀測驗 (占 32 分)

說明：第 36 題至第 51 題，每題請分別根據各篇文章之文意選出最適當的一個選項，請畫記在答案卡之「選擇題答案區」。各題答對者，得 2 分；答錯、未作答或畫記多於一個選項者，該題以零分計算。

第 36 至 39 題為題組

Opened in 1883, the Brooklyn Bridge was the first long-span suspension bridge to carry motor traffic, and it quickly became the model for the great suspension bridges of the following century. Spanning New York's East River, it provided the first traffic artery between Manhattan Island and Brooklyn. Before that, the only transportation was by ferries, which were slow and could be dangerous in winter.

The construction of a bridge over the East River had been discussed since the early 19th century, but the outbreak of the Civil War in 1861 **deflected** all consideration of the project. When the war ended in 1865, the bridge became an important issue once more. In 1867, the New York State legislature passed an act incorporating the New York Bridge Company for the purpose of constructing and maintaining a bridge between Manhattan Island and Brooklyn.

John Augustus Roebling was chosen to design the bridge. Born in Germany in 1806, he held radical views as a student and was listed by the German police as a dangerous liberal. He emigrated to America in 1830 to escape political discrimination.

Roebling proposed a bridge with a span of 1,500 feet (465 m), with two masonry towers in the East River serving as the main piers. The bridge that was actually built is longer—1,597 feet (486 m), the longest suspension bridge at that time.

36. What was the purpose of building the Brooklyn Bridge?
(A) To replace an old bridge.
(B) To set up a model for bridge construction.
(C) To build a suspension bridge for the Civil War.
(D) To provide faster and safer transportation than boats.

37. Which of the following is closest in meaning to "**deflected**" in the second paragraph?
(A) Blocked. (B) Detected. (C) Engaged. (D) Indicated.

38. Which of the following is true about the Brooklyn Bridge?
(A) It was built in 1865. (B) It is shorter than originally planned.
(C) It was first proposed after the Civil War. (D) It was built by the New York Bridge Company.

39. According to the passage, which of the following correctly describes John Augustus Roebling?
(A) He participated in the Civil War and was seriously wounded.
(B) He was chosen to design the bridge because of his radical views.
(C) He was the first person to propose the construction of the bridge.
(D) He moved to America because he was discriminated against in his home country.

第 40 至 43 題為題組

The Japanese have long puzzled public health researchers because they are such an apparent paradox: They have the world's lowest rates of heart disease and the largest number of people that live to or beyond 100 years despite the fact that most Japanese men smoke—and smoking counts as one of the strongest risk factors for heart disease. So what's protecting Japanese men?

Two professors at the University of California at Berkeley hoped to find out the answer. They investigated a pool of 12,000 Japanese men equally divided into three groups: One group had lived in Japan for all their lives, and the other two groups had emigrated to Hawaii or Northern California. It was found that the rate of heart disease among Japanese men increased five times in California and about half of that for those in Hawaii.

The differences could not be explained by any of the usual risk factors for heart disease, such as smoking, high blood pressure, or cholesterol counts. The change in diet, from sushi to hamburgers and fries, was also not related to the rise in heart disease. However, the kind of society they had created for themselves in their new home country was. The most traditional group of Japanese Americans, who maintained tight-knit and mutually supportive social groups, had a heart-attack rate as low as their fellow Japanese back home. But those who had adopted the more isolated Western lifestyle increased their heart-attack incidence by three to five times.

The study shows that the need to bond with a social group is so fundamental to humans that it remains the key determinant of whether we stay healthy or get ill, even whether we live or die. We need to feel part of **something bigger** to thrive. We need to belong, not online, but in the real world of hugs, handshakes, and pats on the back.

40. What is the best title of this passage?
(A) Heart Diseases and Their Causes
(B) The Power of Social Connection
(C) Differences in Japanese Americans
(D) The Sense of Belonging vs. Isolation

41. Which of the following is a finding of the two American professors' study?
(A) Many Japanese men that lived up to 100 years were smokers.
(B) Those who often ate hamburgers and fries were more likely to fall sick.
(C) Japanese immigrants to America usually formed a tight-knit community.
(D) Westernized social life was related to the heart-attack rate of Japanese Americans.

42. Which of the following is an example of "**something bigger**" in the last paragraph?
(A) A family.
(B) A stadium.
(C) The universe.
(D) The digital world.

43. What is the ratio of heart disease between Japanese living in Japan and Japanese Americans in Hawaii?
(A) 1 to 2.5
(B) 1 to 5
(C) 3 to 5
(D) 1.5 to 5

第 44 至 47 題為題組

Bitcoin is an experimental, decentralized digital currency that enables instant payments to anyone, anywhere in the world. Bitcoin uses peer-to-peer technology to operate with no central authority; that is, managing transactions and issuing money are carried out collectively through the network.

Any transaction issued with Bitcoin cannot be reversed; it can only be refunded by the person receiving the funds. That means you should do business with people and organizations you know and trust, or who have an established reputation. Bitcoin can detect typos and usually won't let you send money to an invalid address by mistake.

All Bitcoin transactions are stored publicly and permanently on the network, which means anyone can see the balance and transactions of any Bitcoin address. However, the identity of the user behind an address remains unknown until information is revealed during a purchase or in other circumstances.

The price of a bitcoin can unpredictably increase or decrease over a short period of time due to its young economy, novel nature, and sometimes illiquid markets. Consequently, keeping your savings with Bitcoin is not recommended at this point. Bitcoin should be seen like a high risk asset, and you should never store money that you cannot afford to lose with Bitcoin. If you receive payments with Bitcoin, many service providers can convert them to your local currency.

Bitcoin is an experimental new currency that is in active development. Although it becomes less experimental as usage grows, you should keep in mind that Bitcoin is a new invention that is exploring ideas that have never been attempted before. As such, its future cannot be predicted by anyone.

44. What is the purpose of this article?
(A) To introduce a new currency.
(B) To prove the value of a young economy.
(C) To explore ways to do online transactions.
(D) To explain how to build up a business network.

45. Why is the value of Bitcoin not stable?
(A) Because its use is illegal.
(B) Because it is not a valid investment.
(C) Because it is still developing.
(D) Because its circulation is limited to the youth.

46. Which of the following is true about Bitcoin?
(A) Bitcoin addresses are known only to their owners.
(B) Once a transaction is made, the Bitcoin cannot be refunded.
(C) Bitcoin user's identity is always open to the general public.
(D) When a payment is received, the Bitcoin can be turned into local currency.

47. What advice would the author give to those who are interested in keeping money in Bitcoin?
(A) Better late than never.
(B) Look before you leap.
(C) Make hay while the sun shines.
(D) No pain, no gain.

第 48 至 51 題為題組

Scientists are trying to genetically modify the world in which we live. They are even trying to wipe out diseases via genetic modification. For example, researchers have tried to engineer mosquitoes to kill malaria parasites. The malaria parasite is carried by the female *Anopheles* mosquito. When transmitted to a human, the parasite travels first to the liver and then on to the bloodstream, where it reproduces and destroys red blood cells. An estimated 250 million people suffer from malaria each year, and about one million die—many of them children. There are currently no effective or approved malaria vaccines.

To "kill" malaria, scientists are genetically modifying a bacterium in mosquitoes so that it releases toxic compounds. These compounds are not harmful to humans or the mosquito itself, but they do kill off the malaria parasite, making the mosquito incapable of infecting humans with malaria.

Despite this achievement, scientists are faced with the challenge of giving the modified mosquitoes a competitive advantage so that they can eventually replace the wild population. Complete blockage of the malaria parasite is very important. If some of the parasites slip through the mechanism, then the next generation will likely become resistant to it. And if **that** happens, the scientists are back where they started.

Another challenge for scientists is to gain public approval for this genetic modification regarding mosquitoes and malaria control. Environmental activists have raised concerns about the release of genetically engineered organisms without any clear knowledge of their long-term effect on ecosystems and human health. There is still a long way to go before genetic modification techniques are put to use in disease control.

48. What is the main idea of this passage?

(A) Researchers have found an effective way to halt the spread of insect-borne diseases around the world.

(B) Many people are worried about the effects of genetically modified organisms on the environment.

(C) It takes time to gain public support for the application of genetic modification to disease control.

(D) Genetic engineering looks promising in reducing malaria, though there may be unknown consequences.

49. Which of the following best shows the organization of this passage?

(A) Introduction → Comparison → Contrast

(B) Problem → Solution → Potential difficulties

(C) Proposal → Arguments → Counter-arguments

(D) Definition → Examples → Tentative conclusions

50. According to the passage, which of the following is true about malaria parasites?

(A) They are resistant to genetic modification and vaccines.

(B) They reproduce in the human liver and grow stronger there.

(C) They can be found in only one gender of a class of mosquitoes.

(D) They are transmitted to around one million children each year.

51. What does "**that**" in the third paragraph refer to?

(A) Some malaria parasites escaping from the ecosystems.

(B) Malaria parasites becoming immune to the engineered bacterium.

(C) Modified mosquitoes becoming more competitive than the wild ones.

(D) Transmission of malaria being blocked from mosquitoes to humans.

◆ 第貳部分：非選擇題 (占 28 分)

說明：本部分共有二題，請依各題指示作答，答案必須寫在「答案卷」上，並標明大題號 (一、二)。作答務必使用筆尖較粗之黑色墨水的筆書寫，且不得使用鉛筆。

一、中譯英 (占 8 分)

說明：1. 請將以下中文句子譯成正確、通順、達意的英文，並將答案寫在「答案卷」上。
2. 請依序作答，並標明子題號 (1、2)。每題 4 分，共 8 分。

1. 食用過多油炸食物可能會導致學童體重過重，甚至更嚴重的健康問題。
2. 因此，家長與老師應該共同合作，找出處理這個棘手議題的有效措施。

二、英文作文 (占 20 分)

說明：1. 依提示在「答案卷」上寫一篇英文作文。
2. 文長至少 120 個單詞 (words)。

提示：下圖呈現的是美國某高中的全體學生每天進行各種活動的時間分配，請寫一篇至少 120 個單詞的英文作文。文分兩段，第一段描述該圖所呈現之特別現象；第二段請說明整體而言，你一天的時間分配與該高中全體學生的異同，並說明其理由。

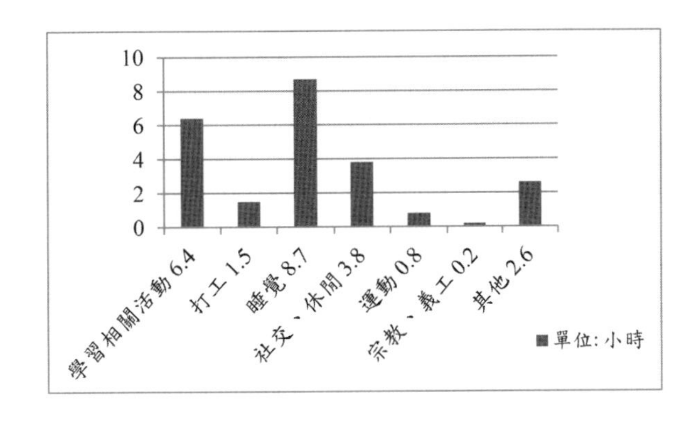

Notes

102 學年度　指考英文試題

◆ 第壹部分：單選題 (占 72 分)

一、詞彙題 (占 10 分)

說明：第 1 題至第 10 題，每題有 4 個選項，其中只有一個是正確或最適當的選項，請畫記在答案卡之「選擇題答案區」。各題答對者，得 1 分；答錯、未作答或畫記多於一個選項者，該題以零分計算。

1. Industrial waste must be carefully handled, or it will ________ the public water supply.
(A) contaminate　(B) facilitate　(C) legitimate　(D) manipulate

2. John's vision was direct, concrete and simple and he recorded ________ the incidents of everyday life.
(A) universally　(B) scarcely　(C) passively　(D) faithfully

3. The government cannot find a good reason to ________ its high expenses on weapons, especially when the number of people living in poverty is so high.
(A) abolish　(B) escort　(C) justify　(D) mingle

4. The writing teacher has found that reading fantasies such as J. K. Rowling's *Harry Potter* may inspire her students to think and write with ________.
(A) creativity　(B) generosity　(C) superstition　(D) foundation

5. Since several child ________ cases were reported on the TV news, the public has become more aware of the issue of domestic violence.
(A) blunder　(B) abuse　(C) essence　(D) defect

6. Helen's doctor suggested that she undergo a heart surgery. But she decided to ask for a second ________ from another doctor.
(A) purpose　(B) statement　(C) opinion　(D) excuse

7. All candidates selected after ________ screening will be further invited to an interview, after which the final admission decision will be made.
(A) preliminary　(B) affectionate　(C) controversial　(D) excessive

8. To prevent terrorist attacks, the security guards at the airport check all luggage carefully to see if there are any ________ items or other dangerous objects.
(A) dynamic　(B) identical　(C) permanent　(D) explosive

9. In the desert, a huge mall with art galleries, theaters, and museums will be constructed to ________ visitors from the heat outside.
(A) convert　(B) defend　(C) shelter　(D) vacuum

10. Judge Harris always has good points to make. Her arguments are very ________ as they are based on logic and sound reasoning.
(A) emphatic　(B) indifferent　(C) dominant　(D) persuasive

二、綜合測驗 (占 10 分)

說明：第 11 題至第 20 題，每題一個空格，請依文意選出最適當的一個選項，請畫記在答案卡之「選擇題答案區」。各題答對者，得 1 分；答錯、未作答或畫記多於一個選項者，該題以零分計算。

第 11 至 15 題為題組

The undersea world isn't as quiet as we thought, according to a New Zealand researcher. Fish can "talk" to each other and make a range of __11__ by vibrating their swim bladder, an internal gas-filled organ used as a resonating chamber to produce or receive sound.

Fish are believed to speak to each other for a number of reasons, such as to attract mates, scare off predators, or give directions to other fish. Damselfish, for example, have been found to make sounds to scare off __12__ fish and even divers. Another discovery about fish sounds is that not all fish are __13__ "talkative." Some species talk a lot, while others don't. The gurnard species has a wide vocal repertoire and keeps up a constant chatter. Codfish, __14__, usually keep silent, except when they are laying eggs. Any goldfish lover who hopes to strike up a conversation with their pet goldfish is __15__. Goldfish have excellent hearing, but they don't make any sound whatsoever. Their excellent hearing isn't associated with vocalization.

11. (A) choices (B) objects (C) accents (D) noises
12. (A) threatened (B) being threatened (C) threatening (D) being threatening
13. (A) merely (B) equally (C) officially (D) favorably
14. (A) by all means (B) for example (C) as a result (D) on the other hand
15. (A) out of luck (B) in the dark (C) off the record (D) on the rise

第 16 至 20 題為題組

The U.S. Postal Service has been struggling financially for some time. It plans to stop delivering mail on Saturdays, __16__ Aug. 1 this year. This decision was announced on Wednesday without congressional approval. __17__ forbidden to do so by the Congress, the agency for the first time will deliver mail only Monday through Friday. It is expected that this __18__ will save about $2 billion a year. In recent years, the postal service has suffered tens of billions of dollars in losses __19__ the increasing popularity of the Internet and e-commerce. The postal service plans to continue Saturday delivery of packages, which remain a profitable and growing part of the delivery business. Post offices would remain open on Saturdays __20__ customers can drop off mail or packages, buy postage stamps, or access their post office boxes. But hours would likely be reduced at thousands of smaller locations.

16. (A) starts (B) started (C) starting (D) to start
17. (A) When (B) Unless (C) Once (D) Lest
18. (A) move (B) round (C) chance (D) fact

19. (A) at	(B) with	(C) under	(D) between
20. (A) so that	(B) as soon as	(C) in case	(D) ever since

三、文意選填 (占 10 分)

說明：第 21 題至第 30 題，每題一個空格，請依文意在文章後所提供的(A)到(L)選項中分別選出最適當者，並將其英文字母代號畫記在答案卡之「選擇題答案區」。各題答對者，得 1 分；答錯、未作答或畫記多於一個選項者，該題以零分計算。

第 21 至 30 題為題組

People who want to experience an overnight stay in arctic-like cold may try the ice hotel—a building of frozen water. Despite the seemingly unattractive prospect of sleeping in a room at minus 15 degrees Celsius, every year about 4,000 people __21__ to an ice hotel in a town in Canada.

The only warm things at the ice hotel are the candles on the bedside tables. The air is so cold that you can see your __22__, which turns to liquid and appears as tiny droplets at the opening of your sleeping bag. The tip of your nose feels numb—almost as though it were __23__. Getting up for a little while—to drink a glass of water or go to the bathroom—seems __24__ without risking death.

Since an adventurous spirit alone is not enough to __25__ more than two hours at the icy hotel, the staff briefs guests on what to wear and how to behave. Normal winter boots and outfits __26__ little protection from the cold. The guests also learn how to __27__ quickly in their arctic sleeping bags and how to prevent eyeglasses from freezing.

For individuals who need to escape the cold for a brief period, there are outdoor hot tubs in the hotel courtyard. You should make sure you have stopped sweating before you go to bed, though, because any __28__ freezes immediately. Guests who are not __29__ can quickly get cold feet and a blocked nose.

Comfort, however, is not the __30__ to stay in the ice hotel. Guests want to feel like polar explorers. For them, the first hot cup of post-expedition coffee is pure delight.

(A) breath	(B) careful	(C) check in	(D) deposit
(E) frozen	(F) impossible	(G) moisture	(H) offer
(I) purpose	(J) sufficient	(K) warm up	(L) withstand

四、篇章結構 (占 10 分)

說明：第 31 題至第 35 題，每題一個空格。請依文意在文章後所提供的(A)到(F)選項中分別選出最適當者，填入空格中，使篇章結構清晰有條理，並將其英文字母代號畫記在答案卡之「選擇題答案區」。各題答對者，得 2 分；答錯、未作答或畫記多於一個選項者，該題以零分計算。

第 31 至 35 題為題組

In the Dutch colonial town later known as Albany, New York, there lived a baker, Van Amsterdam, who was as honest as he could be. He took great care to give his customers exactly what they paid for—not more and not less.

One Saint Nicholas Day morning, when the baker was just ready for business, the door of his shop flew open. ___31___ She asked for a dozen of the baker's Saint Nicholas cookies. Van Amsterdam counted out twelve cookies. But the woman insisted that a dozen is thirteen. Van Amsterdam was not a man to bear foolishness. He refused. The woman turned to go without the cookies but she stopped at the door, saying, "Van Amsterdam! However honest you may be, your heart is small and your fist is tight." Then she was gone.

___32___ His bread rose too high or not at all. His pies were sour or too sweet. His cookies were burnt or doughy. His customers soon noticed the difference and slipped away.

A year passed. The baker grew poorer and poorer. Finally, on the day before Saint Nicholas Day, no customer came to his shop. ___33___

That night, the baker had a dream. He saw Saint Nicholas pulling out gifts from his baskets for a crowd of happy children. No matter how many presents Nicholas handed out, there were always more to give. Then somehow, Saint Nicholas turned into the old woman with the long black shawl!

___34___ He suddenly realized that he always gave his customers exactly what they paid for, "But why *not* give more?"

The next morning, on Saint Nicholas Day, the baker rose early to make cookies. And to his surprise, the cookies were as fine as they could be. When he had just finished, the old woman appeared at his door again. She asked for a dozen of Van Amsterdam's Saint Nicholas cookies. ___35___

When people heard he counted thirteen as a dozen, he had more customers than ever and became wealthy. The practice then spread to other towns as a common custom.

(A) Van Amsterdam awoke with a start.

(B) In walked an old woman wrapped in a long black shawl.

(C) The more he took from the baskets, the more they seemed to hold.

(D) From that day, everything went wrong in Van Amsterdam's bakery.

(E) In great excitement, Van Amsterdam counted out twelve cookies—and one more.

(F) Staring at his unsold Saint Nicholas cookies, he prayed that Saint Nicholas could help him.

五、閱讀測驗 (占 32 分)

說明：第 36 題至第 51 題，每題請分別根據各篇文章之文意選出最適當的一個選項，請畫記在答案卡之「選擇題答案區」。各題答對者，得 2 分；答錯、未作答或畫記多於一個選項者，該題以零分計算。

第 36 至 39 題為題組

All pop artists like to say that they owe their success to their fans. In the case of British band SVM, it's indeed true. The band is currently recording songs because 358 fans contributed the £100,000 needed for the project. The arrangement came via MMC, an online record label that uses Web-based, social-network-style "crowd-funding" to finance its acts.

Here's how it works: MMC posts demos and videos of 10 artists on its website, and users are invited to invest from £10 to £1,000 in the ones they most enjoy or think are most likely to become popular. Once an act reaches £100,000, the financing process is completed, and the money is used to pay for recording and possibly a concert tour. Profits from resulting music sales, concerts, and merchandise are split three ways: investors get to divide 40%; another 40% goes to MMC; the artist pockets 20%. The payoff for investors can be big. One fan in France who contributed £4,250 got his money back 22 times over.

Crowd-funding musical acts is not new. But MMC takes the concept to another level. First of all, investors can get cash rather than just goodies like free downloads or tickets. Also, MMC is a record label. It has the means to get its music distributed around the world and to market artists effectively. "Artists need professional support," says the CEO of MMC's international division.

While digital technology and the Net have created a do-it-yourself boom among musicians, **success is still a long shot**. Out of the 20,000 records released in the U.S. in 2009, only 14 DIY acts made it to the Top 200. Also, with less revenue from recorded music, music companies have become less likely to take risks, which has led to fewer artists receiving funding. The crowd-funding model, however, allows for more records to be made by spreading risk among hundreds of backers. And the social-network aspect of the site helps expand fan bases; that is, investors become a promotional army.

36. Which of the following titles best expresses the main idea of the passage?

(A) Web-based Music Production (B) Fundraising for Music Companies

(C) Music Fans Profiting from Investments (D) Crowd-funding in the Music Industry

37. How much money does a band have to raise via MMC to have their music recorded?

(A) £10. (B) £1,000. (C) £4,250. (D) £100,000.

38. Which of the following statements is true about MMC?

(A) It has helped many do-it-yourself musicians get to the Top 200.

(B) There are works of fourteen artists posted at a time on its website.

(C) It allows fans to provide financial support to the musicians they like.

(D) The biggest share of its profits from a crowd-funding project goes to the musician.

39. What does the author mean by "**success is still a long shot**" in the fourth paragraph?

(A) Success is everlasting in effect.

(B) Success is not easy to achieve.

(C) Success often starts with one big shot.

(D) Success should be every musician's long-term goal.

第 40 至 43 題為題組

In science fiction TV programs such as Star Trek, tractor beams are used to tow spaceships and move objects. For years, scientists have labored to replicate this feat. In 2013, they succeeded. A team of British and Czech scientists, led by Dr. Tomas Cizmar, say they have created a real-life "tractor beam," like the kind from Star Trek, which uses a beam of light to attract objects, at least at a microscopic level.

Light manipulation techniques have existed since the 1970s, but this is thought to be the first time a light beam has been used to draw objects towards a light source. Usually when microscopic objects are hit by a beam of light, they are forced along the direction of the beam. After many years' research, Dr. Cizmar's team discovered a technique that allows for the radiant force of light to be reversed and to use the negative force to draw out certain particles.

Dr. Cizmar says that even though it is a few years away from practical use, the technology has huge potential for medical research. In particular, the tractor beam is highly selective in the particles it can attract, so it can pick up particles that have specific properties, such as size or composition, in a mixture. "Eventually, this could be used to separate white blood cells, for example," Dr. Cizmar told BBC News.

It has been a primary plot device in science fiction TV programs and movies to allow objects like spaceships to be trapped in a beam of light. But Dr. Cizmar said this particular technique would not eventually lead to **that**. A transfer of energy happens in the process. On a microscopic scale that is OK, but on a large scale it would cause huge problems. A large object could be destroyed by the heating, which results from the massive amount of energy necessary to pull it.

40. What is this passage mainly about?
(A) The application of lighting technology in modern society.
(B) The uses and limitations of a scientific invention by a research team.
(C) The adoption of light manipulation techniques in medical treatment.
(D) The influences and effects of scientific developments on science fiction.

41. Which of the following is true about Dr. Cizmar's tractor beam?
(A) It moves big objects as the tractor beam did in Star Trek.
(B) It is the first light beam device that pushes objects forward.
(C) It relies on negative force to pull out specific kinds of particles.
(D) It is currently being used for separating blood cells in medical research.

42. What does "**that**" in the last paragraph refer to?
(A) Transferring a massive amount of energy.
(B) Making science fiction programs and movies.
(C) Burning a large object into ashes.
(D) Capturing spaceships in a beam of light.

43. What is the tone of this passage?
(A) Objective.
(B) Suspicious.
(C) Admiring.
(D) Pessimistic.

第 44 至 47 題為題組

Grace Wambui, a 14-year-old pupil in Nairobi, had never touched a tablet computer. But it took her only about one minute to work out how to use one when such devices arrived at Amaf School in Kawangware, a slum in the Kenyan capital. Teaching used to be conducted with a blackboard and a handful of tattered textbooks. Now children in groups of five take turns to swipe the touch screen of the devices, which are loaded with a multimedia version of Kenya's syllabus.

The tablets at Amaf School are part of a pilot project run by eLimu, a technology start-up. If it and other firms are right, tablets and other digital devices may soon be the rule in African schools. Many are betting on a boom in digital education in Kenya and elsewhere. Some executives even expect it to take off like M-Pesa, Kenya's hugely successful mobile-money service.

Such growth in digital education would be timely. The flood of new pupils has overwhelmed state schools, which were already understaffed, underfunded and poorly managed. The prospect of Africa's 300 million pupils learning digitally has caught the attention of global technology giants. Amazon has seen sales of its Kindle e-readers in Africa increase tenfold in the past year. Intel has been helping African governments buy entry-level computers. In Nigeria, Intel brought together a publisher and a telecom carrier to provide exam-preparation tools over mobile phones, a service that has become hugely popular.

A bigger question is whether digital tools actually improve education. Early results are encouraging. In Ghana, reading skills improved measurably among 350 children that had been given Kindle e-readers. In Ethiopia, in the absence of teachers, children figured out how to use tablets and learned the English ABCs. At Amaf School, average marks in science went from 58 to 73 in a single term.

44. Which of the following is the best title for this passage?
(A) The Bestseller in Africa (B) Problems Plaguing Education in Africa
(C) Schools in Africa Are Going Digital (D) Tablet Computers Are in Great Demand in Kenya

45. What is the author trying to convey in citing Grace Wambui's case?
(A) Grace is a genius in computer skills. (B) The tablet computer is very user-friendly.
(C) The delivery system in Kenya is very poor. (D) Tablet computers are common in Kawangware.

46. According to the passage, what is eLimu?
(A) A company. (B) A computer program.
(C) An e-book. (D) An educational project.

47. According to the passage, which of the following is true about education in Africa?
(A) The number of students keeps dropping in recent years.
(B) There are more than enough teachers for traditional classroom teaching.
(C) Students have received Kindle e-readers donated by Amazon to improve reading.
(D) Early results from use of digital tools in teaching are quite positive in some countries.

第 48 至 51 題為題組

In the Spartathlon, one of the world's toughest ultra-marathons, runners run 245 km, about six marathons, within 36 hours. The runners start in Athens, and run all the way to historical Sparta.

The Spartathlon's heritage goes back to 490 B.C., when Pheidippides, an Athenian, made the journey to Sparta to ask the Spartans for help in fighting the invading Persians. It is recorded that he reached Sparta on the day after he left Athens. In 1982, this story sparked the interest of a British air-force officer and long-distance runner called John Foden, who wondered if it really was possible to run from Athens to Sparta and arrive the next day. With four other officers, Foden decided to see for himself; after a 36-hour slog they arrived in Sparti, as the town is now called. That achievement inspired the organization of the first Spartathlon a year later.

The Spartathlon's attraction has two sources. The first is the difficulty of finishing it. The Spartathlon is not the most difficult race, but it combines lots of different tests. There is the heat of the Greek day, and then the plunge in temperatures when darkness falls. There are climbs: the route includes a series of ascents, among them a 1,200-meter mountain pass in the dead of night. Above all, there is the relentless pressure of the clock. The second reason is that the idea of retracing Pheidippides's footsteps still grips many participants. It feels like racing in history, passing through places where history began.

As finishers receive a laurel wreath and water from schoolgirls, many are overjoyed with emotion. However, **the euphoria is fleeting**. Within a few minutes, their joints and muscles start to seize up: after the race, Sparti resembles the set of a zombie film as participants lumber slowly around on legs that will not bend. But the itch to do it all over again soon appears.

48. What is the second paragraph mainly about?

(A) The background of John Foden.
(B) The route of an ultra-marathon.
(C) The origin of the Spartathlon.
(D) The story of Pheidippides in ancient Athens.

49. Why do ultra-runners choose the Spartathlon?

(A) It is the most classical ultra-marathon in the world.
(B) Runners feel like racing through history.
(C) Their personal problems will be solved in the race.
(D) They have to finish all the tests in one day.

50. What does "**the euphoria is fleeting**" in the last paragraph mean?

(A) The feeling of triumph will last forever.
(B) The race is incomprehensibly difficult to finish.
(C) The fatigue after the race is overwhelming.
(D) The excitement of finishing the race is soon gone.

51. According to the passage, which of the following statements is true about the Spartathlon?

(A) The Spartathlon was first organized in 1983.

(B) The event of the Spartathlon was made into a movie.

(C) After completing the race, many decide not to try it again.

(D) The runners have to endure high temperature day and night.

◆ 第貳部分：非選擇題 (占 28 分)

說明：本部分共有二題，請依各題指示作答，答案必須寫在「答案卷」上，並標明大題號 (一、二)。
作答務必使用筆尖較粗之黑色墨水的筆書寫，且不得使用鉛筆。

一、中譯英 (占 8 分)

說明：1. 請將以下中文句子譯成正確、通順、達意的英文，並將答案寫在「答案卷」上。
2. 請依序作答，並標明子題號 (1、2)。每題 4 分，共 8 分。

1. 對現今的許多學生而言，在課業與課外活動間取得平衡是一大挑戰。

2. 有效的時間管理是每位有責任感的學生必須學習的首要課題。

二、英文作文 (占 20 分)

說明：1. 依提示在「答案卷」上寫一篇英文作文。
2. 文長至少 120 個單詞 (words)。

提示：以下有兩項即將上市之新科技產品：

產品一：隱形披風 (invisibility cloak) 

穿上後頓時隱形，旁人看不到你的存在；同時，隱形披風會保護你，讓你水火不侵。

產品二：智慧型眼鏡 (smart glasses) 

具有掃瞄透視功能，戴上後即能看到障礙物後方的生物；同時能完整紀錄你所經歷過的場景。

如果你有機會獲贈其中一項產品，你會選擇哪一項？請以此為主題，寫一篇至少 120 個單詞的英文作文。文分兩段，第一段說明你的選擇及理由，並舉例說明你將如何使用這項產品。第二段說明你不選擇另一項產品的理由及該項產品可能衍生的問題。

Notes

101 學年度　指考英文試題

◆ 第壹部分：單選題 (占 72 分)

一、詞彙題 (占 10 分)

說明：第 1 題至第 10 題，每題有 4 個選項，其中只有一個是正確或最適當的選項，請畫記在答案卡之「選擇題答案區」。各題答對者，得 1 分；答錯、未作答或畫記多於一個選項者，該題以零分計算。

1. Since it hasn't rained for months, there is a water ________ in many parts of the country.
   (A) resource　(B) deposit　(C) shortage　(D) formula

2. The problem with Larry is that he doesn't know his limitations; he just ________ he can do everything.
   (A) convinces　(B) disguises　(C) assumes　(D) evaluates

3. Agnes seems to have a ________ personality. Almost everyone is immediately attracted to her when they first see her.
   (A) clumsy　(B) durable　(C) furious　(D) magnetic

4. Jason always ________ in finishing a task no matter how difficult it may be. He hates to quit halfway in anything he does.
   (A) persists　(B) motivates　(C) fascinates　(D) sacrifices

5. Poor ________ has caused millions of deaths in developing countries where there is only a limited amount of food.
   (A) reputation　(B) nutrition　(C) construction　(D) stimulation

6. The helicopters ________ over the sea, looking for the divers who had been missing for more than 30 hours.
   (A) tackled　(B) rustled　(C) strolled　(D) hovered

7. One of the tourist attractions in Japan is its hot spring ________, where guests can enjoy relaxing baths and beautiful views.
   (A) resorts　(B) hermits　(C) galleries　(D) faculties

8. When a young child goes out and commits a crime, it is usually the parents who should be held ________ for the child's conduct.
   (A) eligible　(B) dispensable　(C) credible　(D) accountable

9. Since you have not decided on the topic of your composition, it's still ________ to talk about how to write your conclusion.
   (A) preventive　(B) premature　(C) productive　(D) progressive

10. Human rights are fundamental rights to which a person is ________ entitled, that is, rights that she or he is born with.
    (A) inherently　(B) imperatively　(C) authentically　(D) alternatively

二、綜合測驗(占10分)

說明：第11題至第20題，每題一個空格，請依文意選出最適當的一個選項，請畫記在答案卡之「選擇題答案區」。各題答對者，得1分；答錯、未作答或畫記多於一個選項者，該題以零分計算。

第11至15題為題組

The Nobel Peace Center is located in an old train station building close to the Oslo City Hall and overlooking the harbor. It was officially opened on June 11, 2005 as part of the celebrations to __11__ Norway's centenary as an independent country. It is a center where you can experience and learn about the various Nobel Peace Prize Laureates and their activities __12__ the remarkable history of Alfred Nobel, the founder of the Nobel Prize. In addition, it serves as a meeting place where exhibits, discussions, and reflections __13__ to war, peace, and conflict resolution are in focus. The Center combines exhibits and films with digital communication and interactive installations and has already received attention for its use of state-of-the-art technology. Visitors are welcome to experience the Center __14__ or join a guided tour. Since its opening, the Nobel Peace Center has been educating, inspiring and entertaining its visitors __15__ exhibitions, activities, lectures, and cultural events. The Center is financed by private and public institutions.

11. (A) help (B) solve (C) take (D) mark
12. (A) so much as (B) as well as (C) in spite of (D) on behalf of
13. (A) related (B) limited (C) addicted (D) contributed
14. (A) in this regard (B) one on one (C) on their own (D) by and large
15. (A) among (B) regarding (C) including (D) through

第16至20題為題組

In 1985, a riot at a Brussels soccer match occurred, in which many fans lost their lives. The __16__ began 45 minutes before the start of the European Cup final. The British team was scheduled to __17__ the Italian team in the game. Noisy British fans, after setting off some rockets and fireworks to cheer for __18__ team, broke through a thin wire fence and started to attack the Italian fans. The Italians, in panic, __19__ the main exit in their section when a six-foot concrete wall collapsed.

By the end of the night, 38 soccer fans had died and 437 were injured. The majority of the deaths resulted from people __20__ trampled underfoot or crushed against barriers in the stadium. As a result of this 1985 soccer incident, security measures have since been tightened at major sports competitions to prevent similar events from happening.

16. (A) circumstance (B) sequence (C) tragedy (D) phenomenon
17. (A) oppose to (B) fight over (C) battle for (D) compete against
18. (A) a (B) that (C) each (D) their

19. (A) headed for (B) backed up (C) called out (D) passed on

20. (A) be (B) been (C) being (D) to be

三、文意選填 (占 10 分)

說明：第 21 題至第 30 題，每題一個空格，請依文意在文章後所提供的(A)到(L)選項中分別選出最適當者，並將其英文字母代號畫記在答案卡之「選擇題答案區」。各題答對者，得 1 分；答錯、未作答或畫記多於一個選項者，該題以零分計算。

第 21 至 30 題為題組

The Taiwanese puppet show ("Budaixi") is a distinguished form of performing arts in Taiwan. Although basically hand puppets, the __21__ appear as complete forms, with hands and feet, on an elaborately decorated stage.

The puppet performance is typically __22__ by a small orchestra. The backstage music is directed by the drum player. The drummer needs to pay attention to what is going on in the plot and follow the rhythm of the characters. He also uses the drum to __23__ the other musicians. There are generally around four to five musicians who perform the backstage music. The form of music used is often associated with various performance __24__, including acrobatics and skills like window-jumping, stage movement, and fighting. Sometimes unusual animal puppets also appear on stage for extra __25__, especially for children in the audience.

In general, a show needs two performers. The main performer is generally the chief or __26__ of the troupe. He is the one in charge of the whole show, manipulating the main puppets, singing, and narrating. The __27__ performer manipulates the puppets to coordinate with the main performer. He also changes the costumes of the puppets, and takes care of the stage. The relationship between the main performer and his partner is one of master and apprentice. Frequently, the master trains his sons to eventually __28__ him as puppet masters.

Budaixi troupes are often hired to perform at processions and festivals held in honor of local gods, and on happy __29__ such as weddings, births, and promotions. The main purpose of Budaixi is to __30__ and offer thanks to the deities. The shows also serve as a popular means of folk entertainment.

(A) attracted (B) appeal (C) accompanied (D) conduct
(E) director (F) figures (G) occasions (H) succeed
(I) transparent (J) supporting (K) techniques (L) worship

四、篇章結構 (占 10 分)

說明：第 31 題至第 35 題，每題一個空格。請依文意在文章後所提供的(A)到(F)選項中分別選出最適當者，填入空格中，使篇章結構清晰有條理，並將其英文字母代號畫記在答案卡之「選擇題答案區」。各題答對者，得 2 分；答錯、未作答或畫記多於一個選項者，該題以零分計算。

第 31 至 35 題為題組

All advertising includes an attempt to persuade. ___31___ Even if an advertisement claims to be purely informational, it still has persuasion at its core. The ad informs the consumers with one purpose: to get the consumer to like the brand and, on that basis, to eventually buy the brand. Without this persuasive intent, communication about a product might be news, but it would not be advertising.

Advertising can be persuasive communication not only about a product but also an idea or a person. ___32___ Although political ads are supposed to be concerned with the public welfare, they are paid for and they all have a persuasive intent. ___33___ A Bush campaign ad, for instance, did not ask anyone to buy anything, yet it attempted to persuade American citizens to view George Bush favorably. ___34___ Critics of President Clinton's health care plan used advertising to influence lawmakers and defeat the government's plan.

___35___ For instance, the international organization Greenpeace uses advertising to get their message out. In the ads, they warn people about serious pollution problems and the urgency of protecting the environment. They, too, are selling something and trying to make a point.

(A) Political advertising is one example.
(B) To put it another way, ads are communication designed to get someone to do something.
(C) Advertising can be the most important source of income for the media through which it is conducted.
(D) They differ from commercial ads in that political ads "sell" candidates rather than commercial goods.
(E) Aside from campaign advertising, political advertising is also used to persuade people to support or oppose proposals.
(F) In addition to political parties, environmental groups and human rights organizations also buy advertising to persuade people to accept their way of thinking.

五、閱讀測驗 (占 32 分)

說明：第 36 題至第 51 題，每題請分別根據各篇文章之文意選出最適當的一個選項，請畫記在答案卡之「選擇題答案區」。各題答對者，得 2 分；答錯、未作答或畫記多於一個選項者，該題以零分計算。

第 36 至 39 題為題組

A sense of humor is something highly valued. A person who has a great sense of humor is often considered to be happy and socially confident. However, humor is a double-edged sword. It can forge better relationships and help you cope with life, but sometimes it can also damage self-esteem and antagonize others.

People who use bonding humor tell jokes and generally lighten the mood. They're perceived as being good at reducing the tension in uncomfortable situations. They often make fun of their common experiences, and sometimes they may even laugh off their own misfortunes. The basic message they deliver is: We're all alike, we find the same things funny, and we're all in this together.

Put-down humor, on the other hand, is an aggressive type of humor used to criticize and manipulate others through teasing. When it's aimed against politicians, as it often is, it's hilarious and mostly harmless. But in the real world, it may have a harmful impact. An example of such humor is telling friends an embarrassing story about another friend. When challenged about their teasing, the put-down jokers might claim that they are "just kidding," thus allowing themselves to avoid responsibility. This type of humor, though considered by some people to be socially acceptable, may hurt the feelings of the one being teased and thus take a toll on personal relationships.

Finally, in hate-me humor, the joker is the target of the joke for the amusement of others. This type of humor was used by comedians John Belushi and Chris Farley—both of whom suffered for their success in show business. A small dose of such humor is charming, but routinely offering oneself up to be humiliated erodes one's self-respect, and fosters depression and anxiety.

So it seems that being funny isn't necessarily an indicator of good social skills and well-being. In certain cases, it may actually have a negative impact on interpersonal relationships.

36. According to the passage, which group is among the common targets of put-down humor?

(A) Comedians. (B) People who tell jokes.

(C) Politicians. (D) People who are friendly to others.

37. How can people create a relaxing atmosphere through bonding humor?

(A) By laughing at other people's misfortunes.

(B) By joking about experiences that they all have.

(C) By revealing their own personal relationships.

(D) By making fun of unique experiences of their friends.

38. According to the passage, which of the following is true about John Belushi and Chris Farley?

(A) They suffered from over-dosage of anxiety pills.

(B) They often humiliated other people on the stage.

(C) They were successful in their careers as comedians.

(D) They managed to rebuild their self-respect from their shows.

39. What is the message that the author is trying to convey?

(A) Humor deserves to be studied carefully. (B) Humor has both its bright side and dark side.

(C) Humor is a highly valued personality trait. (D) Humor can be learned in many different ways.

第 40 至 43 題為題組

On June 23, 2010, a Sunny Airlines captain with 32 years of experience stopped his flight from departing. He was deeply concerned about a balky power component that might eliminate all electrical power on his trans-Pacific flight. Despite his valid concerns, Sunny Airlines' management pressured him to fly the airplane, over the ocean, at night. When he refused to jeopardize the safety of his passengers, Sunny Airlines' security escorted him out of the airport, and threatened to arrest his crew if they did not cooperate.

Besides that, five more Sunny Airlines pilots also refused to fly the aircraft, citing their own concerns about the safety of the plane. It turned out the pilots were right: the power component was faulty and the plane was removed from service and, finally, fixed. Eventually a third crew operated the flight, hours later. In this whole process, Sunny Airlines pressured their highly experienced pilots to ignore their safety concerns and fly passengers over the Pacific Ocean at night in a plane that needed maintenance. Fortunately for all of us, these pilots stood strong and would not be intimidated.

Don't just take our word that this happened. Please research this yourself and learn the facts. Here's a starting point: www.SunnyAirlinePilot.org. Once you review this shocking information, please keep in mind that while their use of Corporate Security to remove a pilot from the airport is a new procedure, the intimidation of flight crews is becoming commonplace at Sunny Airlines, with documented events occurring on a weekly basis.

The flying public deserves the highest levels of safety. No airlines should maximize their revenues by pushing their employees to move their airplanes regardless of the potential human cost. Sunny Airlines' pilots are committed to resisting any practices that compromise your safety for economic gain. We've been trying to fix these problems behind the scenes for quite some time; now we need your help. Go to www.SunnyAirlinePilot.org to get more information and find out what you can do.

40. According to the passage, what happened to the captain after he refused to fly the aircraft?
(A) He was asked to find another pilot to replace his position.
(B) He was forced to leave the airport by security staff of Sunny Airlines.
(C) He was made to help the Airlines find out what was wrong with the plane.
(D) He was fired for refusing to fly the plane and abandoning the passengers.

41. What is the main purpose of the passage?
(A) To maximize Sunny Airlines' revenues.
(B) To introduce Sunny Airlines' pilot training programs.
(C) To review plans for improving Sunny Airlines' service.
(D) To expose problems with Sunny Airlines' security practices.

42. What happened to the aircraft after the pilots refused to operate the flight?
(A) It was found to be too old for any more flight service.
(B) Its mechanical problem was detected and finally repaired.
(C) It was removed from the airport for a week-long checkup.
(D) Its power component problem remained and no crew would operate the flight.

43. By whom was the passage most likely written?

(A) Sunny Airlines security guards.

(B) Sunny Airlines personnel manager.

(C) Members of Sunny Airlines pilot organization.

(D) One of the passengers of the Sunny Airlines flight.

第 44 至 47 題為題組

Angry Birds is a video game developed by Finnish computer game developer Rovio Mobile. Inspired primarily by a sketch of stylized wingless birds, the game was first released for Apple's mobile operating system in December 2009. Since then, over 12 million copies of the game have been purchased from Apple's App Store.

With its fast-growing popularity worldwide, the game and its characters—angry birds and their enemy pigs—have been referenced in television programs throughout the world. The Israeli comedy *A Wonderful Country*, one of the nation's most popular TV programs, satirized recent failed Israeli—Palestinian peace attempts by featuring the Angry Birds in peace negotiations with the pigs. Clips of the segment went **viral**, getting viewers from all around the world. American television hosts Conan O'Brien, Jon Stewart, and Daniel Tosh have referenced the game in comedy sketches on their respective series, *Conan*, *The Daily Show*, and *Tosh.0*. Some of the game's more notable fans include Prime Minister David Cameron of the United Kingdom, who plays the iPad version of the game, and author Salman Rushdie, who is believed to be "something of a master at *Angry Birds*."

Angry Birds and its characters have also been featured in advertisements in different forms. In March 2011, the characters began appearing in a series of advertisements for Microsoft's Bing search engine. In the same year, Nokia projected an advertisement in Austin, Texas that included the game's characters on a downtown building for its new handset. Later, a T-Mobile advertisement filmed in Spain included a real-life mock-up of the game in a city plaza. Nokia also used the game in Malaysia to promote an attempt to set a world record for the largest number of people playing a single mobile game.

Angry Birds has even inspired works of philosophical analogy. A five-part essay entitled "Angry Birds Yoga—How to Eliminate the Green Pigs in Your Life" was written by Giridhari Dasar in Brazil, utilizing the characters and gameplay mechanics to interpret various concepts of yoga philosophy. The piece attracted much media attention for its unique method of philosophical presentation.

44. What is the purpose of the passage?

(A) To explain how the video game *Angry Birds* was devised.

(B) To investigate why *Angry Birds* has quickly become well-liked.

(C) To introduce *Angry Birds* characters in TV programs and advertisements.

(D) To report on the spread of *Angry Birds* in different media around the world.

45. Which of the following is closest in meaning to the word "**viral**" in the second paragraph?

(A) Apparent. (B) Sarcastic. (C) Exciting. (D) Popular.

46. According to the passage, which of the following people is good at playing *Angry Birds*?

(A) Giridhari Dasar. (B) Conan O'Brien. (C) Salman Rushdie. (D) Daniel Tosh.

47. Which of the following is true about the use of *Angry Birds*, according to the passage?

(A) It has been cited by UK Prime Minister to illustrate political issues.

(B) Its characters are used in advertisements mainly for Apple's products.

(C) Its real-life mock-up has appeared in an advertisement for mobile phones.

(D) It has been developed into a film about the life of a Brazilian yoga master.

第 48 至 51 題為題組

Demolition is the tearing-down of buildings and other structures. You can level a five-story building easily with excavators and wrecking balls, but when you need to bring down a 20-story skyscraper, explosive demolition is the preferred method for safely demolishing the huge structure.

In order to demolish a building safely, blasters must map out a careful plan ahead of time. The first step is to examine architectural blueprints of the building to determine how the building is put together. Next, the blaster crew tours the building, jotting down notes about the support structure on each floor. Once they have gathered all the data they need, the blasters devise a plan of attack. They decide what explosives to use, where to position them in the building, and how to time their explosions.

Generally speaking, blasters will explode the major support columns on the lower floors first and then on a few upper stories. In a 20-story building, the blasters might blow the columns on the first and second floor, as well as the 12th and 15th floors. In most cases, blowing the support structures on the lower floors is sufficient for collapsing the building, but loading explosives on upper floors helps break the building material into smaller pieces as it falls. This makes for easier cleanup following the blast. The main challenge in bringing a building down is controlling the direction in which it falls. To topple the building towards the north, the blasters set off explosives on the north side of the building first. By controlling the way it collapses, a blasting crew will be able to tumble the building over on one side, into a parking lot or other open area. This sort of blast is the easiest to execute, and it is generally the safest way to go.

48. What do the blasters need to do in preparing for the demolition of a building, according to the passage?

(A) Study the structure of the building. (B) Hire an experienced tour guide.

(C) Make a miniature of the building. (D) Consult the original architect.

49. In most cases, where does the explosion start in the building during its destruction?

(A) The topmost layer. (B) The upper floors. (C) The lower levels. (D) The basement.

50. According to the following diagram, which part of the target building should the demolition team explode first to safely bring it down?

(A) The east side. (B) The west side.
(C) The south side. (D) The north side.

51. What is the passage mainly about?

(A) How to execute demolition at the right time.
(B) How to collapse a building with explosives.
(C) How to use explosives for different purposes.
(D) How to destroy a building with minimum manpower.

◆ 第貳部分：非選擇題 (占 28 分)

說明：本部分共有二題，請依各題指示作答，答案必須寫在「答案卷」上，並標明大題號 (一、二)。作答務必使用筆尖較粗之黑色墨水的筆書寫，且不得使用鉛筆。

一、中譯英 (占 8 分)

說明：1. 請將以下中文句子譯成正確、通順、達意的英文，並將答案寫在「答案卷」上。
2. 請依序作答，並標明子題號 (1、2)。每題 4 分，共 8 分。

1. 有些我們認為安全的包裝食品可能含有對人體有害的成分。
2. 為了我們自身的健康，在購買食物前我們應仔細閱讀包裝上的說明。

二、英文作文 (占 20 分)

說明：1. 依提示在「答案卷」上寫一篇英文作文。
2. 文長至少 120 個單詞 (words)。

提示：請以運動為主題，寫一篇至少 120 個單詞的文章，說明你最常從事的運動是什麼。文分兩段，第一段描述這項運動如何進行 (如地點、活動方式、及可能需要的相關用品等)，第二段說明你從事這項運動的原因及這項運動對你生活的影響。

Notes

100 學年度　指考英文試題

◆ 第壹部分：單選題 (占 72 分)

一、詞彙題 (占 10 分)

說明：第 1 題至第 10 題，每題有 4 個選項，其中只有一個是正確或最適當的選項，請畫記在答案卡之「選擇題答案區」。各題答對者，得 1 分；答錯、未作答或畫記多於一個選項者，該題以零分計算。

1. Many people think cotton is the most comfortable ________ to wear in hot weather.
(A) fabric　(B) coverage　(C) software　(D) wardrobe

2. Because of the engine problem in the new vans, the auto company decided to ________ them from the market.
(A) recall　(B) clarify　(C) transform　(D) polish

3. After a day's tiring work, Peter walked ________ back to his house, hungry and sleepy.
(A) splendidly　(B) thoroughly　(C) wearily　(D) vaguely

4. In team sports, how all members work as a group is more important than how they perform ________.
(A) frequently　(B) typically　(C) individually　(D) completely

5. Despite her physical disability, the young blind pianist managed to overcome all ________ to win the first prize in the international contest.
(A) privacy　(B) ambition　(C) fortunes　(D) obstacles

6. Each of the planets in the solar system circles around the sun in its own ________, and this prevents them from colliding with each other.
(A) entry　(B) haste　(C) orbit　(D) range

7. Professor Wang is well known for his contributions to the field of economics. He has been ________ to help the government with its financial reform programs.
(A) recruited　(B) contradicted　(C) mediated　(D) generated

8. Most earthquakes are too small to be noticed; they can only be detected by ________ instruments.
(A) manual　(B) sensitive　(C) portable　(D) dominant

9. With Wikileaks releasing secrets about governments around the world, many countries are worried that their national security information might be ________.
(A) relieved　(B) disclosed　(C) condensed　(D) provoked

10. I'm afraid we can't take your word, for the evidence we've collected so far is not ________ with what you said.
(A) familiar　(B) consistent　(C) durable　(D) sympathetic

二、綜合測驗 (占 10 分)

說明：第 11 題至第 20 題，每題一個空格，請依文意選出最適當的一個選項，請畫記在答案卡之「選擇題答案區」。各題答對者，得 1 分；答錯、未作答或畫記多於一個選項者，該題以零分計算。

第 11 至 15 題為題組

Handling customer claims is a common task for most business firms. These claims include requests to exchange merchandise, requests for refunds, requests that work __11__, and other requests for adjustments. Most of these claims are approved because they are legitimate. However, some requests for adjustment must be __12__, and an adjustment refusal message must be sent. Adjustment refusals are negative messages for the customer. They are necessary when the customer is __13__ or when the vendor has done all that can reasonably or legally be expected.

An adjustment refusal message requires your best communication skills __14__ it is bad news to the receiver. You have to refuse the claim and retain the customer __15__. You may refuse the request for adjustment and even try to sell the customer more merchandise or service. All this is happening when the customer is probably angry, disappointed, or inconvenienced.

11. (A) is correct (B) to be correct (C) is corrected (D) be corrected
12. (A) retailed (B) denied (C) appreciated (D) elaborated
13. (A) at fault (B) on call (C) in tears (D) off guard
14. (A) till (B) unless (C) because (D) therefore
15. (A) by and large (B) over and over (C) at the same time (D) for the same reason

第 16 至 20 題為題組

People may express their feelings differently on different occasions. Cultures sometimes vary greatly in this regard. A group of researchers in Japan, __16__, studied the facial reactions of students to a horror film. When the Japanese students watched the film __17__ the teacher present, their faces showed only the slightest hints of reaction. But when they thought they were alone (though they __18__ by a secret camera), their faces twisted into vivid mixes of anguished distress, fear, and disgust.

The study also shows that there are several unspoken rules about how feelings should be __19__ shown on different occasions. One of the most common rules is minimizing the show of emotion. This is the Japanese norm for feelings of distress __20__ someone in authority, which explains why the students masked their upset with a poker face in the experiment.

16. (A) as usual (B) in some cases (C) to be frank (D) for example
17. (A) of (B) as (C) from (D) with
18. (A) were being taped (B) had taped (C) are taping (D) have been taped
19. (A) rarely (B) similarly (C) properly (D) critically

20. (A) with the help of (B) in the presence of (C) on top of (D) in place of

三、文意選填 (占 10 分)

說明：第 21 題至第 30 題，每題一個空格，請依文意在文章後所提供的(A)到(L)選項中分別選出最適當者，並將其英文字母代號畫記在答案卡之「選擇題答案區」。各題答對者，得 1 分；答錯、未作答或畫記多於一個選項者，該題以零分計算。

第 21 至 30 題為題組

The history of the written word goes back 6,000 years. Words express feelings, open doors into the __21__, create pictures of worlds never seen, and allow adventures never dared. Therefore, the original __22__ of words, such as storytellers, poets, and singers, were respected in all cultures in the past.

But now the romance is __23__. Imagination is being surpassed by the instant picture. In a triumphant march, movies, TV, videos, and DVDs are __24__ storytellers and books. A visual culture is taking over the world—at the __25__ of the written word. Our literacy, and with it our verbal and communication skills, are in __26__ decline.

The only category of novel that is __27__ ground in our increasingly visual world is the graphic novel. A growing number of adults and young people worldwide are reading graphic novels, and educators are beginning to realize the power of this __28__. The graphic novel looks like a comic book, but it is longer, more sophisticated, and may come in black and white or multiple __29__ and appear in many sizes. In fact, some of the most interesting, daring, and most heartbreaking art being created right now is being published in graphic novels. Graphic novels __30__ the opportunity to examine the increasingly visual world of communications today while exploring serious social and literary topics. The graphic novel can be used to develop a sense of visual literacy, in much the same way that students are introduced to art appreciation.

(A) expense (B) fading (C) colors (D) research
(E) replacing (F) offer (G) users (H) rapid
(I) gaining (J) medium (K) circular (L) unknown

四、篇章結構 (占 10 分)

說明：第 31 題至第 35 題，每題一個空格。請依文意在文章後所提供的(A)到(F)選項中分別選出最適當者，填入空格中，使篇章結構清晰有條理，並將其英文字母代號畫記在答案卡之「選擇題答案區」。各題答對者，得 2 分；答錯、未作答或畫記多於一個選項者，該題以零分計算。

第 31 至 35 題為題組

The effect of bullying can be serious and even lead to tragedy. Unfortunately, it is still a mostly unresearched area.

___31___ That year two shotgun-wielding students, both of whom had been identified as gifted and who had been bullied for years, killed 13 people, wounded 24 and then committed suicide. A year later an analysis by the US government found that bullying played a major role in more than two-thirds of the campus violence.

___32___ Numerous dictators and invaders throughout history have tried to justify their bullying behavior by claiming that they themselves were bullied. ___33___ Although it is no justification for bullying, many of the worst humans in history have indeed been bullies and victims of bullying.

Since bullying is mostly ignored, it may provide an important clue in crowd behavior and passer-by behavior. ___34___ Many of them have suggested bullying as one of the reasons of this decline in emotional sensitivity and acceptance of violence as normal. When someone is bullied, it is not only the bully and the victim who are becoming less sensitive to violence. ___35___ In this sense, bullying affects not only the bullied but his friends and classmates and the whole society.

(A) Hitler, for example, is claimed to have been a victim of bullying in his childhood.

(B) Campus bullying is becoming a serious problem in some high schools in big cities.

(C) The friends and classmates of the bully and the victim may accept the violence as normal.

(D) Research indicates that bullying may form a chain reaction and the victim often becomes the bully.

(E) Psychologists have been puzzled by the inactivity of crowds and bystanders in urban centers when crimes occur in crowded places.

(F) The link between bullying and school violence has attracted increasing attention since the 1999 tragedy at a Colorado high school.

五、閱讀測驗(占 32 分)

說明：第 36 題至第 51 題，每題請分別根據各篇文章之文意選出最適當的一個選項，請畫記在答案卡之「選擇題答案區」。各題答對者，得 2 分；答錯、未作答或畫記多於一個選項者，該題以零分計算。

第 36 至 39 題為題組

Since the times of the Greeks and Romans, truffles have been used in Europe as delicacies and even as medicines. They are among the most expensive of the world's natural foods, often commanding as much as US$250 to US$450 per pound. Truffles are actually mushrooms, but unusual ones. They live in close association with the roots of specific trees and their fruiting bodies grow underground. This is why they are difficult to find.

Truffles are harvested in Europe with the aid of female pigs or truffle dogs, which are able to detect the strong smell of mature truffles underneath the surface of the ground. Female pigs are especially sensitive to the odor of the truffles because it is similar to the smell given off by male pigs. The use of pigs is risky, though, because of their natural tendency to eat any remotely edible thing. For this reason, dogs have been trained to dig into the ground wherever they find this odor, and they willingly exchange their truffle for a piece of bread and a pat on the head. Some truffle merchants dig for their prizes themselves when they see truffle flies hovering around the base of a tree. Once a site has been discovered, truffles can be collected in subsequent years.

To enjoy the wonderful flavor of what has been described as an earthly jewel, you must eat fresh, uncooked specimens shortly after they have been harvested. The strength of their flavor decreases rapidly with time, and much of it is lost before some truffles reach the market. To preserve them, gourmet experts suggest putting them in closed glass jars in a refrigerator. Another recommendation is to store them whole in bland oil.

36. Why do some people prefer using dogs than pigs in search of truffles?
(A) Dogs have stronger paws to dig. (B) Dogs usually won't eat the truffles found.
(C) Dogs have a better sense of smell than pigs. (D) Dogs are less likely to get excited than pigs.

37. What is the best way to enjoy truffles as a delicacy?
(A) Eating them cooked with pork. (B) Eating them uncooked with bland oil.
(C) Eating them fresh right after being collected. (D) Eating them after being refrigerated.

38. Which of the following statements is true?
(A) Truffles are roots of some old trees.
(B) Truffles can be found only by dogs and pigs.
(C) Truffles send out a strong odor when they mature.
(D) Truffles cannot be collected at the same place repeatedly.

39. Which of the following can be inferred from the passage?
(A) Truffles sold in glass jars are tasteless.
(B) Truffles taste like fruit when eaten fresh.
(C) Truffles are only used for cooking nowadays.
(D) Truffles are expensive because they are difficult to find.

第 40 至 43 題為題組

In an ideal world, people would not test medicines on animals. Such experiments are stressful and sometimes painful for animals, and expensive and time-consuming for people. Yet animal experimentation is still needed to help bridge vast gaps in medical knowledge. That is why there are some 50 to 100 million animals used in research around the world each year.

Europe, on the whole, has the world's most restrictive laws on animal experiments. Even so, its scientists use some 12 million animals a year, most of them mice and rats, for medical research. Official statistics show that just 1.1 million animals are used in research in America each year. But that is misleading. The American authorities do not think mice and rats are worth counting and, as these are the most common laboratory animals, the true figure is much higher. Japan and China have even less comprehensive data than America.

Now Europe is reforming the rules governing animal experiments by restricting the number of animals used in labs. Alternatives to animal testing, such as using human tissue or computer models, are now strongly recommended. In addition, sharing all research results freely should help to reduce the number of animals for scientific use. At present, scientists often share only the results of successful experiments. If their findings do not fit the hypothesis being tested, the work never sees the light of day. This practice means wasting time, money, and animals' lives in endlessly repeating the failed experiments.

Animal experimentation has taught humanity a great deal and saved countless lives. It needs to continue, even if that means animals sometimes suffer. Europe's new measures should eventually both reduce the number of animals used in experiments and improve the way in which scientific research is conducted.

40. What is the main idea of this passage?
(A) The success of animal experiments should be ensured.
(B) Ban on the use of animals in the lab should be enforced.
(C) Greater efforts need to be taken to reduce the number of lab animals.
(D) Scientists should be required to share their research results with each other.

41. Which of the following statements is true about animals used in the lab?
(A) America uses only about 1.1 million lab animals per year.
(B) Europe does not use mice and rats as lab animals at all.
(C) Britain does not use as many lab animals as China does.
(D) Japan has limited data on the number of lab animals used each year.

42. Which of the following is mentioned as an alternative to replace animal experiments?
(A) Statistical studies. (B) Computer models.
(C) DNA planted in animals. (D) Tissue from dead animals.

43. What usually happens to unsuccessful animal experiments?
(A) They are not revealed to the public.
(B) They are made into teaching materials.
(C) They are collected for future publication.
(D) They are not removed from the research topic list.

第 44 至 47 題為題組

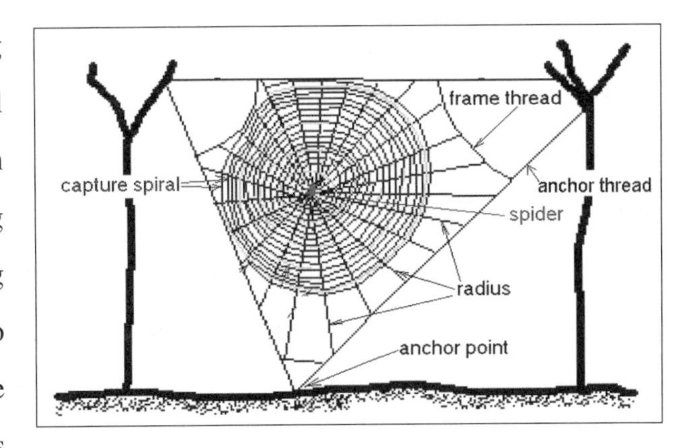

Spider webs are one of the most fascinating examples of animal architecture. The most beautiful and structurally ordered are the orb webs. The main function of the web is to intercept and hold flying prey, such as flies, bees and other insects, long enough for the spider to catch them. In order to do **so**, the threads of the web have to withstand the impact forces from large and heavy prey as well as environmental forces from wind and rain for at least a day in most cases.

The orb web is found to have two main characteristics. The first is its geometry, which consists of an outer frame and a central part from which threads radiate outward. Enclosed in the frame are capture spirals winding round and round from the web center out to the frame. The whole web is in tension and held in place by anchor threads, which connect the frame to the surrounding vegetation or objects. The second and perhaps most important characteristic is the material with which it is built. Spider silk is a kind of natural composite that gives this lightweight fiber a tensile strength comparable to that of steel, while at the same time making it very elastic. Two types of silk threads are used in the web. One is highly elastic and can stretch to almost twice its original length before breaking and, for most types of spiders, is covered in glue. This type is used in the capture spiral for catching and holding prey. The other is stiffer and stronger, and is used for the radius, frames and anchor threads, which allows the web to withstand prey impact and to keep its structural strength through a wide range of environmental conditions.

44. What is this passage mainly about?
(A) The food network in nature. (B) The construction of orb webs.
(C) The network of geometrical studies. (D) The environmental challenges for spider webs.

45. What does the word "**so**" in the first paragraph refer to?
(A) To catch and keep small creatures. (B) To find a good material for the web.
(C) To observe the behavior patterns of spiders. (D) To present a fantastic architecture by animals.

46. Which part of the web is used for supporting the web itself?
(A) The center of the web. (B) The glue on the lines.
(C) The anchor threads. (D) The capture spiral.

47. According to the passage, which statement is true about the silk threads?
(A) They are all sticky and extendable. (B) They are usually strong enough to last for a day.
(C) They remove harmful chemicals from insects. (D) They are made of rare plants in the environment.

第 48 至 51 題為題組

Doctor of Philosophy, usually abbreviated as PhD or Ph.D., is an advanced academic degree awarded by universities. The first Doctor of Philosophy degree was awarded in Paris in 1150, but the degree did not acquire its modern status until the early 19th century. The doctorate of philosophy as it exists today originated at Humboldt University. The German practice was later adopted by American and Canadian universities, eventually becoming common in large parts of the world in the 20th century.

For most of history, even a bachelor's degree at a university was the privilege of a rich few, and many academic staff did not hold doctorates. But as higher education expanded after the Second World War, the number of PhDs increased accordingly. American universities geared up first: By 1970, America was graduating half of the world's PhDs in science and technology. Since then, America's annual output of PhDs has doubled, to 64,000. Other countries are catching up. PhD production has sped up most dramatically in Mexico, Portugal, Italy, and Slovakia. Even Japan, where the number of young people is shrinking, has **churned out** about 46% more PhDs.

Researchers now warn that the supply of PhDs has far outstripped demand. America produced more than 100,000 doctoral degrees between 2005 and 2009, while there were just 16,000 new professorships. In research, the story is similar. Even graduates who find work outside universities may not fare all that well. Statistics show that five years after receiving their degrees, more than 60% of PhDs in Slovakia and more than 45% in Belgium, the Czech Republic, Germany, and Spain are still on temporary contracts. About one-third of Austria's PhD graduates take jobs unrelated to their degrees.

Today, top universities around the world are still picking bright students and grooming them as potential PhDs. After all, it isn't in their interests to turn the smart students away: The more bright students stay at universities, the better it is for academics. But considering the oversupply of PhDs, some people have already begun to wonder whether doing a PhD is a good choice for an individual.

48. In which country did the modern practice of granting doctoral degrees start?
(A) France. (B) Germany. (C) Canada. (D) The U.S.

49. Which of the following words is closest in meaning to "**churned out**" in the second paragraph?
(A) Failed. (B) Warned. (C) Demanded. (D) Produced.

50. Which of the following may be inferred from the third paragraph?
(A) PhD graduates in Austria are not encouraged to work outside university.
(B) Most German PhDs work at permanent jobs immediately after graduation.
(C) It is much easier for American PhD holders to find a teaching position than a research job.
(D) It is more difficult for PhDs to get a permanent job five years after graduation in Slovakia than in Spain.

51. Which of the following best describes the author's attitude toward the increase of PhDs in recent years?

(A) Concerned. (B) Supportive. (C) Indifferent. (D) Optimistic.

◆ 第貳部分：非選擇題 (占 28 分)

說明：本部分共有二題，請依各題指示作答，答案必須寫在「答案卷」上，並標明大題號 (一、二)。作答務必使用筆尖較粗之黑色墨水的筆書寫，且不得使用鉛筆。

一、中譯英 (占 8 分)

說明：1. 請將以下中文句子譯成正確、通順、達意的英文，並將答案寫在「答案卷」上。 2. 請依序作答，並標明子題號 (1、2)。每題 4 分，共 8 分。

1. 日本的核電廠爆炸已經引起全球對核子能源安全的疑慮。
2. 科學家正尋求安全、乾淨又不昂貴的綠色能源，以滿足我們對電的需求。

二、英文作文 (占 20 分)

說明：1. 依提示在「答案卷」上寫一篇英文作文。 2. 文長至少 120 個單詞 (words)。

提示：你認為畢業典禮應該是個溫馨感人、活潑熱鬧、或是嚴肅傷感的場景？請寫一篇英文作文說明你對畢業典禮的看法，第一段寫出畢業典禮對你而言意義是什麼，第二段說明要如何安排或進行活動才能呈現出這個意義。

Notes

99 學年度　指考英文試題

◆ 第壹部分：單選題 (占 72 分)

一、詞彙題 (占 10 分)

說明：第 1 題至第 10 題，每題有 4 個選項，其中只有一個是正確或最適當的選項，請畫記在答案卡之「選擇題答案區」。各題答對者，得 1 分；答錯、未作答或畫記多於一個選項者，該題以零分計算。

1. Chinese is a language with many ________ differences. People living in different areas often speak different dialects.
   (A) sociable　(B) legendary　(C) regional　(D) superior

2. A menu serves to ________ customers about the varieties and prices of the dishes offered by the restaurant.
   (A) appeal　(B) convey　(C) inform　(D) demand

3. Mary and Jane often fight over which radio station to listen to. Their ________ arises mainly from their different tastes in music.
   (A) venture　(B) consent　(C) dispute　(D) temptation

4. The baby polar bear is being ________ studied by the scientists. Every move he makes is carefully observed and documented.
   (A) prosperously　(B) intensively　(C) honorably　(D) originally

5. At twelve, Catherine has won several first prizes in international art competitions. Her talent and skills are ________ for her age.
   (A) comparable　(B) exceptional　(C) indifferent　(D) unconvincing

6. After his superb performance, the musician received a big round of ________ from the appreciative audience.
   (A) vacuum　(B) overflow　(C) applause　(D) spotlight

7. The water company inspects the pipelines and ________ the water supply regularly to ensure the safety of our drinking water.
   (A) exhibits　(B) monitors　(C) interprets　(D) converts

8. This year's East Asia Summit meetings will focus on critical ________ such as energy conservation, food shortages, and global warming.
   (A) issues　(B) remarks　(C) conducts　(D) faculties

9. Having fully recognized Mei-ling's academic ability, Mr. Lin strongly ________ her for admission to the university.
   (A) assured　(B) promoted　(C) estimated　(D) recommended

10. The weatherman has warned about drastic temperature change in the next few days, and suggested that we check the weather on a daily basis and dress ________.
(A) necessarily (B) significantly (C) specifically (D) accordingly

二、綜合測驗 (占 10 分)

說明：第 11 題至第 20 題，每題一個空格，請依文意選出最適當的一個選項，請畫記在答案卡之「選擇題答案區」。各題答對者，得 1 分；答錯、未作答或畫記多於一個選項者，該題以零分計算。

第 11 至 15 題為題組

The sun is an extraordinarily powerful source of energy. In fact, the Earth __11__ 20,000 times more energy from the sun than we currently use. If we used more of this source of heat and light, it __12__ all the power needed throughout the world.

We can harness energy from the sun, or solar energy, in many ways. For instance, many satellites in space are equipped with large panels whose solar cells transform sunlight directly __13__ electric power. These panels are covered with glass and are painted black inside to absorb as much heat as possible.

Solar energy has a lot to offer. To begin with, it is a clean fuel. In contrast, fossil fuels, such as oil or coal, release __14__ substances into the air when they are burned. __15__, fossil fuels will run out, but solar energy will continue to reach the Earth long after the last coal has been mined and the last oil well has run dry.

11. (A) repeats (B) receives (C) rejects (D) reduces
12. (A) supplies (B) has supplied (C) was supplying (D) could supply
13. (A) into (B) from (C) with (D) off
14. (A) diligent (B) harmful (C) usable (D) changeable
15. (A) Otherwise (B) Therefore (C) What's more (D) In comparison

第 16 至 20 題為題組

Signs asking visitors to keep their hands off the art are everywhere in the Louvre Museum, Paris. But one special sculpture gallery invites art lovers to allow their hands to __16__ the works. The Louvre's Tactile Gallery, targeted at the blind and visually __17__, is the only space in the museum where visitors can touch the sculptures, with no guards or alarms to stop them. Its latest exhibit is a __18__ of sculpted lions, snakes, horses and eagles. The 15 animals exhibited are reproductions of famous works found elsewhere in the Louvre. Called "Animals, Symbols of Power," the exhibit __19__ animals that were used by kings and emperors throughout history to symbolize the greatness of their reigns. The exhibit, opened in December 2008, __20__ scheduled to run for about three years. During guided tours on the weekends, children can explore the art with blindfolds on.

16. (A) fix up (B) run over (C) take away (D) knock off
17. (A) impair (B) impairs (C) impaired (D) impairing
18. (A) collection (B) cooperation (C) completion (D) contribution
19. (A) examines (B) protects (C) represents (D) features
20. (A) is (B) being (C) has (D) having

三、文意選填 (占 10 分)

說明：第 21 題至第 30 題，每題一個空格，請依文意在文章後所提供的(A)到(J)選項中分別選出最適當者，並將其英文字母代號畫記在答案卡之「選擇題答案區」。各題答對者，得 1 分；答錯、未作答或畫記多於一個選項者，該題以零分計算。

第 21 至 30 題為題組

Textese (also known as chatspeak, texting language, or txt talk) is a term for the abbreviations and slang most commonly used among young people today. The ___21___ of textese is largely due to the necessary brevity of mobile phone text messaging, though its use is also very common on the Internet, including e-mail and instant messaging.

There are no ___22___ rules for writing textese. However, the common practice is to use single letters, pictures, or numbers to represent whole words. For example, "i <3 u" uses the picture ___23___ of a heart "<3" for "love," and the letter "u" to ___24___ "you." For words which have no common abbreviation, textese users often ___25___ the vowels from a word, and the reader is forced to interpret a string of consonants by re-adding the vowels. Thus, "dictionary" becomes "dctnry," and "keyboard" becomes "kybrd." The reader must interpret the ___26___ words depending on the context in which it is used, as there are many examples of words or phrases which use the same abbreviations. So if someone says "ttyl, lol" they probably mean "talk to you later, lots of love" not "talk to you later, laugh out loud," and if someone says "omg, lol" they most ___27___ mean "oh my god, laugh out loud" not "oh my god, lots of love."

The emergence of textese is clearly due to a desire to type less and to communicate more ___28___ than one can manage without such shortcuts. Yet it has been severely ___29___ as "wrecking our language." Some scholars even consider the use of textese as "irritating" and essentially lazy behavior. They're worried that "sloppy" habits gained while using textese will result in students' growing ___30___ of proper spelling, grammar and punctuation.

(A) quickly (B) criticized (C) likely (D) abbreviated (E) replace
(F) remove (G) standard (H) ignorance (I) popularity (J) symbol

四、篇章結構 (占 10 分)

說明：第 31 題至第 35 題，每題一個空格。請依文意在文章後所提供的(A)到(F)選項中分別選出最適當者，填入空格中，使篇章結構清晰有條理，並將其英文字母代號畫記在答案卡之「選擇題答案區」。各題答對者，得 2 分；答錯、未作答或畫記多於一個選項者，該題以零分計算。

第 31 至 35 題為題組

Do you have trouble getting started in the morning? Do you have problems learning early in the day? If you do, you are not alone. __31__ They learn better at night than they do in the morning.

To investigate when cockroaches learn best, researchers at Vanderbilt University tested the insects for which odor (peppermint or vanilla) they preferred. Most cockroaches preferred the smell of vanilla to that of peppermint at all times. __32__ Therefore, the scientists trained the cockroaches to prefer the peppermint smell by rewarding the insects with a taste of sugar water when they approached a peppermint smell. __33__

When the cockroaches were trained at night, they remembered the new associations (peppermint = sugar water; vanilla = salt water) for up to 48 hours. However, if the cockroaches were trained in the morning, they quickly forgot which smell went with which water. __34__

So, cockroaches learn better at night than they do in the morning. __35__ Because of this, it is likely that information they gather at night will be more useful to them. These experiments provide some clues about the interactions between body rhythms, learning and memory.

(A) When these insects moved toward a vanilla smell, on the other hand, they were punished with a taste of salt.

(B) This result thus shows that the time when they were trained decided the effect of their learning.

(C) They are often more active and tend to search for food during the night.

(D) They were also found to like sugar water, but not salt water.

(E) Cockroaches have the same problem!

五、閱讀測驗 (占 32 分)

說明：第 36 題至第 51 題，每題請分別根據各篇文章之文意選出最適當的一個選項，請畫記在答案卡之「選擇題答案區」。各題答對者，得 2 分；答錯、未作答或畫記多於一個選項者，該題以零分計算。

第 36 至 39 題為題組

The following report appeared in a newspaper in February 2007.

On February 15, 2007, hundreds of people came to New York City's famous railroad station—Grand Central Terminal—to trade in old dollar bills for the new George Washington presidential US $1 coins. The gold-colored coin is the first in a new series by the U.S. Mint to honor former U.S. presidents. The Mint will issue four presidential US $1 coins a year through 2016. These coins will come out in the order in which each president served. The George Washington coin is the first to be released. John Adams, Thomas Jefferson and James Madison coins will come out later this year.

The presidential US $1 coins have a special design. For the first time since the 1930s, there are words carved into the edge of each coin, including the year in which the coin was issued and traditional mottos. Each coin will show a different president on its face, or heads side. It will also show the president's name. The other side of the coin will show the Statue of Liberty and the inscriptions "United States of America" and "$1."

There are some interesting facts about the coins. First, there will be one presidential US $1 coin for each president, except Grover Cleveland. He will have two! Cleveland is the only U.S. president to have served two nonconsecutive terms. The last president now scheduled to get a coin is Gerald Ford. That's because a president cannot appear on a coin when he is still alive. In addition, a president must have been deceased for two years before he can be on a coin.

36. According to the report, how many presidential US $1 coins were scheduled to be released by the end of 2007 altogether?
(A) One. (B) Two. (C) Three. (D) Four.

37. Why did the Mint issue the US $1 coins?
(A) In response to U.S. citizens' requests. (B) In memory of the late U.S. presidents.
(C) To attract more train commuters. (D) To promote the trading of dollar bills.

38. What may you find on the heads side of the new US $1 coin?
(A) The name of a U.S. president. (B) The year when the coin was made.
(C) The Statue of Liberty. (D) English proverbs.

39. Which of the following can be inferred about the presidential coins?
(A) President Gerald Ford's coin was issued in 2008.
(B) The U.S. Mint has issued all the presidential coins by now.
(C) No presidential coin has been released for President Barack Obama.
(D) Every U.S. president had his coin made two years after his term was over.

第 40 至 43 題為題組

Newspapers have tried many things to stop a seemingly nonstop decline in readers. Now France is pushing forward with a novel approach: giving away papers to young readers in an effort to turn them into regular customers. The French government recently detailed plans of a project called "My Free Newspaper," under which 18- to 24-year-olds will be offered a free, year-long subscription to a newspaper of their choice.

Newspaper readership in France has been especially low among young people. According to a government study, only 10 percent of those aged 15 to 24 read a paid-for newspaper daily in 2007, down from 20 percent a decade earlier.

Emmanuel Schwartzenberg, a former media editor of *Le Figaro*, the oldest and second-largest national newspaper in France, said he had strong reservations about the government project. At a time when advertising is in steep decline, he said, newspapers should instead be looking at ways to raise more profits from readers, rather than giving papers away. "This just reinforces the belief that newspapers should be free, which is a very bad idea," Mr. Schwartzenberg said.

French readers, young and old, already have plenty of free options from which to choose, including newspaper websites and the free papers handed out daily in many city centers. Some bloggers said the new program might hold the most appeal to the few young people who do already read, and buy, newspapers.

The French government plans to promote the program with an advertising campaign aimed at young readers and their parents. However, when asked how to attract young readers to the printed press, the government said the primary channel for the ads would be the Internet.

40. Why did the French government decide to launch the free newspaper program?

(A) To fight economic recession. (B) To win approval from youngsters.

(C) To promote newspaper readership. (D) To improve the literacy rate in France.

41. Which of the following can be concluded from the passage?

(A) Everyone considers the government project creative.

(B) Newspaper readership is much higher in other countries.

(C) Research shows young people have no interest in current affairs.

(D) Giving away free papers is not a strong enough incentive to attract readers.

42. What is Mr. Schwartzenberg's attitude toward this program?

(A) Skeptical. (B) Devoted. (C) Optimistic. (D) Indifferent.

43. According to the passage, where would the information about the free newspaper program in France most likely be seen?

(A) In magazines. (B) On blogs. (C) In newspapers. (D) On the Internet.

第 44 至 47 題為題組

Coffee experts are willing to pay large sums of money for high-quality coffee beans. The high-end beans, such as Kona or Blue Mountain, are known to cost extraordinary sums of money. Then there is Kopi Lowak (translated as "Civet Coffee"), the world's most expensive coffee, which sells for as much as US $50 per quarter-pound.

This isn't particularly surprising, given that approximately 500 pounds a year of Kopi Lowak constitute the entire world supply. What is surprising is why this particular coffee is so rare. In fact, it's not the plants that are rare. It's the civet droppings. That's right, the civet droppings—the body waste of the palm civet. Coffee beans aren't Kopi Lowak until they've been digested and come out in the body waste of the palm civet.

Palm civets are tree-dwelling, raccoon-like little animals, native to Southeast Asia and the Indonesian islands. They also have a love for coffee cherries. According to Kopi Lowak suppliers, palm civets eat the fruit whole, but only digest the outer fruit, leaving the beans intact. While the beans are not destroyed, they undergo a transformation in the animal's body. A chemical substance in the digestive system of the palm civet causes some changes to the beans to give them a unique flavor. However, this is not the only explanation why coffee beans retrieved from civet droppings have a special flavor all their own. Another possible reason is that palm civets have an unfailing instinct for picking the coffee cherries at the peak of their ripeness.

Kopi Lowak is reported to have a character in taste unlike any other coffee, complex with caramel undertones and an earthy or gamey flavor. Currently, most of the world's supply of Kopi Lowak is sold in Japan, though a few US markets are also starting to stock up on Kopi Lowak.

44. What does "**This**" in the second paragraph refer to?
(A) Civet Coffee. (B) Blue Mountain coffee.
(C) The high price of Kopi Lowak. (D) The unique taste of Kona.

45. Why is Kopi Lowak expensive?
(A) There is a very limited supply of the beans.
(B) The coffee trees that grow the beans are scarce.
(C) It takes a long time for the coffee beans to ripen.
(D) Only a few experts know how to produce the beans.

46. What is the main point discussed in the third paragraph?
(A) Why palm civets like the coffee beans.
(B) Where Kopi Lowak is mainly harvested.
(C) What chemicals are found in the civet's digestive system.
(D) How palm civets change coffee fruit to Kopi Lowak beans.

47. Which of the following statements is true, according to the passage?
(A) Little palm civets eat only the outer layer of the coffee cherries.
(B) Palm civets somehow know the right time when the coffee fruit ripens.
(C) Kopi Lowak is most popular in Southeast Asia and the Indonesian islands.
(D) Kona and Blue Mountain are the most expensive coffees but only of average quality.

第 48 至 51 題為題組

Gunter Grass was the winner of the 1999 Nobel Prize in Literature. His talents are revealed in a variety of disciplines: He is not only a novelist, poet and playwright, but also a renowned painter and sculptor. As he himself stresses, his creations are closely related to his unique personal history. His father was a German who joined the Nazi party in World War II, while his mother was Polish. As a result, he constantly suffered contradictory feelings: as a Pole who had been victimized, and as someone guilty of harming the Poles. The torment in his heart led him to denounce the Nazis and his political activism has continued throughout his career. His commitment to the peace movement and the environmental movement as well as his unfailing quest for justice has won him praise as "the conscience of the nation."

In the spring of 1996, he was inspired during a trip to Italy to write a poem with his watercolor brush directly on one of his paintings. Before long, a collection of his "water poems" was born. Painting and literature have become his major forms of creativity. For him, painting is a form of creation with concrete, sensual elements, while writing is a hard and abstract process. When he cannot find words to convey his thoughts, painting helps him find the words to express himself. In this way, Grass not only creates simple depictions of the objects he is fond of in life, such as melons, vegetables, fish, and mushrooms, but also uses them as symbols for mental associations of various kinds. For example, to express the complexity of reality, he sometimes places unrelated objects in the same painting, such as a bird and a housefly, or a mushroom and a nail. Grass has depicted a wide variety of natural scenes, animals and plants, and even human artifacts of the German countryside, portraying them in poems, and allowing words to make the paintings rich in literary value.

48. What caused Grass to feel confused and troubled when he was young?
(A) He was the son of a Nazi and a victimized Pole.
(B) He found himself fighting two opposing political parties.
(C) He was trained to be an artist though he wanted to be a poet.
(D) He was born with so many talents that he couldn't choose a direction.

49. Why has Grass been praised as "the conscience of the nation"?
(A) He victimized the Poles and criticized the Nazis.
(B) He has been a strong advocate of peace and justice.
(C) He has shown great sympathy for the Poles through his poems.
(D) He joined the Nazi party and showed great loyalty to his country.

50. Why was Grass's trip to Italy important to him?
(A) He was inspired by a fine arts master in Italy.
(B) He formed a new interest in painting simple objects there.
(C) He developed a new form for creating his poems during the trip.
(D) He found a new way to solve the conflict between the Nazis and the Poles.

51. Which of the following correctly characterizes Grass's poems, according to the passage?
(A) Most of his poems depict the cruelty of the Nazis.
(B) The theme of his poems won him the Nobel Peace Prize.
(C) The poems on his paintings are often not related to objects in the real world.
(D) The ideas in his poems are expressed more thoroughly with the help of his paintings.

◆ 第貳部分：非選擇題 (占 28 分)

說明：本部分共有二題，請依各題指示作答，答案必須寫在「答案卷」上，並標明大題號 (一、二)。
作答務必使用筆尖較粗之黑色墨水的筆書寫，且不得使用鉛筆。

一、中譯英 (占 8 分)

說明：1. 請將以下中文句子譯成正確、通順、達意的英文，並將答案寫在「答案卷」上。
2. 請依序作答，並標明子題號 (1、2)。每題 4 分，共 8 分。

1. 近二十年來我國的出生率快速下滑。
2. 這可能導致我們未來人力資源的嚴重不足。

二、英文作文 (占 20 分)

說明：1. 依提示在「答案卷」上寫一篇英文作文。
2. 文長至少 120 個單詞 (words)。

提示：在你的記憶中，哪一種氣味 (smell) 最讓你難忘？請寫一篇英文作文，文長至少 120 字，文分兩段，第一段描述你在何種情境中聞到這種氣味，以及你初聞這種氣味時的感受，第二段描述這個氣味至今仍令你難忘的理由。

Notes

指考英文模擬實戰一

◆ 第壹部分：單選題 (占 72 分)

一、詞彙題 (占 10 分)

說明：第 1 題至第 10 題，每題有 4 個選項，其中只有一個是正確或最適當的選項，請畫記在答案卡之「選擇題答案區」。各題答對者，得 1 分；答錯、未作答或畫記多於一個選項者，該題以零分計算。

1. Penelope had a ________ grin on her face when she tried to play a joke on her sister.
(A) mischievous (B) knowledgeable (C) feminine (D) tremendous

2. As the cost of housing ________, people can't afford to buy houses and apartments anymore.
(A) strengthens (B) refreshes (C) flickers (D) escalates

3. The actor whose secret affair had recently been caught on camera was ________ by a bunch of reporters outside his apartment.
(A) converted (B) ambushed (C) illustrated (D) exposed

4. The botanist traveled into the heart of the Amazon River, hoping to collect more ________ of rare species.
(A) incentives (B) acquaintances (C) specimens (D) distributions

5. As the cold front approaches, the temperature is expected to ________ below zero degree.
(A) plunge (B) loosen (C) expire (D) diminish

6. Most people were surprised to find this foreigner able to speak the local language with such ________.
(A) meditation (B) insistence (C) gratitude (D) fluency

7. The prime minister's latest remark does not ________ to his previous action, which is quite bizarre.
(A) incline (B) abide (C) correspond (D) beware

8. Ancient Egyptians were able to perfect the ________ of dead bodies by making them into mummies, thus preventing them from rotting.
(A) inference (B) morality (C) preservation (D) shortage

9. The online shopping website is very popular, for it promises top-quality merchandise and ________ delivery.
(A) ample (B) prompt (C) miraculous (D) supreme

10. To most westerners, wedding vows play a(n) ________ part in a wedding because they bear witness to the love the couple share.
(A) superficial (B) passionate (C) obstinate (D) indispensable

二、綜合測驗 (占 10 分)

說明：第 11 題至第 20 題，每題一個空格，請依文意選出最適當的一個選項，請畫記在答案卡之「選擇題答案區」。各題答對者，得 1 分；答錯、未作答或畫記多於一個選項者，該題以零分計算。

第 11 至 15 題為題組

Hippos are well-known for their large size, aggressive natures and for rolling about in the water all day. But, something else that is ___11___ unique to hippos is their red "sweat," which led western explorers to name it "blood sweat." However, the reddish substance is not actually sweat. Humans and other animals sweat to prevent their bodies from overheating, whereas this "blood sweat" has two other unique purposes.

The soft hairless skin of a hippo while perfect for swimming is quite sensitive to the harsh African sun, ___12___ is why hippos prefer to stay in water throughout the day, only to go out at night to feed. Sometimes, though, a hippo will need to leave the ___13___ of the water for more food during the day. The "blood sweat" ___14___ natural sunscreen, protecting a hippo's skin from burning.

The other interesting trait of the "sweat" is that it has quite powerful antibacterial properties. When hippos are not lounging about in the water, they are usually fighting with each other. Their aggression has even given them a reputation as the most dangerous African animal to people, ___15___ more human deaths than any other large animal. Serious injuries are inevitable in the life of a hippo and the "blood sweat" helps to prevent them from dying of infection after being wounded.

11. (A) fortunately	(B) particularly	(C) scarcely	(D) roughly
12. (A) that	(B) what	(C) which	(D) whose
13. (A) invasion	(B) realm	(C) obstacle	(D) protection
14. (A) acts as	(B) blends into	(C) tosses aside	(D) wraps around
15. (A) suitable for	(B) responsible for	(C) subject to	(D) opposed to

第 16 至 20 題為題組

When it comes to massive video game franchises (系列作), what is the first that comes to mind? Is it Nintendo's *Mario* or *Zelda*? What about the *Call of Duty* series? And let's not forget about the wildly popular game, *League of Legends*. It is not unreasonable to assume that one of these franchises ___16___ having the best-selling game of all time. Actually, it is none of these. ___17___, the best-selling video game is a modest little puzzle title called *Tetris*.

Tetris was written by the Russian game designer, Alexey Pajitnov, and was first released in 1984. The game revolves around trying to complete lines by dropping and rotating random four square shapes. ___18___ lines disappear, preventing the screen from filling up with shapes and ending the game. The players gain points from completing multiple lines at once as well as surviving for as long as possible.

This simple yet extremely addictive game did not ___19___ until the launch of the Nintendo

Gameboy in 1989, through which *Tetris* became one of the most popular games ever. It is estimated that over 170 million copies of the game have been sold worldwide, making it the best-selling game ever as well as the best-selling mobile game __20__ over 100 million paid downloads. It just goes to show that it is often the simple ideas that sell the best.

16. (A) boasts (B) resumes (C) flatters (D) interprets
17. (A) After all (B) As a result (C) Under the circumstances (D) In fact
18. (A) Transformed (B) Marked (C) Completed (D) Corrected
19. (A) fade out (B) go away (C) blow up (D) take off
20. (A) with (B) by (C) in (D) besides

三、文意選填 (占 10 分)

說明：第 21 題至第 30 題，每題一個空格，請依文意在文章後所提供的(A)到(L)選項中分別選出最適當者，並將其英文字母代號畫記在答案卡之「選擇題答案區」。各題答對者，得 1 分；答錯、未作答或畫記多於一個選項者，該題以零分計算。

第 21 至 30 題為題組

Few animals are more intimidating than scorpions. With eight legs, including sharp pincers and a segmented poisonous tail, scorpions truly are __21__. However, behind their frightening appearance lies plenty of medicinal uses and vast untapped knowledge to __22__ the field of medicine.

Scorpions catch their prey by using the stingers on their tails to inject a cocktail of toxins, or venom, that will either __23__ or kill their target. It is this venom that possesses a wide range of unique compounds which are used to __24__ medicines. Some venoms are so valuable that large scorpions found in Pakistan can sell for more than US$50,000 dollars each.

Perhaps the most significant research into scorpion venom has been done on Chlorotoxin, which is found in the venom of the Deathstalker scorpion. Chlorotoxin has allowed the development of a number of __25__ to be employed for the diagnosis and treatment of some cancers, such as breast cancer. Another important venom comes from the Mesobuthus eupeus and has been found to contain highly effective antimicrobial compounds as well as other proteins that specifically kill malaria, making these __26__ promising candidates to be used for new anti-malarial drugs.

Each species of scorpion creates their own unique blend of toxins specifically __27__ to their diet and it was only the Buthidae family of scorpions that had been extensively researched. Twelve other families had yet to be studied. However, recently in Australia, the venom of over 1,500 scorpions has been __28__ by a team of researchers in an effort to discover more useful substances and many of the compounds in the venoms are unlike anything that has been seen before. Some of them cause __29__ and could be used to create new forms of painkillers. Others cause __30__ pain and may allow us to understand the way pain works better. Many exciting breakthroughs are sure to be just around the corner.

(A) manufacture	(B) adapted	(C) techniques	(D) substances
(E) recover	(F) advance	(G) paralysis	(H) collected
(I) extreme	(J) terrifying	(K) disable	(L) disappointing

四、篇章結構 (占 10 分)

說明：第 31 題至第 35 題，每題一個空格。請依文意在文章後所提供的(A)到(F)選項中分別選出最適當者，填入空格中，使篇章結構清晰有條理，並將其英文字母代號畫記在答案卡之「選擇題答案區」。各題答對者，得 2 分；答錯、未作答或畫記多於一個選項者，該題以零分計算。

第 31 至 35 題為題組

On December 8, 2015, Douglas Tompkins, the founder of clothing giants, The North Face and Esprit, was kayaking on Lake General Carerra on the border of Chile and Argentina. The lake surrounded on all sides by mountains possessed its own microclimate of unpredictable weather conditions with summer temperatures rarely surpassing 4°C. __31__ A sudden shift in the 60 km/h winds caused his kayak to overturn, leaving Tompkins in the freezing lake waters for over an hour before he was rescued. __32__

While being most known for his business ventures in the fashion industry, Tompkins was an important advocate for ecological conservation ever since he sold his holdings in his Esprit franchise back in 1989. __33__ In 1990, he founded the Foundation of Deep Ecology, which promotes environmental activism and in 1992 he formed The Conservation of Land Trust, which aims to protect the natural environment across many areas of Chile and Argentina.

Tompkins used his wealth to purchase vast stretches of wild lands in an effort to conserve them against human activity. __34__ Despite resistance, Tompkins persisted in his aims of establishing natural parks free of human interference, such as the Pumalin Park, an 800,000-acre area of the Valdivian temperate rainforest and the Corcovado National Park, which was over 200,000 acres of native forest originally intended for logging.

__35__ The day following his death, the Chilean government announced that Pumalin Park would become a national park, truly a gesture to encourage optimism about the future of our planet.

(A) Such a kayaking endeavor would not have been easy for a hardy and youthful adventurer, but for Tompkins, at age 72, it was no small feat indeed.

(B) Over his lifetime, Tompkins bought more than 2 million acres of land over 12 parks throughout Chile and Argentina, a worthy legacy for such a dedicated man.

(C) Tompkins spent the years between 1960 and 1962 ski racing and rock climbing in Colorado, Europe, and South America.

(D) His focus was on southern South America, where he had taken many trips: climbing, kayaking, and skiing.

(E) He had stopped breathing before he could reach the hospital and was pronounced dead soon after.

(F) These acts were quite controversial within Chile and Argentina as they were viewed as handicapping the economic activity of the local inhabitants.

五、閱讀測驗 (占 32 分)

說明：第 36 題至第 51 題，每題請分別根據各篇文章之文意選出最適當的一個選項，請畫記在答案卡之「選擇題答案區」。各題答對者，得 2 分；答錯、未作答或畫記多於一個選項者，該題以零分計算。

第 36 至 39 題為題組

If you were asked which body in our solar system was most likely to harbor life, what would you say? Most would answer Mars. While Mars is certainly similar to Earth in a lot of ways, after numerous observations from telescopes, spacecraft, and robots, the prospect of life on Mars does not seem likely.

Many scientists now consider, Europa, a moon orbiting the gas giant, Jupiter, to be the most likely candidate to support life. Even though Europa is much smaller and farther from the sun than Earth, it possesses the three fundamental properties imperative to life: liquid water, chemical building blocks and a source of energy.

The surface of Europa is covered in a sheet of ice several kilometers thick, but beneath the crust, it is thought there exists a layer of liquid water over one hundred kilometers deep. Additionally, similar to the ion-rich solution of our own oceans, Europa's waters are also rich in dissolved ions, such as magnesium, sodium, potassium, and chlorine.

It is believed that life on Earth originated from chemical building blocks that were randomly formed by chemical reactions during the Earth's early history. The ice on the surface of Europa is constantly being bombarded with radiation from Jupiter, allowing the formation of these very building blocks, namely oxygen, hydrogen peroxide, carbon dioxide and sulfur dioxide. The presence of these compounds in the subsurface oceans could react with the rocks on the ocean floor to free other life supporting nutrients.

Finally, all life requires energy to move and reproduce. Europa's orbit around Jupiter is oval in shape and as such the moon is constantly moving closer and farther away from Jupiter. **This** combined with the huge gravitational field that Jupiter projects results in the moon warping, creating internal friction and therefore heat within Europa. This heat could potentially be what prevents its ocean from freezing as well as supporting life there.

There you have it. Europa meets the three primary criteria for supporting and sustaining life. Only time will tell if there really are alien species swimming about in its waters.

36. According to the passage, which of the following is true about Europa?
(A) It is a moon of Jupiter in our solar system. (B) It is about the same size as Earth.
(C) Europe is very similar to Earth in many ways. (D) The heat on Europa comes from the outside.

37. How does the author start the passage?
(A) By mentioning a recent discovery made on Mars.
(B) By talking about the unlikelihood of life forms on Mars.
(C) By refuting the claim that there is life in the solar system outside of Earth.
(D) By pointing out the fact that scientists believe in the existence of life on Mars.

38. What does "**this**" in the fifth paragraph refer to?
(A) The energy that all life requires. (B) The huge gravitational field of Jupiter.
(C) The oval-shaped orbit of Europa. (D) The internal friction and heat within Europa.

39. Which of the following is true about the theory of the possible life forms on Europa?
(A) They probably do not breathe in oxygen.
(B) They probably rely on the solar energy from the sun.
(C) They probably live on land like the life forms on Earth.
(D) They probably live in liquid water under a very thick layer of ice.

第 40 至 43 題為題組

In 1971, the psychologist, Philip Zimbardo, constructed a psychological experiment to study the effects of perceived power by playing out the dynamic between guard and prisoner in what is now called the Stanford Prison Experiment. To carry out the experiment, Zimbardo created a mock prison in the basement of the Stanford University's psychology department. The participants were selected from a pool of 70 college students responding to a local ad. After being interviewed and taking a personality test to eliminate candidates with mental problems, medical issues, and a history of drug abuse, 24 applicants had been chosen to participate.

Volunteers were separated into two roles: guards and prisoners. On the first day of the experiment, prisoners were, without warning, "arrested," taken to the "prison," and processed by the guards. Each prisoner was stripped, shaved and taken blindfolded to their cells wearing only a gown. Guards were given uniforms and asked to do whatever was necessary to maintain order within the prison without the use of violence.

Surprisingly, each group took to their new roles quickly, especially the guards who within hours of the start of the experiment began to harass the prisoners. The prisoners were insulted and made to do pointless tasks. The prisoners soon after began acting the part. They talked about prison issues, told on other prisoners to the guards and took the rules of the prison very seriously.

By the second day of the experiment, the prisoners rebelled by fortifying their cells. The guards responded with force. After they broke into the cells, they stripped each prisoner, took their beds, and placed the leaders in solitary confinement. After 36 hours, one prisoner was released after an apparent mental breakdown. Though the experiment was intended to last two weeks, it was stopped after only six days when Zimbardo's girlfriend, after seeing the experiment on tape, threatened to go to the authorities.

The Stanford Prison Experiment demonstrated how readily people conform to social roles when they are expected to, highlighting how good normal people can do evil given a change in circumstances. The experiment was also subject to significant ethical criticism, especially regarding its lack of fully informed consent and ultimately responsible for tougher regulations in the way psychological experiments could be conducted.

40. Which of the following about the Stanford Prison Experiment is **NOT** mentioned in the passage?
(A) The subjects of the experiment. (B) The safety rules of the experiment.
(C) The procedures of the experiment. (D) The conclusion of the experiment.

41. How was the experiment forced to stop prematurely?
(A) The prisoners escaped the prison cells by force.
(B) The principal of the university stepped in and shut it down.
(C) One student had a mental breakdown and this caught media's attention.
(D) The psychologist's girlfriend thought the experiment had gone out of control.

42. According to the passage, what was the Stanford Prison Experiment mostly criticized for?
(A) The students involved weren't told everything about what could have gone wrong.
(B) The students were not selected properly and had some character flaws.
(C) It was conducted privately without the approval of the university.
(D) There was not enough supervision and management in the mock prison.

43. Which of the following is true about the Stanford Prison Experiment?
(A) The participants were selected from more than a hundred applicants.
(B) The prisoners never rebelled and no one was released from the prison.
(C) The guards were never told not to use violence.
(D) The experiment showed how social roles were taken seriously by people.

第 44 至 47 題為題組

For a lot of people, bees mean two things: stings and delicious honey. While honey may be one of life's pleasures, the absence of bees from our planet would not only spell the end of our favorite breakfast spread but a total collapse of the world's food production and perhaps the end of humanity itself.

The reason for this is the dependence of the majority of the world's crops on bees to grow the fruits and seeds we consume. To reproduce and therefore bear fruit, many kinds of trees and plants need to be cross-pollinated, which is the transfer of pollen from one plant to another of the same species. Some of this is achieved via the wind, but mostly by insects and most often it is bees that cross-pollinate the overwhelming majority of plants.

To thirty-five of the world's most important fruits, nuts, and vegetables, including apples, almonds, and pumpkins, bees are either greatly important or absolutely essential to their production. Without bees, these crops would either be terribly rare or extinct. The yields of many other crops, such as coffee, strawberries, and coconuts, also benefit significantly from the presence of bees. Without a doubt, the extinction of bees would cause a worldwide famine.

This is troubling because reports are showing a stark decline in worldwide bee populations. It is estimated that there are less than half as many bees as there were after World War II and that number is dropping every year. But why? Studies blame a range of causes, such as shrinking habitats, viruses and parasites, but it is the overuse of pesticides that is causing the most problems for bees. Ironically, protecting our crops from insects may ultimately lead to their and our **demise**.

With so much at stake, it is important to get involved in protecting global bee populations. This could be as little as planting bee friendly flowers in your backyard or as much as politically advocating for stricter pesticide laws in your region. Bees are far too important to humanity to ignore.

44. What is the purpose of this passage?
   (A) To emphasize the importance of bee protection.
   (B) To promote environmentally-friendly products.
   (C) To inform the readers about some facts of bees.
   (D) To urge the scientists to find alternatives to bees.

45. Which of the following is closest in meaning to "**demise**" in the fourth paragraph?
   (A) Survival. (B) Protection. (C) Doom. (D) Resistance.

46. What is the third paragraph mainly about?
   (A) Another reason why bees play an important role in nature.
   (B) The ways famines take place and how they affect crops.
   (C) The many important fruits and crops that rely on bees' cross-pollination.
   (D) The types of plants that might survive without bees' cross-pollination.

47. Which of the following is **NOT** mentioned as one of the reasons why global bee populations are decreasing?
   (A) The disappearance of the natural environment for bees to live in
   (B) Diseases caused by virus are threatening the bee populations
   (C) The fact that we use too many chemicals to kill pests and insects
   (D) The lack of biodiversity among bee species and populations.

第 48 至 51 題為題組

Forty years ago, as part of a plan for economic recovery, the small Nordic nation of Finland underwent drastic educational reforms. By the year 2000, the results of the Programme for International Student Assessment (PISA), a standardized test given to 15-year-olds globally, revealed Finland as having the best young readers in the world. Then three years later, the nation came top in math and in 2006, they were leading in science as well. Perhaps what is most interesting about Finland's educational success is the unusual system they use.

Compared with a majority of the world, Finland's education system stands out for not creating a competitive environment. Finnish children start school as late as seven years old and are not assessed for the first six years of their school life. Students are only given one standardized test throughout their entire education at the age of sixteen. Furthermore, children are not separated into different classes based on ability. They are also given 75 minutes of recess each day. It is ironic that Finland ranks so highly for reading, science, and math despite Finnish education's lack of pressure toward high performance. Finland's example seems to indicate that children respond better to a stress-free learning environment.

Another reason for Finland's success may be due to its teachers. All teachers in Finland are required to have a master's degree and are selected from the top ten percent of graduates. Despite being paid less than teachers from the US, the job is highly sought-after. In 2010, 6,600 people applied for elementary school training slots out of the 660 available. This is not surprising though, as teachers in Finland are afforded the same social status as doctors and lawyers.

Another remarkable aspect of Finnish education is its dedication to making sure all students are not left behind. Teachers are given educational guidelines, not a curriculum, which means they have the freedom to tune their teaching to each unique set of children. Furthermore, thirty percent of students are given extra help in their first nine years of school. The rest of the world could learn a lot from Finland's schooling.

48. How does the author prove that Finland probably has one of the best education systems in the world?

(A) By quoting experts and scholars

(B) By listing the features Finland education.

(C) By emphasizing the economic success Finland has.

(D) By comparing education in Finland with that in the US.

49. According to the passage, which of the following is true about the teachers in Finland?

(A) A master's degree is optional for a Finnish teacher.

(B) Teachers in Finland are paid more than their counterparts in the US.

(C) Teachers in Finland are expected to receive training regularly.

(D) Teachers in Finland are highly respected by the public.

50. How is a stress-free environment created in schools in Finland?
  (A) Assessments do not take place very often.
  (B) Students can choose freely what they want to do at school.
  (C) No homework is given to students during the first six years.
  (D) Students are encouraged to take part in extracurricular activities.

51. Why are there 30 percent students given extra help in the first nine years of school?
  (A) Because they are exceptional students who should aim higher.
  (B) Because their parents are too busy to help them with schoolwork.
  (C) Because they do not perform as well and need extra help.
  (D) Because private schools offer more schooling to privileged children.

◆ 第貳部分：非選擇題 (占 28 分)

說明：本部分共有二題，請依各題指示作答，答案必須寫在「答案卷」上，並標明大題號 (一、二)。作答務必使用筆尖較粗之黑色墨水的筆書寫，且不得使用鉛筆。

一、中譯英 (占 8 分)

說明：1. 請將以下中文句子譯成正確、通順、達意的英文，並將答案寫在「答案卷」上。 2. 請依序作答，並標明子題號 (1、2)。每題 4 分，共 8 分。

1. 因為網路的便利與人們習慣的改變，人們不像以前一樣常看報紙。
2. 即便如此，我的父母仍訂閱報紙來掌握世界潮流與殺時間。

二、英文作文 (占 20 分)

說明：1. 依提示在「答案卷」上寫一篇英文作文。 2. 文長至少 120 個單詞 (words)。

提示：每個人都有受挫或失敗的經驗，如何成熟的面對挫折不被打倒是人生的重要課題，請就這個主題，寫一篇英文作文，文長至少 120 個單詞。文分兩段，第一段說明遇到挫折或不如意時，應該如何面對與處理，第二段則就自身經驗加以闡述。

指考英文模擬實戰二

◆ 第壹部分：單選題 (占 72 分)

一、詞彙題 (占 10 分)

說明：第 1 題至第 10 題，每題有 4 個選項，其中只有一個是正確或最適當的選項，請畫記在答案卡之「選擇題答案區」。各題答對者，得 1 分；答錯、未作答或畫記多於一個選項者，該題以零分計算。

1. To ________ for the benefits from the government, a family needs to fall within the income threshold.
(A) qualify (B) relieve (C) bulge (D) impose

2. As a modern dance lover, I have long had a ________ for contemporary dance styles over traditional classical ballet.
(A) paradox (B) pension (C) posture (D) preference

3. The ________ lines in this poem are the reason why it's open to interpretation.
(A) eloquent (B) ambiguous (C) superficial (D) robust

4. To cater to the public's taste, news these days is often filled with ________ and distortions. Consequently, fact checking and research skills are now more crucial to readers than ever before.
(A) ripples (B) superstitions (C) distractions (D) exaggerations

5. Several whales were found ________ along the coast and many efforts were put in to save them from dying.
(A) revived (B) fiddled (C) stranded (D) possessed

6. One of a teacher's tasks is to ignite a ________ of interest in a student's learning, paving the way for a lifetime's pursuit of knowledge.
(A) herald (B) hedge (C) spark (D) remark

7. Two decades of laboring in the mines has ________ Stephen's skin and turned his hair gray, resulting in him looking a lot older than his real age.
(A) blurred (B) clutched (C) wrinkled (D) elevated

8. ________ of the sales clerk's real intention, the guard refused to open the door for him and sent him away.
(A) Beneficial (B) Suspicious (C) Envious (D) Dreadful

9. This new start-up launched a(n) ________ product this year that changed the face of the industry.
(A) revolutionary (B) enthusiastic (C) straightforward (D) authentic

10. This new strain of flu is highly ________, so the Central Disease Control Bureau has warned the public and urged everyone to get a flu shot.
(A) compatible (B) cumulative (C) contagious (D) customary

二、綜合測驗 (占 10 分)

說明：第 11 題至第 20 題，每題一個空格，請依文意選出最適當的一個選項，請畫記在答案卡之「選擇題答案區」。各題答對者，得 1 分；答錯、未作答或畫記多於一個選項者，該題以零分計算。

第 11 至 15 題為題組

Good Friday, also referred to as Holy Friday, is a Christian holiday observed throughout the world that signifies Jesus Christ's crucifixion, or his death on the cross. It is the Friday that precedes Easter Sunday, the date of which varies ___11___ and there is a great deal of disagreement about how it should be calculated. Good Friday forms a part of Holy Week, which commemorates the Passion of the Christ before he came back to life on Easter Sunday. The Thursday celebrates the last supper and Jesus's ___12___ betrayal by Judas for 30 pieces of silver. The Friday remembers Jesus's crucifixion and the Saturday is the day Jesus "rested" in his tomb ___13___ on the Sunday.

Different branches of the Church celebrate the day differently, but for many churches, it is a day of fasting and many prayers, singing, and ceremony in remembrance of Jesus Christ's crucifixion and death. Good Friday is ___14___ a national holiday in many countries with a strong Christian tradition and some traditions are practiced even among secular families. In England and Australia, many people eat Hot Cross Buns, a raisin bread roll with a cross ___15___ on top. Many also refrain from consuming meat except fish on Good Friday and most shops are required by law to be closed.

11. (A) from dawn to dusk (B) from top to bottom (C) from time to time (D) from year to year
12. (A) subtle (B) subconscious (C) suburban (D) subsequent
13. (A) before raising (B) before rising (C) after raising (D) after rising
14. (A) renowned for (B) spent on (C) recognized as (D) replaced by
15. (A) marked (B) marking (C) to be marked (D) to mark

第 16 至 20 題為題組

Everyone has heard and probably used Wikipedia. It is the world's largest and most comprehensive encyclopedia. Not to be confused with it, there exists another "encyclopedia" called Uncyclopedia. As you may have guessed by the "un" ___16___ "en," it is not actually an encyclopedia at all but a website that makes fun of Wikipedia.

Founded on January 5th, 2005, by Jonathon Huang, Uncyclopedia attempts to mock Wikipedia in almost every conceivable way: from its articles to its layout, projects, and its code of conduct. Nothing is left ___17___. The website contains over 30,000 articles in English based on Wikipedia articles of the same name.

Uncyclopedia encourages its articles to humorously parody Wikipedia while also attempting to ___18___ the truth, such as in the case of its article on Satan, calling him "the primary antagonist in the best-selling novel, the Bible." In the article on pandas where it is stated that "It is widely accepted that hamsters and panda bears were once the same species." However, many often ___19___ the mark by using false information together with absurd humor. Rather than being rated on the credibility of their sources and conciseness of their writing, Uncyclopedia's articles are ___20___ their humor, overall presentation, and the images used. If you are in the mood for an amusing read instead of intellectual stimulation, then perhaps uncylopedia.wikia.com is the place to go.

16. (A) on top of (B) instead of (C) along with (D) except for
17. (A) untouched (B) unfinished (C) uncovered (D) unlocked
18. (A) conclude (B) hide (C) reverse (D) resemble
19. (A) manage to hit (B) fail to hit (C) succeed in hitting (D) insist in hitting
20. (A) labeled as (B) lobbied for (C) informed about (D) judged on

三、文意選填 (占 10 分)

說明：第 21 題至第 30 題，每題一個空格，請依文意在文章後所提供的(A)到(L)選項中分別選出最適當者，並將其英文字母代號畫記在答案卡之「選擇題答案區」。各題答對者，得 1 分；答錯、未作答或畫記多於一個選項者，該題以零分計算。

第 21 至 30 題為題組

From their biology to their lifestyle, hummingbirds are certainly one of the most interesting bird species on the planet. Small and colorful, hummingbirds ___21___ their name to the humming noise they make due to the speed they flap their wings as they fly.

Native to the Americas, there are as many as 325 different species of hummingbirds, one of which, the ruby throat, is the smallest bird in the world, ___22___ just three grams. Hummingbirds characteristically have long tapered beaks with which they use to lick nectar from flowers. While feeding, hummingbirds can lick up to 15 times per second. Depending on the population of ___23___ and the conditions of their habitat, hummingbirds live on average from 3 to 12 years.

Hummingbirds have the highest wing beat of any bird, flapping on average 50 beats every second. This allows them to ___24___ mid-air to feed. What enables them to flap their wings so quickly is their incredibly high metabolism. Their hearts beat on average 1,200 times a minute and they take over 250 ___25___ every minute. To maintain this huge metabolism, they need to feed constantly and when food is ___26___ or at night, they enter torpor, a state of reduced activity and metabolism.

Despite their small stature, hummingbirds can be quite ___27___, regularly attacking much larger birds that intrude on their territory. It is not uncommon to see hummingbirds chase crows or other birds that wander close by.

Historically, hummingbirds were ___28___ for their feathers. These days, however, they are most threatened by the ___29___ and loss of their habitats as each species is uniquely adapted to a specific environment. Because of this, hummingbirds are classified as a(n) ___30___ species. Fortunately, hummingbirds benefit from being adored by many homeowners across the Americas. Many people set up hummingbird feeders in their backyards to help them during long migrations in the summer.

(A) scarce	(B) aggressive	(C) hover	(D) amounting
(E) hunted	(F) endangered	(G) owe	(H) destruction
(I) breaths	(J) weighing	(K) surroundings	(L) predators

四、篇章結構 (占 10 分)

說明：第 31 題至第 35 題，每題一個空格。請依文意在文章後所提供的(A)到(F)選項中分別選出最適當者，填入空格中，使篇章結構清晰有條理，並將其英文字母代號畫記在答案卡之「選擇題答案區」。各題答對者，得 2 分；答錯、未作答或畫記多於一個選項者，該題以零分計算。

第 31 至 35 題為題組

On October 30th, 1938, as a Halloween special, an adaption of H.G. Wells' famous novel, *The War of the Worlds*, was aired over the Columbia Broadcasting System. __31__ Later, panic erupted. Many people fled their homes and reports were coming in of people smelling poison gas or seeing flashes of light in the distance.

__32__ A number of employees working in a dressmaking department of a U.S. textile factory started to fall ill with numbness, nausea, dizziness, and vomiting. Rumor had it that there was a bug living in the factory spreading this mysterious disease, and it wasn't long before 62 women were showing the same symptoms. Research by the Public Health Service Communicable Disease Center concluded that while a bug may have bitten a few of the workers, the cause of the symptoms for the rest of the women was anxiety. __33__

Mass hysteria is the phenomenon associated with the collective manifestation of symptoms or behaviors caused by a common anxiety and is particularly prevalent when a group believes they are suffering from the same disease, such as in the case of the previously mentioned June Bug Epidemic.

__34__ However, it is generally believed among experts that a combination of heightened stress and group pressure is the basis for such episodes. Stress creates stress in others, which in turn creates more panic until the mind takes over. People begin misinterpreting normal phenomena as something more evil. __35__ Many of the women working in the factory feared being bitten by the same bug that plagued their colleagues, resulting in the symptoms to psychologically manifest across 62 other people.

(A) In extreme cases, the brain can even create physical symptoms.
(B) Very little is still known about the mechanisms that create these incidents.
(C) Mass hysteria is an ancient disease, first described in Egyptian medical texts in the 15th century BC.
(D) In 1962, another strange incident occurred.
(E) Both of these events were cases of what is known as mass hysteria.
(F) For people who had only listened to a portion of the broadcast, it sounded like actual real news announcement.

五、閱讀測驗(占 32 分)

說明：第 36 題至第 51 題，每題請分別根據各篇文章之文意選出最適當的一個選項，請畫記在答案卡之「選擇題答案區」。各題答對者，得 2 分；答錯、未作答或畫記多於一個選項者，該題以零分計算。

第 36 至 39 題為題組

Ever since the beginning of the Internet, for many, the days of the public library were numbered. When you can Google any question your mind ponders, it certainly seems that these once important public institutions of free information are doomed to decline into irrelevance. However, for a few, there is hope for the future of our libraries, not as spaces filled with rows of bookcases, but transformed into something that meets the demands of the modern information age.

David Pescovitz, research director at the Institute for the Future, a collective think-tank that makes predictions about our world, believes that libraries will become an all-in-one space for learning, sharing, creating, and even experiencing. In addition to providing a means of accessing information, libraries, as we move further into the 21st century, will emphasize **connectivity**, reflecting our use of social media and streaming services.

In some regards, this is already happening. There are libraries with 3D printers, laser cutters and other gadgets that expand the definition of a library to a place of not just learning, but creation, too. "I think the library as a place of access to materials, physical and virtual, becomes increasingly important," says Pescovitz. That is not all, though. He even imagines a future where people can check out "experiences" from the library, such as exploring another planet or looking into the past, using cutting-edge virtual reality technology.

Another thing libraries have going for them is their physicality. Libraries could act as community hubs, bringing people together, enabling those with common interests to engage in their hobbies in a social way. Libraries are already starting to facilitate the cultural growth of their communities by providing resource centers and art spaces.

Furthermore, there is more and more focus on enhancing the learning process and helping people know what information they need to find. Gaining the right knowledge is not as easy as simply going to Google. You have to know what question to ask or what search to make. Libraries and their librarians can act as guides, directing people to the information they need as effortlessly as possible. Although they may change, libraries still have their place in society.

36. What is the best title of this passage?

(A) Libraries of Tomorrow　(B) The Limitations of Libraries

(C) Libraries Embrace Information Technology　(D) Libraries as Community Hubs

37. What does the author mean by "**connectivity**" in the second paragraph?

(A) People can connect to the library websites at any time.

(B) People can use the Wi-Fi service in the library to access information.

(C) Social networking and streaming service will become a part of resources in libraries.

(D) People can create things in libraries, using tangible or virtual materials provided there.

38. How does the author present his or her ideas?

(A) By using lots of real-life examples.

(B) By making a list of his ideas.

(C) By citing figures and statistics to support his ideas.

(D) By focusing on the pros and cons.

39. According to the passage, which of the following is **NOT** one of the features libraries already have?

(A) 3D printers. (B) Resources centers.

(C) Rows of bookcases. (D) Cutting-edge virtual reality technology.

第 40 至 43 題為題組

Have you ever bought a tray of large bright red tomatoes from your local grocery store only to find they were bland and watery? As Sanwen Huang, the deputy director of the Agricultural Genome Institute in Shenzhen, once said, "Consumers complain that the modern tomato has little flavor. It's like a 'water bomb.'" This is a common experience for many consumers around the globe, but why are our tomatoes becoming more and more tasteless?

The answer to that question, as you would expect, has to do with money. Growers care most about crop yields, and achieving these high yields comes at the cost of taste. The varieties of tomatoes most known for the size of their harvest tend to the least flavorful. That is not the only reason, though. Tomato variants are also chosen for their size and their firmness. Consumers prefer to buy large fruit and firmer tomatoes are much easier to transport. As such, the taste of the tomato is often overlooked.

A study, co-led by Huang, that tried to determine the genetic basis for a tomatoes taste researched 398 varieties of tomatoes by sequencing each of their genomes. The study then narrowed down 33 compounds as being responsible for tomatoes' flavor after a focus group of 100 participants judged each tomato based on "overall liking" and "flavor intensity." The study concluded that most store-bought tomatoes contained significantly less of these flavor compounds. Furthermore, larger tomatoes generally have less sugar, which is another factor making store-bought tomatoes less desirable.

However, there is hope for a better tomato as Huang's and his colleague's findings could prove instrumental in helping tomato cultivators and breeders create new, tastier varieties of store-bought tomatoes. By working together, "We can provide a better-flavored tomato," Huang said.

40. Where is this passage most likely taken from?

(A) Spam. (B) TV guide. (C) Encyclopedia. (D) Newspaper.

41. According to the passage, who is to blame for tomatoes' tastelessness?
 (A) Huang's researcher team. (B) Growers.
 (C) Consumers. (D) Both growers and consumers.

42. Which of the following statement is true about Huang's study in the third paragraph?
 (A) He was the sole leader of the study.
 (B) He realized that there were about 398 compounds that determine tomatoes' flavor.
 (C) He concluded that store-bought tomatoes contained more flavor compounds.
 (D) Generally speaking, the larger tomatoes are, the less sweet they are.

43. What can be inferred about Huang's attitude toward his findings?
 (A) Optimistic. (B) Pessimistic. (C) Neutral. (D) Indifferent.

第 44 至 47 題為題組

It was a time of struggle and hardship. For nearly ten years in the 1930s, the Great Plains of America's mid-west had been ravaged by drought and terrifying dust storms. Farmers had in the preceding years transformed the land into farmland that promised to ensure prosperity for generations to come. That was not to be, however. One by one, the families of the region were forced to give up after persevering as long as they could through failed crops and choking black clouds of dust. Many moved west to California, hoping to find work there in what is known as the Dust Bowl Migration.

A series of wet years in the 1920s had misled many farmers to believe that the plains of Oklahoma, Texas, and Arkansas were suitable for yearly plowing for wheat production, but the region was actually quite dry, receiving only on average 250 mm of rain per year. The extensive deep plowing of the plains' virgin topsoil had removed the native deep-rooted grasses that held the soil in place. The droughts that followed dried out the earth, which made it vulnerable to wind erosion and ultimately became largely infertile.

The winds carried the dust, creating huge black clouds named "black blizzards" that often traveled as far as the east coast of the U.S. They were so thick that visibility in them was as little as 1 meter. These dust storms caused widespread damage to buildings and made residents sick with sore throats and coughs. As many as 350 houses would have to be torn down from one storm alone.

Failed farms, unemployment, and foreclosures led to homelessness and tens of thousands of families were forced to migrate out in search of livelihood. It is estimated that over 500,000 Americans were left homeless and around 3.5 million people moved out of the Great Plains region with most of them going to California. Unfortunately, Californian farms typically only hired workers seasonally and America was in the midst of the Great Depression. Many who had come in search of new opportunities were no better off than where they had left.

44. What does the Dust Bowl Migration refer to?

(A) Farmers moving to California from America's mid-west in search for a better life.

(B) Farmers persevering through failed crops and choking clouds of dust in the mid-west.

(C) Unemployment and failed farming attempts in the mid-west in the 1930s.

(D) A large amount of dust blown from America's mid-west to California.

45. Besides the droughts, what also contributed to the farmland in the mid-west becoming barren?

(A) The good years preceding the droughts. (B) The deep-rooted grasses.

(C) The migration of farmers. (D) The Great Depression.

46. Which of the following words is best in describing the Great Plains in the 1930s?

(A) Miserable. (B) Ridiculous. (C) Promising. (D) Picturesque.

47. Which of the following statements is true about the dust storms?

(A) They could only be seen in the middle and western part of the US.

(B) People could barely see anything once caught in them.

(C) They didn't have an influence on people's health and well-being.

(D) They were so destructive that they killed thousands of people.

第 48 至 51 題為題組

The Internet brought about a huge shift in the entertainment media that people consume. First came user created video content, supported by platforms like YouTube, then came on-demand television services, such as Netflix, and now there is live streaming or more specifically video game streaming.

"Streamers," as they are called, play video games and broadcast live to hundreds or even thousands interested viewers. However, it is not as simple as just playing a game. To maintain a large audience, streamers have to entertain as they play. This could be as straightforward as being exceptionally good at a game or more subtle as having an interesting personality. In any case, constantly communicating is important for any successful streamer and that often means requiring the use of a webcam to be visible to their audience.

The growth and popularity of video game streaming on platforms like Twitch has meant that, for a lucky few, streaming is more than just a hobby. It is a job and it can pay well. The biggest streamers attract between 20 to 30 thousand concurrent viewers each day they go live, but moderate streams of a few thousand viewers can be more than big enough to turn streaming into a career.

Streamers **leverage** their audience to generate revenue through a variety of means, the most obvious of which is monthly subscriptions and private donations. A subscription is basically a five-dollar monthly donation that affords the subscriber unique privileges. The top streamers consistently hold between 10 and 20 thousand "subs," which translates to more than US$600,000 in annual revenue from subscriptions alone. Then there are private donations which can be significant. Ranging from two-dollar tips to large sums in the thousands, these donations constantly pop up throughout the streams duration from appreciative fans.

Another way streamers earn money is via sponsorship and advertising by promoting their sponsor on stream and interspersing the broadcast with ad breaks. Many large gaming and tech companies routinely utilize streamers to market their products. Similar to sports in the 20th century, gaming is fast on its way to becoming just as huge.

48. According to the passage, besides the ability to play well, what is also important for a successful streamer?
(A) An attractive appearance.
(B) Devotion to gaming.
(C) A charming personality.
(D) Expensive equipment.

49. Which of the following is closest in meaning to "**leverage**" in the fourth paragraph?
(A) Control.
(B) Monitor.
(C) Utilize.
(D) Neglect.

50. According to the passage, how do streamers make money?
(A) Through subscriptions.
(B) Through gaming companies.
(C) Through tips from the fans.
(D) All of the above.

51. What can we infer from the conclusion?
(A) Gaming is going to become as popular as sports.
(B) Gaming is simply a fad that will lose its appeal soon.
(C) Gaming is a career that has its risks and should be treated carefully.
(D) Gaming is never going replace sports in entertainment.

◆ 第貳部分：非選擇題 (占 28 分)

說明：本部分共有二題，請依各題指示作答，答案必須寫在「答案卷」上，並標明大題號 (一、二)。作答務必使用筆尖較粗之黑色墨水的筆書寫，且不得使用鉛筆。

一、中譯英 (占 8 分)

說明：1. 請將以下中文句子譯成正確、通順、達意的英文，並將答案寫在「答案卷」上。
2. 請依序作答，並標明子題號 (1、2)。每題 4 分，共 8 分。

1. 隨著近年來空氣品質的惡化，呼吸新鮮空氣成為少數人才能享有的特權。
2. 為了保護下一代，政府應立即採取行動防止更多的廢氣被排放。

二、英文作文 (占 20 分)

說明：1. 依提示在「答案卷」上寫一篇英文作文。
2. 文長至少 120 個單詞 (words)。

提示：每個人或多或少都有對某樣物品或某種活動愛不釋手甚至上癮 (addiction) 的經驗；有的人每天都要喝咖啡、有的人手機不離身、也有人喜歡健身或玩電動。請以此為主題寫一篇英文作文，文長至少 120 個單詞，文分兩段，第一段說明你對事物上癮的想法，第二段則就自身經驗加以描述。

Notes

指考英文模擬實戰三

◆ 第壹部分：單選題 (占 72 分)

一、詞彙題 (占 10 分)

說明：第 1 題至第 10 題，每題有 4 個選項，其中只有一個是正確或最適當的選項，請畫記在答案卡之「選擇題答案區」。各題答對者，得 1 分；答錯、未作答或畫記多於一個選項者，該題以零分計算。

1. After retirement, the former executive went back to his hometown alone and began a(n) ________ life of a farmer who grows organic vegetables.
(A) alternative (B) explicit (C) solitary (D) solid

2. Severe flooding not only stopped car engines but also sent drivers ________ to the top of their cars.
(A) hurling (B) scrambling (C) stalking (D) haunting

3. The locals are advised to stay away from the chemical factory until the toxic fumes have ________.
(A) commuted (B) circulated (C) transmitted (D) dispersed

4. Changing our scheduled travel plans has been a real ________ because we also have to change our flight and accommodations.
(A) nightmare (B) stake (C) sentiment (D) drizzle

5. Standing in the heart of bustling New York City like a quiet sanctuary in the midst of chaos, Central Park serves as a(n) ________ for many people.
(A) oasis (B) ally (C) pirate (D) harmony

6. Since it contains many cancer-fighting ________, green tea is beneficial to our health.
(A) components (B) divisions (C) recessions (D) pollutants

7. This latest evidence the detective found cast ________ on the suspect's versions of the events.
(A) anticipation (B) suspension (C) suspicion (D) participation

8. The president's plan to ________ revise the long-standing health care bill has sparked much controversy.
(A) superficially (B) substantially (C) thoughtfully (D) occasionally

9. The nation is in mourning for the much ________ film director, who had received numerous awards throughout her career.
(A) esteemed (B) whined (C) subscribed (D) proceeded

10. Continuous rain has caused flooding in mountainous regions. It is estimated at least 10,000 people have been ________.
(A) retrieved (B) exaggerated (C) evacuated (D) fostered

二、綜合測驗（占 10 分）

說明：第 11 題至第 20 題，每題一個空格，請依文意選出最適當的一個選項，請畫記在答案卡之「選擇題答案區」。各題答對者，得 1 分；答錯、未作答或畫記多於一個選項者，該題以零分計算。

第 11 至 15 題為題組

Weather events, like El Niño, cause a lot of damage. When we think about weather events, the first thing that comes to our minds are floods and damaged buildings.

However, researchers have noticed that ___11___ El Niño occurs, the cholera cases in eastern Africa increase tremendously. Now scientists believe that getting prepared against cholera before El Niño happens would improve the lives of millions of people.

El Niño happens all across the world and occurs every two to seven years and can be predicted six to twelve months ___12___. When El Niño happens, the Pacific Ocean's surface temperature near South America becomes warmer than usual. This usually happens in December. About 9 or 10 months later, this warming spreads to the western Pacific, ___13___ extreme flooding and droughts.

Cholera spreads when water supplies are contaminated. This usually happens when sewage water mixes with drinking water. Flooding is a common cause of the spread. ___14___ a drought, the water supply is so scarce that people might use contaminated water because they have no other choice. These situations increase the number of cholera cases by up to 50,000 when El Niño occurs.

Cholera is a highly dangerous and deadly disease. By knowing that a weather event can cause the spread of cholera bacteria can help health workers get prepared ___15___. They can supply clean drinking water and save lives.

11. (A) wherever (B) whatever (C) however (D) whenever
12. (A) at all times (B) ahead of time (C) for the time being (D) behind the times
13. (A) causes (B) causing (C) caused (D) to cause
14. (A) Judging from (B) With regard to (C) In the case of (D) Regardless of
15. (A) in advance (B) on purpose (C) for effect (D) to spare

第 16 至 20 題為題組

In the near future, humans might be the only type of primate that is left in the world. Scientists believe many primates, including orangutans, gorillas, and lemurs, will no longer be found in the wild.

Scientist Jo Setchell says that we have 60% of primates ___16___ extinction within the next few decades. Our children will most likely see the last primates if their numbers decrease ___17___. There will be no primates left by the time our grandchildren are born.

Humans are ___18___ for primate extinction. Human activities such as cutting down trees are destroying tropical forests, which are the main habitat for most primates. And the problem is even bigger than most scientists had imagined.

Most primate species live in Brazil, Indonesia, Madagascar, and the Democratic Republic of Congo. These countries try to protect the primates __19__ in their forests, but usually, there aren't enough money or scientists to make significant improvements for these animals. For example, Madagascar has more than 100 primate species, 94% of __20__ are at risk of extinction. 90% of Madagascar's forests have already been cut down.

Scientists believe that the only way to save primates is to protect the areas they live in. If humans protect primates and the forests they live in, we still might have a chance to save them.

16. (A) compelled (B) threatened (C) scattered (D) displaced
17. (A) in the long run (B) in the course of time (C) at this rate (D) to this end
18. (A) to blame (B) being blamed (C) to be blamed (D) blaming
19. (A) living (B) to live (C) lived (D) live
20. (A) those (B) them (C) who (D) which

三、文意選填 (占 10 分)

說明：第 21 題至第 30 題，每題一個空格，請依文意在文章後所提供的(A)到(L)選項中分別選出最適當者，並將其英文字母代號畫記在答案卡之「選擇題答案區」。各題答對者，得 1 分；答錯、未作答或畫記多於一個選項者，該題以零分計算。

第 21 至 30 題為題組

NASA has been flying people into space since 1961, and it's the only group to ever send someone to the Moon. It is surely one of the world's most __21__ organizations. Right now, one of its main focuses is putting an astronaut on Mars. Despite having such a big and important goal, NASA still has time for a __22__ matter. It proved that in April of 2011 when it took the strange decision to use six armed officials to track down and __23__ a friendly old woman.

The story began when 75-year-old Joann Davis contacted the space agency to ask for its help in selling two paperweights. One of them __24__ a tiny piece of moon rock, and the other held a small piece of an old spaceship. Davis's first husband, who died in 1986, was given the items as a reward for his work as a NASA engineer, and Davis wanted to sell them because she __25__ needed the money. She was in financial troubles. Her son struggled with illness for years and she had to pay his medical bills, and later, that son and Davis's youngest daughter died, leaving her with grandchildren to __26__.

NASA chiefs weren't happy that Davis had a piece of moon rock, as there's a law in the US that says anything taken from the moon belongs to the government. So, even though Davis had told the agency she wanted to sell the paperweights __27__, they sent six officers with guns to meet her. Once they arrived, they __28__ seized objects and restrained the elderly woman for two hours. They wouldn't even let her use the bathroom. She had to __29__ urinate in her pants. Her treatment was so __30__ that a US court has said that she will be able to sue the organization.

The lesson here for NASA: Aim for the stars, not little old ladies.

(A) registered (B) trifling (C) desperately (D) inspirational
(E) forcibly (F) contained (G) humiliating (H) spacious
(I) legally (J) detain (K) embarrassedly (L) attend

四、篇章結構 (占 10 分)

說明：第 31 題至第 35 題，每題一個空格。請依文意在文章後所提供的(A)到(F)選項中分別選出最適當者，填入空格中，使篇章結構清晰有條理，並將其英文字母代號畫記在答案卡之「選擇題答案區」。各題答對者，得 2 分；答錯、未作答或畫記多於一個選項者，該題以零分計算。

第 31 至 35 題為題組

Priscilla Chan, physician, educator, and wife of Facebook CEO Mark Zuckerberg, was born on February 24, 1985. Her parents, Chinese immigrants from Vietnam, did not go to college and worked hard to provide for their children. __31__ In high school, she was captain of the tennis and robotics teams, graduated top of her class, and was admitted to Harvard University in 2003.

At Harvard, Chan majored in biology and volunteered in an after-school mentoring program. __32__ Through this, she realized that tutoring alone could not solve the bigger problem she perceived. Children need to feel safe, happy, and healthy growing up in order to succeed, she thought. This idea would go on to shape her life and career goals. __33__ The couple moved to California and married in 2012, the same year Chan earned her medical degree from UC San Francisco and began her residency at San Francisco General Hospital.

In 2015, Chan and Zuckerberg pledged to donate 99% of their Facebook shares to charitable causes. __34__ Chan is currently director of The Primary School, which serves 50 families in the East Palo Alto area. __35__ Chan is combining two areas that have long been important to her. Through the efforts of The Primary School, she hopes to combat the effects of poverty on children and families who are most at risk. With Chan leading the way, chances are great that she will succeed once again.

(A) With the help of scholarships, Priscilla Chan soon finished her studies at Harvard Medical School.
(B) It provides both K–8 education as well as health care services.
(C) Dennis and Yvonne Chan wanted their children to do better and have more opportunities, so Priscilla worked hard not to disappoint them.
(D) She worked with disadvantaged kids from one of Boston's poorer neighborhoods.
(E) Education is one area they are targeting.
(F) While at Harvard, Chan also met Zuckerberg and the two soon began dating.

五、閱讀測驗 (占 32 分)

說明：第 36 題至第 51 題，每題請分別根據各篇文章之文意選出最適當的一個選項，請畫記在答案卡之「選擇題答案區」。各題答對者，得 2 分；答錯、未作答或畫記多於一個選項者，該題以零分計算。

第 36 至 39 題為題組

Throughout the United States, prisons are full of people who have made poor choices during their lives. Yet, while being put in prison is first and foremost a punishment, it is also a place where one can turn one's life around. When Angel Sanchez was sentenced to prison for fifteen years, he decided to use his time locked up to reflect on his choices and also prepare for his future on the outside.

As a young boy, Sanchez spent most of his boyhood on the streets of Miami's Little Havana. He carried a gun as a way to protect himself and win some respect as well. His mother was crack-addicted and his Cuban immigrant father spoke poor English and drove a tow truck to raise his son. His father often told him the importance of education. By 16, he had been arrested four times because of a long list of crimes. It was his final arrest that landed him in prison. While in prison, he decided to make some changes for a wasted life. As he knew once he was released, he would go back to his old life and die on the street one day. Accordingly, he began to read books in the prison law library and earned his GED, which is equivalent to a high school diploma. He dreamed that once he was out of prison, he could practice law to help others.

Later, he was released from jail, and he applied to numerous schools and was finally admitted to Valencia College. He has been an exceptional student with a 4.0 GPA. Luckily enough, a charitable foundation, the Jack Kent Cooke Scholarship, awarded to just 85 students a year, chose Angel Sanchez as one of the recipients. The scholarship allowed him to finish his college without financial worries. He still has some work to do to become a lawyer. Since he is a former **perpetrator**, he will need to petition the courts to even have the opportunity to practice law.

Sanchez's story tells us that with hard work, determination, and persistence, dreams can come true.

36. According to the passage, what is true about Angel Sanchez?
   (A) Both of his parents were addicts and lack of responsibility.
   (B) He had killed many people to secure his position as a gang leader.
   (C) He had a humble beginning and a rough start in life.
   (D) He had applied for many colleges, but because of his past disgrace, only one accepted him.

37. When Angel Sanchez was studying in college, what happened?
   (A) He passed all his subjects with flying colors.
   (B) He won the Jack Kent Cooke Scholarship because of his Cuban background.
   (C) The court had already granted him to practice law.
   (D) He specialized in dealing with the legal cases of gang members.

38. Which of the following is closest in meaning to "**perpetrator**" in the fourth paragraph?
   (A) Criminal. (B) Ambassador. (C) Intruder. (D) Beggar.

39. What is the tone of this passage?
   (A) Skeptical. (B) Motivational. (C) Bitter. (D) Ironic.

第 40 至 43 題為題組

When talking about environmental conservation, protecting natural resources is often the focus of conversations. However, numerous animals and plants are suffering the consequences of human pollution as well as poaching. Nepal's one-horned rhino is one such example.

Throughout Nepal, one-horned rhinos used to be extremely prevalent. But, due to poaching as well as people driving the animals off their land, their population is on the decrease drastically. From numbers that were once in the thousands, one-horned rhinos were reduced to just over 100 by the end of the twentieth century. However, conservation efforts have been put into place and the rhino population is increasing.

During the last ten years, the one-horned rhino population has increased to more than 600 and was even able to be removed from the International Union for Conservation of Nature's endangered species list. One way that their numbers have been able to increase is due to the efforts to relocate rhinos to safe areas where they cannot be poached. However, the task of relocating these rare animals is difficult and unpredictable. Furthermore, such a task must be replicated at least numerous times over the next few years. One-horned rhinos are large creatures and cannot be moved easily. It requires large teams of people, including vets, riding atop elephants to move around the animals swiftly and quietly in order to tranquilize them for their long journey. Once sedated, they will be taken into specially made cages and lifted to large trucks to their new homes away from poachers and other threats. Yet, moving the rhinos to safe zones is not the end of the work that needs to be done.

The illegal trade of rhino horns, which are prized in China and Southeast Asia for their supposed medicinal properties, remains a real threat. Even though the growing population of one-horned rhinos is a good sign, poachers will still return if we let our guard down. Thus, the public needs more education on the importance of protecting animal species from extinction.

40. What is the best title of this passage?
 (A) Nepal's Vulnerable Rhinos on the Road to Recovery
 (B) The Extinction of One-horned Rhinos in Nepal
 (C) The Greed of Human Beings are the Danger to One-horned Rhinos
 (D) Awareness of One-horned Rhinos Needed

41. Which of the following is **NOT** a contributing factor to the decrease of one-horned rhino population?
 (A) Human pollution. (B) Illegal hunting. (C) Shrinking habitats. (D) Pesticide overuse.

42. According to the passage, what is required to relocate huge creatures?
 (A) A huge cage, elephants, horns, and fires. (B) Elephants, tranquilizers, horns, and a huge cage.
 (C) Vets, horns, tranquilizers, and a truck. (D) Tranquilizers, elephants, vets, and a huge truck.

43. What can be inferred from the last paragraph?
 (A) Poachers will still try to catch rhinos if possible.

(B) The burden of conservation is on the government alone.

(C) Alternatives have been found to replace the one-horned rhinos for medicine.

(D) The public shows little concerns about the once-endangered species.

第 44 至 47 題為題組

The concept of self-driving cars has been around for years and many technology corporations like Google, Uber, Tesla, and Apple are already experimenting and testing with driverless technology for years. The first stage of self-driving cars seems quite sound. They can already change lanes, control speed, and warn drivers of potential hazards in the road. However, drivers will need to be willing to give up control of their car in order to enjoy these and other benefits.

The most obvious area in which we would benefit from driverless technology is safety. While driving a car, distractions are everywhere and a distracted driver is a dangerous driver. With driverless cars, the car itself would be able to recognize dangerous road conditions and make real-time adjustments in order to keep everyone safe. Our cars spend most of their time every day parked in a parking lot or on the street. With a driverless car, we could develop ride sharing programs where a car could take one person to work, and then go pick someone else up and take them to the supermarket. This would reduce the number of cars on the road, which would, in turn, reduce pollution.

Although there are many benefits, there are a few downfalls of driverless technology. Because safety is the primary concern, the fatalities and casualties happening on the roads and highways will drop. Thus, people working at insurance industry and hospitals may suffer job losses. Other driving-related jobs would be hurt as well. The release of self-driving cars might also pose a threat to truck drivers, taxi drivers, delivery drivers and bus drivers.

With new driverless features being created all the time, the future is looking bright for self-driving cars. However, we must continue to work on developing these features to make them as safe as possible. Maybe in the near future, we will all be driven to work or school by cars and buses without drivers.

44. What is the best title of this passage?

(A) How will self-driving technology change our lives?

(B) What are the pros and cons of the self-driving vehicles?

(C) How hazardous might self-driving cars be once they hit the roads?

(D) Will many people working in auto industry lose their jobs soon?

45. According to the passage, which of the following is **NOT** a feature of a driverless car?

(A) Road recognition. (B) Speed adjustment. (C) Danger warning. (D) Voice control.

46. If self-driving cars are mass-produced, which companies might reduce staff?

(A) An insurance company. (B) An express company.

(C) A taxi company. (D) All of them.

47. According to the passage, which of the following is a benefit of driverless cars to the people?

(A) Casualty rate on the streets will be reduced.

(B) Commuters will be able to shorten their commute time.

(C) Businesses can expect a reduction in operating costs.

(D) Taxi drivers will be able to do their job more easily.

第 48 至 51 題為題組

When hearing a news story about a kidnapping or a hostage story, it is often natural to immediately put yourself in that situation and think about what you would do. Many will often wonder why someone didn't try to run away or fight back. Usually fear prevents people from acting. However, in some situations, hostages may choose not to act not out of fear, but because they sympathize or even support their captors. While it may seem unbelievable, this phenomenon has been named the Stockholm syndrome.

It received its name after a bank hostage situation in Stockholm, Sweden during 1973. Four people were taken hostage and held inside the bank for six days before police were able to release them. While the people of Sweden were happy to see the hostages released, the hostages themselves had mixed emotions. They had developed a bond with their captor and wanted to be released with him. Furthermore, they also refused to work together with the authorities to identify the captors.

Instead of being angry or having resentment, they believed their captor to be kind for allowing them to live and for giving them food and water. The captives reverted back to an almost childlike state and saw their captor as a person of authority that could give them the best chance to survive. But this mind alteration was not exclusive to the captives.

While talking about Stockholm syndrome, we most often talk about how hostages are affected by their time of confinement. However, captors also go through a change of behavior and attitude toward their prisoners. Because the captives often fear for their lives, they are obedient toward the people holding them hostage. This makes it harder for the captors to then harm their hostages or put them in any danger. They become very protective of their prisoners and want to make sure they stay safe.

While Stockholm syndrome is a term that gets thrown around a lot when talking about a hostage situation, it is in fact very rare. It is important to remember that when people are faced with incredible danger, the will to survive will take over.

48. What is the second paragraph mainly about?

(A) How the phrase "Stockholm Syndrome" was coined.

(B) How the four hostages escaped from their captors.

(C) How the traumas the hostages suffered affected their lives.

(D) How the hostages braved the kidnappers fearlessly.

49. According to the passage, which of the following is **NOT** mentioned about the victims of "Stockholm Syndrome"?
(A) They firmly believe in the good side of the captors.
(B) They are sympathetic to the captors.
(C) They are reluctant to cooperate with the authorities.
(D) They are prone to developing a split personality.

50. From where can this article probably be found?
(A) A scientific journal. (B) A literary magazine. (C) A fashion magazine. (D) A psychology journal.

51. According to the passage, why do the captors develop a protective feeling toward their captives?
(A) Because the captors feel a strong sense of guilt.
(B) Because the captives are usually very obedient.
(C) Because the captives' minds are filled with hatred and revenge.
(D) Because the captors are afraid that the hostages may take revenge on them.

◆ 第貳部分：非選擇題 (占 28 分)

說明：本部分共有二題，請依各題指示作答，答案必須寫在「答案卷」上，並標明大題號 (一、二)。
作答務必使用筆尖較粗之黑色墨水的筆書寫，且不得使用鉛筆。

一、中譯英 (占 8 分)

說明：1. 請將以下中文句子譯成正確、通順、達意的英文，並將答案寫在「答案卷」上。
2. 請依序作答，並標明子題號 (1、2)。每題 4 分，共 8 分。

1. 全世界有三分之一的成年人和小孩體重過重。
2. 同時，他們因為肥胖而產生健康問題。

二、英文作文 (占 20 分)

說明：1. 依提示在「答案卷」上寫一篇英文作文。
2. 文長至少 120 個單詞 (words)。

提示：前美國總統 Obama 的女兒 Malia Obama 決定去哈佛就讀之前，先辦休學一年。給自己空檔來思考未來的方向和確認志趣所在。Malia 的決定獲得 Obama 的支持；這一年叫做 gap year。如果你也有類似的機會，你將會如何安排這一年呢？你想將時間用於國內外旅遊、打工、做志工、上一些自己想要上的課程還是其他選項？你要如何規畫你的 gap year？請寫一篇作文，文分兩段，第一段詳述要如何安排一個充實的 gap year，第二段說明如何藉由這樣的安排來更加確立自己未來方向，並幫助自己成長；過個更充實的四年大學生活。

Notes

指考英文模擬實戰四

◆ 第壹部分：單選題 (占 72 分)

一、詞彙題 (占 10 分)

說明：第 1 題至第 10 題，每題有 4 個選項，其中只有一個是正確或最適當的選項，請畫記在答案卡之「選擇題答案區」。各題答對者，得 1 分；答錯、未作答或畫記多於一個選項者，該題以零分計算。

1. The comedian's ________ performances on stage and TV shows are a sight to behold. No wonder many critics call him the master of comedy.
(A) harsh (B) dreadful (C) witty (D) controversial

2. When Dennis was about to reach the mountaintop, he decided to take a selfie. All of a sudden, he lost his footing and ________ down the slope.
(A) tumbled (B) stammered (C) flipped (D) spoiled

3. Thomas Edison took ________ methods in planning. He would make careful drawings of his ideas and inventions.
(A) ridiculous (B) rigorous (C) turbulent (D) hasty

4. The hospitalized singer found great ________ in all the cards and letters he had received from his fans.
(A) conspiracy (B) substitution (C) eternity (D) consolation

5. The long-haul flight severely ________ Philip's biological clock and thus he got really bad jet lag.
(A) disturbed (B) disconnected (C) discriminated (D) distracted

6. The sole survivor of the flooding ________ to the press how he narrowly survived being buried alive by the mudslide.
(A) aroused (B) awakened (C) detailed (D) enlightened

7. Being public figures, Catherine and Prince William have no choice but to get used to being ________ by vicious rumors.
(A) revived (B) troubled (C) corrupted (D) postponed

8. The notorious landlady ________ denied all accusations against her despite being in the wrong.
(A) extremely (B) logically (C) alternately (D) emphatically

9. The ________ facilities were destroyed in the disaster area. The villagers urgently needed clean food and water.
(A) sanitation (B) medication (C) military (D) research

10. The hearing-impaired clerk claimed that the way she had been treated at work had caused her much ________ physically and mentally.
(A) recession (B) awe (C) distress (D) entertainment

二、綜合測驗 (占 10 分)

說明：第 11 題至第 20 題，每題一個空格，請依文意選出最適當的一個選項，請畫記在答案卡之「選擇題答案區」。各題答對者，得 1 分；答錯、未作答或畫記多於一個選項者，該題以零分計算。

第 11 至 15 題為題組

Irenie Ekkeshis had serious eye pain the morning she woke up in January 2011. Originally, she ___11___ the pain, so she went to a pharmacy and picked up some eye drops. However, a few days later, it turned out that things were about to get much worse. She couldn't stand seeing bright lights. She found herself in a(n) ___12___ pain, and she couldn't see clearly. She went to her local eye hospital and found out that she had Acanthamoeba Keratitis, which is a serious eye infection.

Ekkeshis had to quit her job as a travel company director due to the loss of her eyesight. The acute pain in her eye started to ___13___ after months of treatment. However, her vision ___14___ blurred. In 2013, she had a corneal transplant (角膜移殖), but the operation still did little to regain her eyesight. Doctors also gave her the second operation on her eye, but unfortunately, one eye is permanently blind. Nowadays, she works hard on spreading ___15___ about this infection and urges people to be more careful. Please be reminded that your eyes are very sensitive, and could be easily harmed if you do not clean your contact lenses carefully.

11. (A) took little heed of (B) took its toll on (C) took it on the chin (D) took a fall for
12. (A) blunt (B) vital (C) intact (D) exquisite
13. (A) heal (B) ease (C) reveal (D) recover
14. (A) remained (B) retained (C) sustained (D) contained
15. (A) harness (B) bitterness (C) awareness (D) tidiness

第 16 至 20 題為題組

Oceans are fascinating. Yet, they are, at the same time, ___16___ places for humans. Our sea bed is covered with internet cables, high-tech machinery, and tunnels that make our lives better. Scientists, engineers and maintenance people who work in the ocean put themselves ___17___ on a daily basis. But with technological advancements, these brave individuals can work in a safer environment.

Norwegian engineers have invented a new snake-like robot that can swim in the ocean. The company that produces the robot hopes that it can repair underwater structures. This robot is ___18___ cameras and sensors. The parts, such as the cleaning brush, could be changed according to the user's needs. The best part is that it can squeeze into tiny spaces that humans are unable to.

Other inventions, like the driverless boat and the micro-submarine, can help scientists do research and gather information about the ocean. These vehicles are operated with the help of a remote-control. That way they can stay dry and away from danger. Both the boat and the micro-submarine are ___19___. Their inventors hope to minimize pollution by using clean energy and recyclable materials.

And finally, sea batteries are improving ocean research. Deep-sea devices can now run on better batteries that can ___20___ low temperatures and high pressure. This can help scientists send machines down the ocean for longer periods.

Hopefully, these new robots will help scientists and engineers understand the ocean much better.

16. (A) jealous (B) dangerous (C) eligible (D) valiant
17. (A) at risk (B) at large (C) at random (D) at hand
18. (A) equipped with (B) connected with (C) linked to (D) occupied with
19. (A) family-friendly (B) student-oriented (C) eco-friendly (D) child-oriented
20. (A) consist (B) insist (C) persist (D) resist

三、文意選填 (占 10 分)

說明：第 21 題至第 30 題，每題一個空格，請依文意在文章後所提供的(A)到(L)選項中分別選出最適當者，並將其英文字母代號畫記在答案卡之「選擇題答案區」。各題答對者，得 1 分；答錯、未作答或畫記多於一個選項者，該題以零分計算。

第 21 至 30 題為題組

People say that it's impossible to escape the ravages of time. However, that may not be ___21___ true. According to the latest scientific studies, you can quite easily just run away from it.

Researchers have been ___22___ the benefits of various forms of exercise, and they've found that runners generally live three additional years than non-runners. Furthermore, the advantages that running can bring about are present even when runners ___23___ in unhealthy activities such as smoking and drinking. It also doesn't matter runners run slowly or ___24___. Running, it seems, will always help people ___25___ their life span. Scientists arrived at this conclusion after ___26___ data from a large trove of medical studies. They found that although many ___27___ of exercise do help people live longer lives, nothing works as well as running.

As little as five minutes of running every day can make an impact on a person's health, and ___28___, an hour of running statistically lengthens life expectancy by seven hours, the researchers report. Of course, the more you run, the smaller those gains become, but no matter how much running you do, the activity will never ___29___ impact your health.

Doctors are not sure why running is so ___30___ for people, but they believe that part of the reason is that it combats high blood pressure and lowers body fat. So, if you want to live a long, healthy, and happy life, you know what to do—just put on your sneakers, and go for a run.

(A) looking into (B) on occasion (C) extend (D) on average
(E) types (F) helpful (G) combing through (H) entirely
(I) partial (J) engage (K) negatively (L) frames

四、篇章結構 (占 10 分)

說明：第 31 題至第 35 題，每題一個空格。請依文意在文章後所提供的(A)到(F)選項中分別選出最適當者，填入空格中，使篇章結構清晰有條理，並將其英文字母代號畫記在答案卡之「選擇題答案區」。各題答對者，得 2 分；答錯、未作答或畫記多於一個選項者，該題以零分計算。

第 31 至 35 題為題組

As the old saying goes, no one among us is perfect. __31__. For example, two soccer players are running quickly to kick the ball when one player tackles the other and breaks his or her leg. Or a driver looks down to adjust the radio, doesn't see that the car in front of them has stopped, and suddenly hits it. In cases like these, we have to make a moral judgment by weighing the damage that was caused and the mental state of the person who caused it. __32__

Of course, this idea has been examined using psychology before, but an international team of scientists from Italy, Austria, and the U.S. has recently looked at it from the perspective of our anatomy. __33__ Do the volume and structure of certain areas of the brain help explain differences in moral judgment? To determine this, the team first presented a number of stories with four possible outcomes to participants in the study. __34__ The team analyzed the data and found that the more developed the area of the brain known as the left STS region (左顳上溝) is, the more likely the participant was to forgive someone for a mistake, even one that caused serious harm.

In conclusion, this study gives clues about what happens inside our brain when we make moral judgments and forgive. __35__ In doing so, they hope to unlock more secrets of how the brain works.

(A) Building on these results, the team hopes to conduct more experiments with different, more realistic scenarios and more diverse subjects in the future.

(B) Through this process, we then determine whether we can forgive this person or not.

(C) Everyone makes mistakes on occasion, and sometimes the damage we cause can be significant.

(D) They then measured the participants' brain activity while they contemplated forgiveness.

(E) They wondered what actually goes on inside of the brain when we are making moral judgments.

(F) The brain is one of the most complex and magnificent organs in the human body.

五、閱讀測驗 (占 32 分)

說明：第 36 題至第 51 題，每題請分別根據各篇文章之文意選出最適當的一個選項，請畫記在答案卡之「選擇題答案區」。各題答對者，得 2 分；答錯、未作答或畫記多於一個選項者，該題以零分計算。

第 36 至 39 題為題組

Every year, hundreds of thousands of seals are killed by hunters in the Arctic region of Canada. The seals are not killed out of necessity for food, though. Instead, they are slaughtered mostly for their pelts, which is the skin of the animals that contains fur. Some of the fat of the seals, called blubber, is also taken and used to produce seal oil, which is then used in nutritional supplements.

The seal hunt is very controversial, but it is fully legal. The Canadian government sets a limit on the number of seals that can be taken each year in the hunt. The annual hunt takes place in March and April, and for the hunters, it brings in much-needed income. During the hunt, the hunters make up to 35 percent of their annual income.

Those who condemn the seal hunt do so because they feel it is inhumane. Since the most valuable part of the seal is the pelt, the vast majority of them are **clubbed** to death. This method allows the hunters to kill the seal without harming the pelt. However, as reported in the *Daily Mail*, veterinarians that examined the corpses of the seals found evidence that many of the seals were not dead at the time they were skinned. This could mean that they were still able to feel pain when their pelts were taken.

In recent years, many world governments have begun to ban seal products that come as a result of this commercial hunt. People opposed to the seal hunt see this as a positive development, as without a market for seal products, the practice of hunting them loses its economic value for the hunters.

The annual seal hunt in Canada shines a spotlight on the problem of making progress in a world that still relies on a traditional practice for people to make a living. The lives of the seals matter, but the lives of the hunters do, too. It will likely take time and compromise to find a solution that satisfies all.

36. According to the first paragraph of the passage, which of the following is true?

(A) Seals are killed because of overpopulation.

(B) Though seal hunting is brutal, it is highly profitable.

(C) Hunters heavily rely on the income from slaughtering seals, which accounts for all of their annual income.

(D) The Canadian government allows hunters to kill seals because of food shortages.

37. Which of the following is closest in meaning to "**clubbed**" in the third paragraph?

(A) pierced. (B) beaten. (C) stabbed. (D) slashed.

38. What is the best title of this passage?

(A) Seal Hunt: The Problematic Balance between Profit and Humanity

(B) Seal Hunt: The Problematic Balance between the Savage and the Civilized

(C) Seal Hunt: The Problematic Balance between Government and People

(D) Seal Hunt: The Problematic Balance between News and Reality

39. According to the passage, which of the following statements is true?

(A) Seal slaughters last for as long as four months each year.

(B) Besides their skin, seals' blubber is also a commodity.

(C) According to statistics, all of the seals were dead before they were skinned.

(D) The demand for seal products worldwide has been shrinking.

第 40 至 43 題為題組

If you are a wildlife lover with plans to visit the Southern Hemisphere, Kangaroo Island is a fine place to visit. Not far from the Australian mainland, this island keeps more than a third of its land as protected nature preserves. Thus, it is filled with native Australian animals such as kangaroos, koalas, echidnas, and sea lions. For bird watchers, there are hundreds of species that can be spotted, from water birds and game birds to species like parrots that have bright, colorful feathers. Birds of prey such as owls, falcons, and hawks can also be found, and along the shores, there are even penguin colonies.

Put simply, Kangaroo Island is filled with wildlife. However, people also live on the island, but the population is small, with fewer than 5,000 residents. Due to the island being such an unspoiled place, it does have great value as a tourist destination for nature lovers. Nevertheless, all the comforts that travelers want and need are still available.

During the day, visitors can tour the nature preserves and snap pictures of the amazing wildlife on Kangaroo Island. They can visit beaches to see pelicans flying and sea lions lying in the sun. Much of the sightseeing is done on foot, as the island is filled with hiking trails. One particular trail spans three nature preserves and takes 5 days to finish. If you plan to take this trail, you'd best be prepared to do a lot of walking!

When nighttime rolls around, visitors can eat at luxurious restaurants serving all sorts of gourmet food. Seafood and fine wines are on the menu, and those who like to eat will love what the island's restaurants have to offer.

When you're ready for bed, Kangaroo Island offers something for everyone. You can stay in a cottage by the shore or in a five-star hotel room. If you are on a budget, campgrounds are available as well. In so many ways, Kangaroo Island is a paradise just waiting to be discovered!

40. According to the passage, who may **NOT** like this animal haven?
(A) Extreme sports lovers. (B) Gourmets. (C) Bird-watchers. (D) Amateur photographers.

41. According to the passage, which statement is **NOT** true about Kangaroo Island?
(A) The accommodations provided cover a wide range of choices.
(B) The total population of animals outnumbers that of locals.
(C) More than two-thirds of its land is designated as preserves.
(D) Most animals are only native to Australia.

42. According to the third paragraph of the passage, which of the following is true?
(A) Visitors can go hunting at daytime and enjoy shopping at the mall when night falls.
(B) The longest trail runs as long as the whole island.
(C) Visitors can buy feed and feed birds and animals.
(D) Visitors can take a stroll on trails either ambitiously or casually.

43. What kinds of animals are mentioned in the passage?
(A) Falcons, hawks, parrots, pandas. (B) Kangaroos, game birds, water birds, and koalas.
(C) Koalas, owls, kangaroos, lions, buffalos. (D) Pelicans, owls, koalas, whales.

第 44 至 47 題為題組

For paleontologists—the scientists who study fossils—2015 was an exciting year. It was at this time that they made a discovery of a fossil of a Teleocrater in Tanzania. The finding is changing the way paleontologists have looked at different types of ancient creatures such as archosaurs and dinosaurs. The discovery was important enough to merit a news report in *The New York Times*, after the much more scientific report of the findings was published in the journal *Nature*.

To understand why the discovery is important, one must look at the scientific understanding of evolution. There were fossils discovered in the 1930s that were not classified until the 1950s. It was at this time that the name Teleocrater was created by the paleontologist Alan Charig. Although he had classified the creature, there was still not enough evidence to support the classification. Thus, even though the Teleocrater was named, it was never placed in the evolutionary family tree of dinosaurs.

The discovery in 2015 changed all this. It provided evidence for Teleocrater, and it also made another important discovery at the same time. Teleocrater was an archosaur, a type of reptile. About 250 million years ago, archosaurs split into two different branches on the evolutionary tree. One branch was the dinosaurs, which eventually became the birds that we see today. The other branch went in another direction and became crocodiles and alligators. What is strange about Teleocrater is that it has characteristics of both branches. It has some features of birds, but it has ankle bones that are similar to crocodiles. It is a very significant find because it shows what was happening at the time the archosaurs were branching off.

Of all the fossils that have been found and classified, this recent finding shows that there is much to discover in paleontology. Each new discovery helps fill in a piece of the puzzle of evolution and allows our understanding of the prehistoric world to grow. What new discoveries **lie in store** for future generations of paleontologists? We'll just have to wait and see!

44. According to the passage, which of the following statement is **NOT** true?

(A) There is proof showing Teleocrater belongs in the evolutionary tree of dinosaurs.

(B) Dinosaurs are ancestors of the modern birds.

(C) One branch of archosaurs developed into reptiles.

(D) Alan Charig and his research team found the Teleocrater fossil.

45. Which of the following is closest in meaning to the phrase "**lie in store**"?

(A) Going to happen.
(B) Hitting the sack.
(C) Available to buy at a store.
(D) Having enough storage.

46. Why was 2015 a significant year in paleontology?

(A) Alan Charig named the fossil Teleocrater in this year.

(B) Scientists found a fossil linking birds and reptiles.

(C) *The New York Times* published a highly scientific report about Teleocrater.

(D) Paleontologists gained a complete understanding of Teleocrater.

47. Which of the following statements about archosaurs is true?

(A) They evolved into dinosaurs only.
(B) They existed about 300 million years ago on Earth.
(C) They usually had characteristics of birds.
(D) They are closely related to present-day reptiles.

第 48 至 51 題為題組

When you comb or brush your hair, you probably discard any stray hairs that become separated from your scalp. In one culture, saving these strands of hair is a tradition that is carried on by women and girls. The particular culture that does this is a small minority in the Guizhou Province of China called the Long-horned Miao.

The headdresses are woven around wooden ornaments that resemble the horns of a cow. In an article in the *Daily Mail*, an expert in Chinese minority culture stated that the wooden ornaments probably came from an older tradition that held the cow as a sacred animal. The Miao live in rural areas, and cows were probably honored for their usefulness to humans. Eventually, the tradition evolved into a tradition that honored human ancestors rather than cows.

To make the headdresses, hair from ancestors is wrapped with wool and linen around a wooden clip. This, in turn, is tied together with a long white ribbon. All of the materials used to make the headdresses are used and passed down through each generation.

The headdresses are not the only special thing the Miao wear. They also dress in colorful clothing with intricate patterns. The patterns are embroidered, which means they are sewn into the cloth using colored thread. The main colors are red, orange, white, and black.

One of the special festivals where the clothing and headdresses are worn is the Flower Dancing Festival. It is the most popular festival for the young people in Miao society, and it is where the single girls of one village dance and sing to entertain boys from other villages. If there is an attraction between a boy and a girl, then a long engagement may result. To get married in Miao society is not an easy thing, and it can take many months before an agreement is reached between two families.

The special headdresses are not worn on a daily basis, though. Instead, they are only worn on special occasions and for the amusement of tourists. Unfortunately, the tradition is slowly dying out, as the younger generation of Miao is leaving the rural areas where they grew up for greater opportunities in other parts of China.

48. Why are Miao people called "The Long-horned" Miao?

(A) They transmit messages by blowing horns in mountainous areas.
(B) The ornaments they wear on their heads look like the horns of cows.
(C) They weave their stray hairs into the shape of a horn to keep them tidy.
(D) They think a horn is a sacred object to send their prayers to their gods.

49. According to the passage, which of the following is true about the traditions of the Miao people?
(A) Women and girls collect their own stray hairs and never throw them away.
(B) Women and girls cut cows' hair to decorate themselves.
(C) Mothers are asked to save their daughters' hair since childhood.
(D) Their ancestors pass down their stray hairs to their female descendants.

50. On what occasions can females wear the special headdresses?
(A) As long as they want to.
(B) When they are doing chores.
(C) When the girls want to entertain boys and draw their attention.
(D) When a harvest celebration is held.

51. Why is the tradition of wearing the long-horned headdresses dying out?
(A) Young girls are moving to urban cities to seek better working opportunities.
(B) The local government banned the Miao females from wearing such weird hairstyles.
(C) Females think that those inherited stray hairs are very unhygienic.
(D) Females gradually lose their interest in preserving such a tradition.

◆ 第貳部分：非選擇題 (占 28 分)

說明：本部分共有二題，請依各題指示作答，答案必須寫在「答案卷」上，並標明大題號 (一、二)。作答務必使用筆尖較粗之黑色墨水的筆書寫，且不得使用鉛筆。

一、中譯英 (占 8 分)

說明：1. 請將以下中文句子譯成正確、通順、達意的英文，並將答案寫在「答案卷」上。
2. 請依序作答，並標明子題號 (1、2)。每題 4 分，共 8 分。

1. 在日益競爭的勞力市場，台灣的年輕人正在面臨低薪的困境。更慘的是，很多人還有負債。
2. 為了有更好的出路和更優渥的薪水，越來越多的大學畢業生決定要到國外找工作。

二、英文作文 (占 20 分)

說明：1. 依提示在「答案卷」上寫一篇英文作文。
2. 文長至少 120 個單詞 (words)。

提示：前一陣子在美式的知名大賣場發生顧客因不滿工作人員的服務態度，而對她拳腳相向。此事引起社會軒然大波。有人認為服務業就是要「顧客至上」，要以消費者的權益為最優先的考量；有人則認為顧客不一定是對的，消費者也是需要被教育學習尊重服務人員。身為消費者的你認為怎樣才是服務業者應有的態度呢？請寫一篇作文，文分兩段，第一段描述根據自己被服務過的經驗或是你親眼所見他人被服務的經驗。 第二段請就此經驗來說明你認為什麼才是服務業者應有的態度。

加碼贈送

107 108 學年度 指考英文 試題與詳解

三民書局

108 學年度　指考英文試題

◆ 第壹部分：單選題 (占 72 分)

一、詞彙題 (占 10 分)

說明：第 1 題至第 10 題，每題有 4 個選項，其中只有一個是正確或最適當的選項，請畫記在答案卡之「選擇題答案區」。各題答對者，得 1 分；答錯、未作答或畫記多於一個選項者，該題以零分計算。

1. The sign in front of the Johnsons' house says that no one is allowed to set foot on their ________ without permission.
(A) margin　(B) shelter　(C) reservation　(D) property

2. Instead of giving negative criticism, our teachers usually try to give us ________ feedback so that we can improve on our papers.
(A) absolute　(B) constructive　(C) influential　(D) peculiar

3. A study shows that the chance of an accident is much higher for drivers who are ________ in phone conversations while driving.
(A) contained　(B) engaged　(C) included　(D) located

4. Mike trembled with ________ and admiration when he saw the magnificent view of the waterfalls.
(A) awe　(B) plea　(C) oath　(D) merit

5. Ms. Chen has a large collection of books and most of them are quite heavy; she needs a bookshelf ________ enough to hold all of them.
(A) coarse　(B) vigorous　(C) portable　(D) sturdy

6. The athlete rolled up his sleeves to show his ________ forearms, thick and strong from years of training in weight-lifting.
(A) barren　(B) chubby　(C) ragged　(D) muscular

7. Suffering from a serious financial crisis, the car company is now on the edge of ________, especially with the recent sharp decrease in its new car sales.
(A) graduation　(B) capacity　(C) depression　(D) bankruptcy

8. After the rain, the meadow ________ under the sun with the droplets of water on the grass.
(A) rippled　(B) shattered　(C) glistened　(D) mingled

9. The Great Wall of China was originally built to ________ the northern border of the country against foreign invasion.
(A) fortify　(B) rehearse　(C) diminish　(D) strangle

10. A mad scientist in a novel is often portrayed as a wild-eyed man with crazy hair, working ________ in a lab full of strange equipment and bubbling test tubes.
(A) contagiously　(B) distinctively　(C) frantically　(D) tremendously

二、綜合測驗 (占 10 分)

說明：第 11 題至第 20 題，每題一個空格，請依文意選出最適當的一個選項，請畫記在答案卡之「選擇題答案區」。各題答對者，得 1 分；答錯、未作答或畫記多於一個選項者，該題以零分計算。

第 11 至 15 題為題組

The fashion industry in Africa has witnessed tremendous growth in recent years. African fashion design has caught the eyes of international celebrities including former US first lady, Michelle Obama, Rihanna, and Beyoncé, __11__. Global demand for African-inspired fashion has led to incredible sales for some African designers and brands.

Folake Folarin—Coker, founder of Tiffany Amber, is one of the best-known fashion designers in both the African and global fashion industry. Born in Lagos, Nigeria, she received her education in Europe, __12__ she got an opportunity to interact with various cultures at a young age. __13__, she has a master's degree in law from Switzerland, but as fate would have it, her passion for fashion led her into fashion design.

Folake's tasteful and colorful creations have earned her global __14__, making her the first African fashion designer to showcase her talent at the New York Mercedes Fashion Week for two consecutive years. She has also been widely __15__ in international media such as CNN. In 2013, she was listed as one of the Forbes Power Women in Africa.

11. (A) if any (B) among others (C) in short (D) at best
12. (A) where (B) there (C) that (D) whether
13. (A) Generally (B) Ideally (C) Relatively (D) Interestingly
14. (A) recognition (B) motivation (C) supervision (D) preparation
15. (A) believed (B) announced (C) featured (D) populated

第 16 至 20 題為題組

When we stream the latest TV series, or download high-resolution photos, we are probably unaware that the data behind them is speeding around the world in cables under the sea.

These cable systems, faster and cheaper than satellites, carry most of the intercontinental Internet traffic. Today, there are over 420 submarine cables __16__, stretching over 700,000 miles around the world. It is not a new phenomenon, __17__. The first transcontinental cable—laid in 1854—ran from Ireland to Newfoundland, and made telegraph communication possible between England and Canada. Currently, the world's highest-capacity undersea Internet cable is a 5,600–mile link between the US and Japan. __18__ named "FASTER," the cable connects Oregon in the US with Japan and Taiwan.

The submarine cables require extra __19__ to install. They must generally be run across flat surfaces of the ocean floor, and stay clear of coral reefs, sunken ships, fish beds, and other general __20__. The fiber-optic cables are also very fragile, so they are surrounded with layers of tubing and steel to prevent damage.

16. (A) at large (B) in service (C) by contrast (D) under control
17. (A) then (B) still (C) instead (D) though
18. (A) Suitably (B) Constantly (C) Vitally (D) Mockingly
19. (A) speed (B) light (C) care (D) link
20. (A) directions (B) obstacles (C) aquariums (D) circulations

三、文意選填 (占 10 分)

說明：第 21 題至第 30 題，每題一個空格。請依文意在文章後所提供的(A)到(L)選項中分別選出最適當者，並將其英文字母代號畫記在答案卡之「選擇題答案區」。各題答對者，得 1 分；答錯、未作答或畫記多於一個選項者，該題以零分計算。

第 21 至 30 題為題組

The Getty Center sits more than 800 feet above sea level, towering above the city of Los Angeles. A 0.75–mile-long tramway takes visitors to the top of the hill. At the top, four exhibit pavilions and a visitor center form the heart of an eleven-building complex. The museum was originally constructed to __21__ the vast art collection belonging to oil tycoon J. Paul Getty. Today, it is stocked with so many art works that the exhibit arenas can show just a part of them at a time, making the __22__ special exhibitions a highlight of any visit to the Getty.

The Center's award-winning architect, Richard Meier, did an outstanding job of creating a public space that has __23__ many visitors. Visitors go to the Getty thinking they are visiting a museum with works of art on the inside. What they discover instead is a work of art with a museum inside. The idea is interesting: The outdoor space can be a completely satisfying __24__ experience.
Meier took a few basic __25__: metal, stone and glass. Working with a billion-dollar budget, he combined them to create a work of architecture that can excite visitors as much as the art collection inside does. Around every corner and at every __26__, there is a new view to enchant guests. And then, just when they think they have seen it all, a new fountain or landscape pops up.
The building stone is travertine, __27__ from Italy, the same source as for the historic buildings in Rome. A special cutting process exposes the fossils long buried inside the stone, which reveals the delicate treasures __28__ under the rough surface. Some of them are set as "feature" stones scattered about the site, waiting to __29__ those who find them. The most fantastic one is on the arrival plaza wall, across from the tram station.
In addition to museum tours, the Getty also provides various free on-site tours, including tours of the gardens. These __30__ are a must for anyone interested in learning more about Meier's techniques and ideas.

(A) delight (B) explorations (C) turn (D) surprised

(E) imported　(F) over-emphasized　(G) artistic　(H) hidden

(I) foundations　(J) materials　(K) house　(L) ever-changing

四、篇章結構 (占 10 分)

說明：第 31 題至第 35 題，每題一個空格。請依文意在文章後所提供的(A)到(F)選項中分別選出最適當者，填入空格中，使篇章結構清晰有條理，並將其英文字母代號畫記在答案卡之「選擇題答案區」。各題答對者，得 2 分；答錯、未作答或畫記多於一個選項者，該題以零分計算。

第 31 至 35 題為題組

Copernicus, founder of modern astronomy, was born in 1473 to a well-to-do merchant family in Torun, Poland. He was sent off to attend university in Italy, studying mathematics and optics, and canon law. Returning from his studies abroad, Copernicus was appointed to an administrative position in the cathedral of Frauenburg. There he spent a sheltered and academic life for the rest of his days.

__31__ He made his observations from a tower situated on the protective wall around the cathedral. His observations were made with the "bare eyeball," so to speak, as a hundred years were to pass before the invention of the telescope. In 1530, Copernicus completed his famous work *De Revolutionibus*, which later played a major role in changing the philosophical view of humankind's place in the universe. __32__

Copernicus died in 1543 and was never to know what a stir his work would cause. In his book, he asserted that the Earth rotated on its axis once daily and traveled around the Sun once yearly. __33__ People then regarded the Earth as stationary, situated at the center of the universe, with the Sun and all the planets revolving around it. Copernicus' theory challenged the long-held belief that God created the Heavens and the Earth, and could overturn the core values of the Catholic world. __34__ Other ministers quickly followed suit, saying of Copernicus, "This fool wants to turn the whole art of astronomy upside down."

Ironically, Copernicus had dedicated his work to Pope Paul III. __35__ The Church ultimately banned *De Revolutionibus*, and the book remained on the list of forbidden reading material for nearly three centuries thereafter.

(A) Meanwhile, Copernicus was a lifelong member of the Catholic Church.

(B) The book, however, wasn't published until two months before his death.

(C) If this act was an attempt to seek the Catholic Church's approval, it was of no use.

(D) This went against the philosophical and religious beliefs held during medieval times.

(E) Religious leader Martin Luther voiced his opposition to the sun-centered system model.

(F) In his spare time, Copernicus studied the stars and the planets, applying his math knowledge to the mysteries of the night sky.

五、閱讀測驗 (占 32 分)

說明：第 36 題至第 51 題，每題請分別根據各篇文章之文意選出最適當的一個選項，請畫記在答案卡之「選擇題答案區」。各題答對者，得 2 分；答錯、未作答或畫記多於一個選項者，該題以零分計算。

第 36 至 39 題為題組

Tempeh (or *tempe*), a traditional soy product from Indonesia, is hailed as the country's "gift to the world," like *kimchi* from Korea or *miso* from Japan.

A stable, cheap source of protein in Indonesia for centuries, *tempeh* is a fermented food originating from the island of Java. It was discovered during tofu production when discarded soybean residue caught microbial spores from the air and grew certain whitish fungi around it. When this fermented residue was found to be edible and tasty, people began producing it at home for daily consumption across the country. This has given rise to many variations in its flavor and texture throughout different Indonesian regions.

Tempeh is high in protein and low in fat, and contains a host of vitamins. In fact, it is the only reported plant-based source of vitamin B12. Apart from being able to help reduce cholesterol, increase bone density, and promote muscle recovery, *tempeh* has a lot of polyphenols that protect skin cells and slow down the aging process. Best of all, with the same protein quality as meat and the ability to take on many flavors and textures, *tempeh* is a great meat substitute—something the vegetarian and vegan communities have been quick in adopting.

In addition to its highly nutritional makeup, *tempeh* has diverse preparation possibilities. It can be served as a main course (usually in curries) or a side dish to be eaten with rice, as a deep-fried snack, or even blended into smoothies and healthy juices. Though not yet a popular food among international diners, you may find *tempeh*-substituted BLTs (bacon, lettuce, tomato sandwiches) in San Francisco as easily as you can find vegetarian burgers with *tempeh* patties in Bali.

For the people of Indonesia, *tempeh* is not just food but also has cultural value. With the Indonesian traditional fabric *batik* being recognized by UNESCO as "Intangible Cultural Heritage of Humanity," *tempeh* has great potential for this honor as well.

36. What is the passage mainly about?
    (A) The preparation of a health food.
    (B) A traditional delicacy from Java.
    (C) A gourmet guide for vegetarians.
    (D) The cultural heritage of Indonesia.

37. According to the passage, which of the following is true about *tempeh*?
    (A) It is mainly served as a side dish.
    (B) It is discarded when fungi grow around it.

(C) It is formed from fermented soybeans.

(D) It has the same nutritional benefits as *kimchi*.

38. What aspects of *tempeh* are discussed in paragraphs 2 to 4?

(A) Origin → nutrition → cuisine.

(B) Origin → cuisine → marketing.

(C) Cuisine → nutrition → marketing.

(D) Distribution → cuisine → nutrition.

39. Which of the following can be inferred from this passage?

(A) Senior citizens will eat *tempeh* as vitamin supplement.

(B) *Tempeh* will soon be more popular than *kimchi* or *miso*.

(C) The nutrition of *tempeh* will be reduced with mass production.

(D) *Tempeh* is likely to be recognized as an international cultural symbol.

第 40 至 43 題為題組

When Dr. David Spiegel emerged from a three-hour shoulder surgery in 1972, he didn't use any pain medication to recover. Instead, he hypnotized himself. It worked—to the surprise of everyone but Spiegel himself, who has studied hypnosis for 45 years.

Hypnosis is often misunderstood as a sleep-like state in which a person is put to sleep and does whatever he is asked to do. But according to Dr. Spiegel, it is a state of highly focused attention and intense concentration. Being hypnotized, you tune out most of the stimuli around you. You focus intently on the subject at hand, to the near exclusion of any other thought. This trance-like state can be an effective tool to control pain, ease anxiety, and deal with stress.

Not all people, however, are equally hypnotizable. In a recent study, Dr. Spiegel and his colleagues found that people who are easily hypnotized tend to be more trusting of others, more intuitive, and more likely to get caught up in a good movie. The research team compared people who were highly hypnotizable with those low in hypnotizability. Both groups were given fMRI scans during several different conditions: at rest, while recalling a memory, and during two sessions of hypnotism. The researchers saw some interesting changes in the brain during hypnosis—but only in the highly hypnotizable group. Specifically, there was a drop in activity in the part of the brain which usually fires up when there is something to worry about.

This helps explain how hypnosis can have powerful effects, including reducing stress, anxiety, pain, and self-consciousness. Spiegel hopes that the practice can be used to replace painkillers. His own previous research has shown that when people in pain were taught self-hypnosis, they needed half the pain medication and suffered half the pain of those who were only given access to painkillers. However, more needs to be learned about hypnosis in order to harness its potential effects.

40. How does the author begin the passage?

(A) By giving a definition.

(B) By mentioning an incident.

(C) By providing statistics.

(D) By comparing people's responses.

41. According to the passage, what is the goal of Dr. Spiegel's work?

(A) To explain the real causes of pain.

(B) To help people concentrate on their job.

(C) To explore how hypnosis can be used as a medical treatment.

(D) To strengthen the brain's functions to reduce psychological problems.

42. According to Dr. Spiegel, which of the following is true when people are hypnotized?

(A) They recall only happy memories.

(B) Their mind is fixed only on what they are doing.

(C) They do whatever they are told to do.

(D) They have greater awareness of things around them.

43. What can be inferred about highly hypnotizable people?

(A) They tend to be isolated from the society.

(B) They are more likely to fall asleep during the day.

(C) They may easily identify themselves with characters in fictions.

(D) They are more trustworthy than people who are less hypnotizable.

第 **44** 至 **47** 題為題組

In many languages, such as English, there is no straightforward way to talk about smell. For **want** of dedicated odor terminology, English speakers are often forced to use odor-sources such as "flowery" and "vanilla" and metaphors like "sweet" and "oriental" in their descriptions of smell.

But the difficulty with talking about smell is not universal. The Maniq, a group of hunter-gatherers in southern Thailand, can describe smells using at least fifteen different terms, which express only smells and are not applicable across other sensory domains. In addition to Maniq, researchers found that there are also a dozen words for various smells in Jahai, a language spoken by a neighboring hunter-gatherer population.

Interestingly, the difficulty for English speakers to translate smell directly into words seems to have very little to do with the nose's actual capabilities. According to findings of a recent study, English speakers are capable of discriminating more than a trillion different odors. Then, why is there a gap between their ability to discriminate scent and their vocabulary? The researchers suggest that surroundings may play a significant role.

Maniq and Jahai speakers live in tropical rainforest regions with a hunting-gathering lifestyle, and these two ethnic groups evaluate their surroundings through their noses to survive in nature. In an environment that is still largely untouched by humans, they are surrounded by smells at all times. They need to use their sense of smell to identify animals that they can hunt, and to recognize objects or events, such as spoiled food, that can pose a danger. Unlike the Maniq and the Jahai, many English speakers inhabit the post-industrial west and do not rely on smells to survive in their environment. This difference may explain the interesting linguistic phenomenon discussed above.

44. What is the purpose of this passage?
(A) To evaluate the languages used by different ethnic groups.
(B) To prove how civilization slows down language development.
(C) To describe how terms of smell are found in different languages.
(D) To point out the link between language use and the environment.

45. What does the word "**want**" in the first paragraph most likely mean?
(A) Lack. (B) Growth. (C) Loss. (D) Search.

46. Which of the following is true about the Maniq?
(A) They live in a different climate zone from the Jahai.
(B) Their ability to smell is stronger than that of the Jahai.
(C) They use smell terms to describe how food looks and tastes.
(D) Their living environment is similar to that in earlier human history.

47. Why is it difficult for English speakers to describe smells directly?
(A) They cannot distinguish the smells around them.
(B) The sense of smell is not critical for their survival.
(C) They consider it uncivilized to talk about smells directly.
(D) There are not many sources of odor in their surroundings.

第 48 至 51 題為題組

The okapi is a mammal living above the equator in one of the most biodiverse areas in central Africa. The animal was unknown to the western world until the beginning of the 20th century, and is often described as half-zebra, half-giraffe, as if it were a mixed-breed creature from a Greek legend. Yet its image is prevalent in the Democratic Republic of Congo—the only country in the world where it is found living in the wild. The okapi is to Congo what the giant panda is to China or the kangaroo to Australia.

Although the okapi has striped markings resembling those of zebras', it is most closely related to the giraffe. It has a long neck, and large, flexible ears. The face and throat are greyish white. The coat is a chocolate to reddish brown, much in contrast with the white horizontal stripes and rings on the legs and white ankles. Overall, the okapi can be easily distinguished from its nearest relative. It is much smaller (about the size of a horse), and shares more external similarities with the deer than with the giraffe. While both sexes possess horns in the giraffe, only males bear horns in the okapi.

West got its first **whiff** of the okapi in 1890 when Welsh journalist Henry Morton Stanley had puzzled over a strange "African donkey" in his book. Other Europeans in Africa had also heard of an animal that they came to call the "African unicorn." Explorers may have seen the fleeting view of the striped backside as the animal fled through the bushes, leading to speculation that the okapi was some sort of rainforest zebra. Some even believed that the okapi was a new species of zebra. It was only later, when okapi skeleton was analyzed, that naturalists realized they had a giraffe on their hands.

1987, the Okapi Wildlife Reserve was established in eastern Congo to protect this rare mammal. But decades of political turbulence has seen much of the Congo's natural resources spin out of the government's control, and okapi numbers have fallen by 50 percent since 1995. Today, only 10,000 remain.

48. Which of the following is a picture of an okapi?

(A) 
(B) 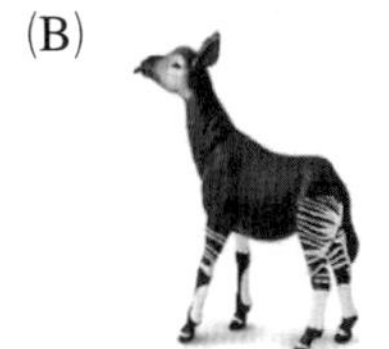
(C) 
(D) 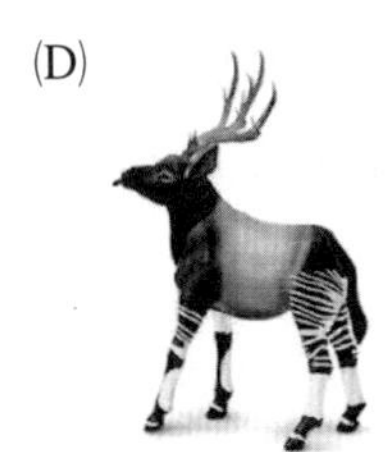

49. Which of the following descriptions is true about the okapi?
(A) It is an important symbol of Congo.
(B) It is a mystical creature from a Greek legend.
(C) It has been well protected since 1987.
(D) It is more closely related to the zebra than the giraffe.

50. What does the word "whiff" most likely mean in the third paragraph?
(A) Firm belief. (B) Kind intention. (C) Slight trace. (D) Strong dislike.

51. Which of the following can be inferred about Henry Morton Stanley?
(A) He was the first European to analyze okapi skeleton.
(B) He had found many new species of animals in Africa.
(C) He did not know the "African donkey" in his book was the okapi.
(D) He had seen the backside of an okapi dashing through the bushes.

◆ 第貳部分：非選擇題 (占 28 分)

說明：本部分共有二題，請依各題指示作答，答案必須寫在「答案卷」上，並標明大題號 (一、二)。
作答務必使用筆尖較粗之黑色墨水的筆書寫，且不得使用鉛筆。

一、中譯英 (占 8 分)

說明：1. 請將以下中文句子譯成正確、通順、達意的英文，並將答案寫在「答案卷」上。
　　　2. 請依序作答，並標明子題號 (1、2)。每題 4 分，共 8 分。

1. 創意布條最近在夜市成了有效的廣告工具，也刺激了買氣的成長。
2. 其中有些看似無意義，但卻相當引人注目，且常能帶給人們會心的一笑。

二、英文作文 (占 20 分)

說明：1. 依提示在「答案卷」上寫一篇英文作文。
　　　2. 文長至少 120 個單詞 (words)。

提示：右表顯示美國 18 至 29 歲的青年對不同類別之新聞的關注度統計。請依據圖表內容寫一篇英文作文，文長至少 120 個單詞。文分二段，第一段描述圖表內容，並指出關注度較高及偏低的類別；第二段則描述在這六個新聞類別中，你自己較為關注及較不關注的新聞主題分別為何，並說明理由。

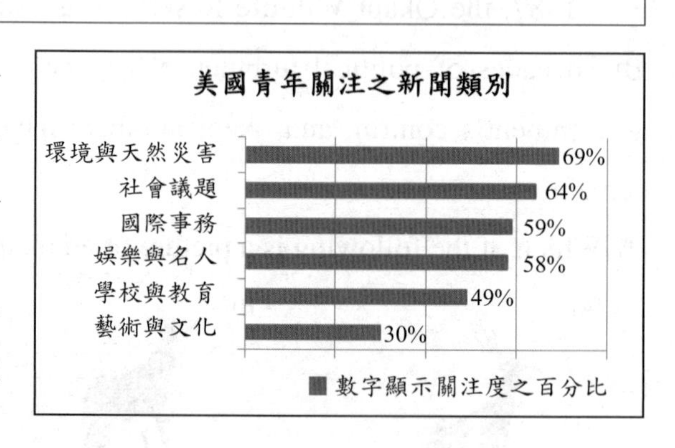

108 學年度　指考英文試題詳解

◆ 第壹部分：選擇題

一、詞彙題

(D) 1. Johnson 家房子前面的標誌寫著：未經允許，任何人不得進入他們的地產。

(A) 邊緣　(B) 避難處
(C) 預約　(D) 地產

解析

❶ 本題可由 house 聯想到(D) property。

❷ 本題也可由文意與常識判斷：Johnson 家門前的標誌寫著：未經允許不可進入他們的地產，故選(D) property。

補充

set foot on/in 進入 (某地) (※較常用 in)
without permission 未經允許

(B) 2. 我們的老師們經常試著給我們有建設性的回饋，而不是給負面的批評，好讓我們能改善我們的論文。

(A) 絕對的　(B) 有建設性的
(C) 有影響力的　(D) 怪異的

解析

❶ 本題由搭配詞 constructive feedback (有建設性的回饋) 得知本題選(B) constructive。

❷ 本題亦可由文意解答。由 instead of (不…，反而…) 可知前後句文意相反，由此推知與 negative 相對的形容詞為 constructive。

(B) 3. 一項研究顯示：駕駛邊開車邊忙著講電話，發生意外的機率會比平常高出許多。

(A) 含有的　(B) 忙於…的
(C) 包含的　(D) 位於…

解析

從文意駕駛遭逢意外的危險大增，可推知是邊開車邊忙著講電話，故選(B) engaged。

補充

❶ be engaged in 忙於…

❷ much 可修飾比較級，相同用法的有 even、far、a lot。

(A) 4. 當 Mike 看見壯觀的瀑布景色時，他既敬畏又讚嘆地微微顫抖。

(A) 讚嘆　(B) 懇求
(C) 宣誓　(D) 優點

解析

❶ 本題可直接由搭配詞 tremble with awe 選出答案(A) awe。

❷ 本題亦可從文意得知答案：當 Mike 看到壯觀的瀑布景色時，他敬畏與讚嘆地微微顫抖。

補充

tremble with fear/rage/anger/hunger 因恐懼 / 暴怒 / 生氣 / 飢餓而發抖

(D) 5. 陳老師有大量的藏書，而且它們大多很重；她需要一個夠堅固而能裝得下所有藏書的書架。

(A) 粗糙的　(B) 活力充沛的
(C) 手提的　(D) 堅固的

解析

❶ 由文意陳老師有大量的藏書，大部分都很重，推論她需要堅固的書架放書，故選(D) sturdy。

❷ 本句原為 Ms. Chen has . . . ; she needs a bookshelf which is sturdy enough to hold . . . ，which is sturdy enough to hold . . . 為形容詞子句，省略 which is 後，變成形容詞片語修飾 a bookshelf。

補充

adj. / adv. + enough to V 夠…而能…

(D) 6. 這名運動員捲起袖子，為了展示他肌肉發達的前臂，它們的粗壯來自好幾年的舉重訓練。

(A) 貧瘠的　(B) 圓胖的
(C) 襤褸的　(D) 肌肉發達的

解析

本題從關鍵字 athlete、thick and strong、weight-lifting 可聯想到形容詞 muscular，由文意可知：運動員捲起袖子是為了露出數年舉重訓練產生的健壯肌肉，故選(D) muscular。

補充

此句的 from 意為「因為」。

(D) 7. 這家汽車公司正遭受嚴重的財務危機，尤其是最近新車款的銷售急遽減少，現在瀕臨破產。

(A) 畢業　(B) 能力
(C) 憂鬱　(D) 破產

解析

❶ 前句指出某汽車公司遭受嚴重的財務危機，後句表示最近銷售急遽減少，可推知該公司應該遭受財務困難，瀕臨破產，故選(D) bankruptcy。

❷ 本題亦可由 financial crisis、sharp decrease in car sales 聯想到(D) bankruptcy。

補充

on the edge of 瀕於…。

(C) 8. 雨後，因為陽光照射草上的水珠，草地在太陽下閃閃發亮。

(A) 如波浪般起伏　(B) 粉碎
(C) 閃閃發亮　(D) 使混合

解析
本題可從線索 the sun 、 the droplets of water 推知在雨後草地因為被陽光照射的水珠而閃閃發亮，故選(C) glistened。

補充
此句的 with 意為「因為」。

(A) 9. 中國的萬里長城原本是為了增強北方邊界，以對抗外國入侵而建造。
(A) 增強　(B) 排練
(C) 減弱　(D) 勒死

解析
從 against 與 foreign invasion 可推測，萬里長城的建造目的是為了要增強北邊的防禦，故選(A) fortify。

(C) 10. 在小說裡，瘋狂科學家通常被描寫成有一頭亂髮、狂熱的男人，在充滿奇異設備與冒泡試管的實驗室裡拚命地工作。
(A) 有感染力地　(B) 獨特地
(C) 拚命地　(D) 非常地

解析
❶ 本題可由 mad、wild-eyed (狂熱的)、crazy，可聯想到熱衷於研究的科學家，故選(C) frantically。

❷ 本題也可直接由搭配詞 work frantically(拚命地工作) 選出答案(C) frantically。

補充
be portrayed as 被描寫成

二、綜合測驗

11–15 為題組

近年來，非洲的時尚產業已有巨幅的成長，非洲的時裝設計引起了國際知名人士的注意，包括美國前第一夫人蜜雪兒・歐巴馬 (Michelle Obama) 、 蕾哈娜 (Rihanna)、碧昂絲 (Beyoncé) 都在 11.其中。全世界對非洲風時尚的需求，造就了一些非洲設計師跟非洲品牌驚人的銷售量。

富雷克・科克爾 (Folake Folarin－Coker) 是蒂芬妮・安柏 (Tiffany Amber) 這個品牌的創辦人，也是非洲與全球時尚產業知名的服裝設計師。她出生於奈及利亞的拉哥斯 (Lagos)，在歐洲受教育，12.在那裡，她年紀輕輕就獲得和各種文化交流的機會。13.有趣的是，她在瑞士拿到法學碩士的學位，但因為命運的安排，對時尚的熱愛引領她踏進了時尚設計圈。

富雷克 (Folake) 既雅致又繽紛的作品為她贏得了全球的 14.讚譽，這使她成為首位連續兩年在賓士紐約時裝週發表作品的非洲服裝設計師 。許多像是 CNN 的國際媒體廣泛地 15.以她為特色報導過她 ；在 2013 年，《富比世雜誌》更把她列為非洲最有影響力的女性之一。

(B) 11. (A) 如有　(B) 其中
(C) 簡而言之　(D) 最多

解析
本題測驗慣用語的意思。本句指出近年來非洲的時裝設計受到國際知名人士的注意，包括美國前第一夫人蜜雪兒・歐巴馬、蕾哈娜、碧昂絲，可知她們均在國際知名人士中，故答案選(B) among others。

(A) 12. (A) 在那裡　(B) 在那裡
(C) 那個　(D) 是否

解析
前句文意表示「她出生於奈及利亞的拉哥斯，在歐洲受教育」，空格後面接完整子句，得知本格應選有連接功能的選項以連接前後句，四個答案中只有關係副詞 where 適合，答案選(A) where。

補充
◆關係副詞等於「介系詞 + which」，依據先行詞不同 (時間 / 地點 / 原因)，使用 when/where/why，後面接完整子句。

例 ： Sandy took a trip to Kenting, where she enjoyed much sunshine and water sports.

◆關係代名詞代替先行詞 ，依據先行詞不同 (人 / 事物)，使用 who/which/that，後面接不完整子句。

例 ： The hostess of the talk show had an interesting conversation with the singer, who had just released his new album.

(D) 13. (A) 通常　(B) 理想上
(C) 相對的　(D) 有趣的是

解析
前文提到富雷克・科克爾是時尚品牌的創辦人，空格後句卻提到她在瑞士拿到法學碩士學位，時尚與法學二者沒有直接相關、落差較大，因此選(D) Interestingly。

(A) 14. (A) 讚譽　(B) 動機
(C) 監督　(D) 準備

解析
由後句「這使她成為首位連續二年在賓士紐約時裝週發表作品的非洲設計師」，可反推富雷克既雅致又繽紛的作品為她贏得了全球的讚譽，答案選(A) recognition。

(C) 15. (A) 被相信　(B) 被宣告
(C) 以…為特色　(D) 居住

解析
後句指出在 2013 年，她被《富比世雜誌》列為非洲最有影響力的女性之一，回推她應常受到國際媒體的特別報導，由文意選出(C) featured。

16–20 為題組

當我們在收看最新的電視影集或下載高解析度的照片時，我們或許不會察覺到其背後的數據資料正在世界各地的海底電纜內快速傳輸著。

這些纜線系統比衛星的傳輸速度更快、造價更便宜，負責洲際網路大部分的傳輸工作。現在有超過420條海底電纜在16.使用中，全球長度達70多萬英里。17.但是這並非是什麼新現象。第一條跨洲電纜在1854年鋪設，連接愛爾蘭和紐芬蘭島(Newfoundland)，讓英格蘭和加拿大之間得以利用電報聯繫。目前世界最高容載量的海底網路電纜長達5,600英里，連接美國跟日本。18.適如其名為「神速」，這條纜線將美國的奧勒岡州 (Oregon) 與日本和臺灣連接起來。

海底電纜的鋪設需要格外19.小心。纜線必須鋪設於平坦的海床上，並避開珊瑚礁、沉船、魚窩等一般20.障礙物。光纖電纜也非常脆弱，所以外面還會包覆層層的管子和鋼材以防受損。

(B) 16. (A) 一般地 (B) 使用中
(C) 相較之下 (D) 在控制之下

解析

由關鍵字 Today 可知本句談論到海底電纜現今的情形，文意應為「現在有超過420條海底電纜在使用中」，故選(B) in service。

(D) 17. (A) 然後 (B) 仍然
(C) 反而 (D) 但是

解析

本題的前一句提到目前在使用中的海底電纜超過420條，涵蓋範圍超過70多萬英里，後一句則談到第一條跨洲電纜在1854年鋪設，可回推這並非新現象，故選表轉折語氣的「但是」，答案為(D) though。

比較

❶ though 置於句首時，解釋為「雖然」，意義與用法等同 although。
例：Though the task is challenging, Gabriel is determined to complete it.

❷ though 置於句尾時，解釋為「但是」，意義與用法等同 however。
例：The steak is delicious. I doubt Ian, who is a picky eater, will like it, though.

(A) 18. (A) 適當地 (B) 一直
(C) 絕對 (D) 嘲笑地

解析

前句提到目前世界最高容載量的網路電纜長達5,600英里，連接美國與日本。本格後面提到電纜名為"FASTER"，由前述資訊可知，此條電纜的長度如此長，要有足夠的網路速度才能快速傳輸，可知名字取為"FASTER"十分貼切，故選(A) Suitably。

(C) 19. (A) 速度 (B) 光線
(C) 小心 (D) 連結

解析

由後一句描述鋪設海底電纜的許多條件，由此推知需要格外小心，故選(C) care。

(B) 20. (A) 方向 (B) 障礙物
(C) 水族箱 (D) 循環

解析

本句描述鋪設海底電纜的條件為遠離珊瑚礁、沉船、魚窩等，這些都會讓電纜處於非平坦的狀態，都是需要避開的障礙物，故選(B) obstacles。

三、文意選填

21–30 為題組

蓋蒂中心 (the Getty Center) 坐落於海拔八百多英尺高，俯看整個洛杉磯。遊客可以搭乘全長零點七五英里的輕軌電車至山頂。四間展覽館和遊客中心是山頂上的十一棟建築物群的中心建築。裡頭的博物館起初是建來21.收藏石油大亨保羅・蓋蒂 (J. Paul Getty) 龐大的藝術珍藏品。如今博物館充滿了藝術品，展覽區一次只能展出一小部分，因此22.不斷改變的展覽品也就成了遊覽蓋蒂中心的重頭戲。

蓋蒂中心的建築師理查・麥爾 (Richard Meier) 是得過獎的建築師，創造的公共空間十分出色，讓許多訪客23.倍感驚訝。遊客會以為自己要參觀的是展示藝術品的博物館，但隨即便會發覺整棟建築物就是裡面有個博物館的藝術品。這個構想非常引人入勝：戶外空間可以是個欣賞24.藝術的愜意體驗。

麥爾挑選了基本的25.建築材料：金屬、石頭、玻璃。他運用十億美金的預算，靠這些建材蓋出建築界的藝術品來，遊客看了內心澎湃不已，不亞於觀看裡頭的藝術品。蓋蒂中心的每個角落、每個26.轉角處的景色都不同，讓遊客沉醉其中。正當遊客以為已經沒什麼可看的了，突然間又會有座沒看過的噴泉，或是陌生的景色映入眼簾。

建築石材用的是義大利27.進口的洞石，羅馬的古蹟也是用同樣的石頭蓋的。特殊的切割過程會讓長久以來埋藏在洞石裡的化石得以重見天日，顯露出28.隱藏在粗糙表面的精緻珍寶。蓋蒂中心把一些洞石當作「特色」石擺放在中心的各處，等著讓發現的人感到驚喜29.開心。最奇特的那顆則置於中心入口廣場的牆上，跟輕軌電車的車站遙遙相望。

除了博物館有導覽外，蓋蒂中心還提供多種免費的現場導覽，包括花園導覽。對想多了解麥爾的建築手法跟理念的人，這些30.探索可是絕對必要的。

(A) 使高興 *vt.*	(B) 探索 *n.* [C]
(C) 轉角 *n.* [C]	(D) 使驚訝 *vt.*
(E) 進口 *vt.*	(F) 過度強調的 *adj.*
(G) 藝術的 *adj.*	(H) 隱藏的 *adj.*
(I) 地基 *n.* [C]	(J) 建築材料 *n.* [C]
(K) 收藏 *vt.*	(L) 不斷改變的 *adj.*

解析

(K) 21. The museum was originally constructed to ______ the vast art collection ...，本空格在不定詞 to 之後，應填原形動詞，可能的選項有 delight (可當名詞或動詞)、turn (可當名詞或動詞)、house (可當名詞或動詞)。空格後為廣大藝術收藏品，可搭配的動詞應為 house (收藏)，由文意得知蓋蒂中心原本是建造來儲藏石油大亨 J. Paul Getty 的廣大藝術品，故空格應填(K) house。

(L) 22. ... making the ______ special exhibitions a highlight，本空格在名詞組 special exhibitions 之前，應填形容詞修飾，可能選項有 over-emphasized、artistic 或 ever-changing。前句說明蓋蒂博物館的館藏太多以致於一次只能展出一部分，可知展覽的內容不斷更換改變，故選(L) ever-changing。

(D) 23. creating a public space that has ______ many visitors，本空格前有 has，時態為完成式，此格應為過去分詞，可能選項有 surprised、imported、over-emphasized、hidden。本格前的文意指出，蓋蒂中心是其建築師的傑出之作，後一句表示蓋蒂中心的訪客看似參觀收藏藝術品的博物館，實則是參觀內含博物館的藝術建築，回推本格應表達蓋蒂中心的美讓許多訪客倍感驚訝，故答案為(D) surprised。

(G) 24. The outdoor space can be a completely satisfying ______ experience.，本空格在名詞 experience 前，應填形容詞。由前文對蓋蒂中心的描述，可推知戶外空間的設計也充滿了藝術感，提供訪客感受藝術的經驗，故答案應選(G) artistic。

(J) 25. Meier took a few basic ______: metal, stone and glass.，本格前有 a few 與形容詞，應填複數名詞，又後有冒號說明空格內容為金屬、石頭、玻璃，判斷應與其相關，三樣均為建築材料，故選(J) materials。

(C) 26. Around every corner and at every ______, ...，本格前有 every，應填單數名詞，由介系詞 at，可知搭配的為 turn，本句文意為「每個角落、每個轉角處的景色都不同，讓遊客沉醉其中」，答案為(C) turn。此外 at every turn 為片語，故可從搭配字推論答案。

(E) 27. The building stone is travertine, ______ from Italy, ...，本空格前為完整句子，可知本格應為修飾語或分詞片語，由 from Italy 可推知是指石材進口自義大利，故選(E) imported。本句可還原為 The building stone is travertine, which is imported from Italy，省略關係代名詞 which 與 is 後，成為分詞片語 imported from Italy。

(H) 28. ...which reveals the delicate treasures ______ under the rough surface.，本空格前有名詞 treasures，應為其修飾語或分詞片語，由 reveal 與 under 可聯想到 hidden，從文意「特殊的切割過程會讓長久以來埋藏在洞石裡的化石得以重見天日，顯露出隱藏在粗糙表面的精緻珍寶」判斷，得知答案為(H) hidden。本句原為 ...which reveals the delicate treasures that are hidden under the rough surface.。

(A) 29. ..., waiting to ______ those who find them，本空格在不定詞 to 之後，應填原形動詞，由文意「擺放在中心的各處，等著讓發現的人感到驚喜」，得知應選(A) delight。

(B) 30. These ______ are a must for anyone interested in learning more about Meier's techniques and ideas.，本空格在 These 之後，應填複數名詞，由文意「對想多了解麥爾的建築手法跟理念的人，這些探索可是絕對必要的」可選出(B) explorations。

四、篇章結構

31–35 為題組

哥白尼 (Copernicus) 是創立現代天文學的人，1473 年生於波蘭托倫的商人家，家境優渥。家人送他到義大利讀大學，他主修數學、光學、教會法。他學成歸國以後，奉派到弗龍堡的大教堂做行政的工作，他在那裡備受呵護，只管做學問，就這樣度過了後半生。

31.哥白尼會在閒暇之餘研究恆星與行星，運用自己的數學知識來解夜空裡的謎團。哥白尼在教堂防風牆上的一座塔裡觀測天象，他只憑肉眼觀察群星，畢竟望遠鏡還要再過一百年才問世。1530 年，哥白尼完成了名著《天體運行論 (*De Revolutionibus*)》，往後世人的哲學觀變得不同，重新看待人類在宇宙中的地位，這本書在這方面起了重大的作用。32.然而，這本著作一直到他過世前二個月才出版。

1543 年，哥白尼與世長辭，他到死前都料想不到自己寫的書會引發軒然大波。他在書裡斷言地球每天繞著自己的軸轉動一次，每年則繞著太陽轉動一次，33.這個說法牴觸了中世紀的哲學觀跟宗教信仰，當時的人認為地球是靜止且位在宇宙中央的，而太陽以及所有的行星都繞著地球轉。長久以來，大家都認定上帝創造了蒼穹和地球，哥白尼提出的理論不僅質疑了這種看法，還有可能推翻天主教世界的核心價值。34.宗教領袖馬丁・路德 (Martin Luther) 就反對太陽中心論，不久，其他神職人員也跟進，一提到哥白尼便說：「這傻蛋想要顛覆天文學啊。」

諷刺的是，哥白尼把《天體運行論》獻給了教宗保祿三世 (Pope Paul III)。35.他若是想要尋求天主教會的認可，此舉根本徒勞無功。教會最後禁了《天體運行論》，且一禁就禁了將近三百年之久。

解析

(F) 31. 第一段的最後一句提到哥白尼後半生都住在大教堂進行學術研究，本格後句說明他在高塔中做觀察，由後句的主詞為代名詞 He 回推，本格應為有指示對象的主詞，且依據描述，主詞應為哥白尼，檢視(F)選項與前句的關聯，Copernicus 與 He 對應，studied the stars 與 made his observations 對應，兩句也均有提及 cathedral、there。由選項文意「哥白尼會在閒暇之餘研究恆星與行星，運用自己的數學知識來解夜空裡的謎團」，可確定答案為(F)。

(B) 32. 第二段提到哥白尼完成名著《天體運行論》，本格後句提到哥白尼於 1543 年逝世，不知道他的著作會引發軒然大波，可見討論重點為其著作，檢視(B)選項與前後句的關聯，The book 與 his work 對應、death 與 died 對應，選項文意「然而，這本著作一直到他過世前二個月才出版」，可確定文意連貫，因此答案為(B)。

(D) 33. 本格前句提到哥白尼宣稱地球每天自轉，一年繞太陽公轉一圈，後句表示當時的人認為地球是宇宙的中心，可知他的主張與當時的信仰相牴觸，檢視(D)選項。went against 與前後句文意呼應、during medieval times 與後句的 then 對應，故答案為(D)「這個說法牴觸了中世紀的哲學觀跟宗教信仰」。

(E) 34. 本格後句後的主詞為 Other ministers，且他們稱哥白尼為傻瓜，由 other 可回推本格的主詞應為同樣身份的一員，且反對哥白尼的主張，考慮(E)選項。選項(E)的 Religious leader 與 Other ministers 呼應、voiced his opposition 與 This fool 呼應、the sun-centered system model 與哥白尼「地球繞太陽轉」的看法呼應，故(E)為答案。

(C) 35. 本格前句表示哥白尼將他的著作獻給教宗，後句說明教會最後卻將《天體運行論》列為禁書，前後行為相反，考慮(C)選項。選項的 this act 與哥白尼獻出著作的行為呼應、it was of no use 與書被禁用的結果呼應，推知(C)為答案，「他若是想要尋求天主教會的認可，此舉根本徒勞無功」。

五、閱讀測驗

36–39 為題組

天貝是印尼的傳統黃豆製品。與韓國的泡菜，還有日本的味噌一樣，被譽為是印尼「送給世人的大禮」。

天貝是發酵食物，源於爪哇島，數百年來在印尼是穩定、便宜的蛋白質來源。當地人發現在製作豆腐時，丟掉的黃豆殘渣在接觸了空氣中的細菌孢子後，周圍長了某些灰白色的真菌。等到有人發現這發酵的殘渣不僅可以吃，味道還很不錯，印尼各地的人們便在家裡自行製作，供每天食用。如此一來，印尼各地的天貝都有不同的風味及口感。

天貝富含蛋白質，熱量低，又有多種維生素。其實，據報導，天貝是唯一的純素維生素 B12 來源。除了有助於降低膽固醇、增加骨質密度、促進肌肉復原以外，還含有大量多酚，能保護皮膚細胞、減緩老化。最棒的是，天貝的蛋白質堪比肉類，又能做成多種不同口味及口感，拿來代替肉品再好不過——素食者與全素主義者早就將天貝納入飲食了。

天貝除了成分組成極具營養價值以外，料理的方式也很多元。可以當成主食 (搭配咖哩)，也可以油炸當作配菜，與米飯一同享用，甚至還能跟奶昔以及健康果汁混著食用。雖然天貝還不是國際餐廳裡的熱門菜色，但要在舊金山買到以天貝來代替培根的三明治，跟在峇里島買個夾了天貝的素漢堡一樣容易。

在印尼人眼中，天貝不單單只是食物，還具有文化價值。聯合國教科文組織已把印尼的傳統蠟染花布列為人類非物質文化遺產，天貝也深具潛力能獲此殊榮。

(B) 36. 本文主旨為何？

(A) 健康食物的料理方法。
(B) 爪哇島的傳統佳餚。
(C) 素食者的美食指南。
(D) 印尼的文化遺產。

說明

本文整篇在介紹印尼的傳統食物天貝，由第二段可知天貝來自爪哇島，答案應選(B)。

(C) 37. 根據本文，下列關於天貝的敘述何者為真？
(A) 它主要被當作配菜。
(B) 當周圍長出真菌時，它就會被扔掉。
(C) 它是從發酵的黃豆製成。
(D) 它有跟泡菜一樣的營養效益。

說明

根據第二段，天貝源於豆腐製造過程中的黃豆殘渣，長出真菌後經過發酵後可以食用，可知答案選(C)。

(A) 38. 第二到四段提到天貝的什麼部分？
(A) 起源 → 營養 → 烹調。
(B) 起源 → 烹調 → 行銷。
(C) 烹調 → 營養 → 行銷。
(D) 分布 → 烹調 → 營養。

說明

第二段提到天貝起源於爪哇島，第三段主要討論天貝的營養價值與效益，第四段則講述天貝的烹調方式，因此正確答案為(A)。

(D) 39. 下列何者可由本文推論而出？
(A) 年長者會吃天貝作為維生素補充品。
(B) 天貝很快將會比泡菜或味噌受歡迎。
(C) 在大量製造下，天貝的營養會流失。
(D) 天貝可望在國際上成為文化的象徵。

說明

(A) 天貝是唯一的純素維生素 B12 來源，但並未提及年長者會將其作為維生素補充品，此為錯誤選項；(B) 文內並無做此比較，此為錯誤選項；(C) 文內並無提及大量製造會產生的影響，此為錯誤選項；(D) 第五段的末句指出「聯合國教科文組織已把印尼的傳統蠟染花布列為人類非物質文化遺產，天貝也深具潛力能獲此殊榮」，可知答案選(D)。

40–43 為題組

1972 年，大衛・史皮格爾 (David Spiegel) 博士的肩膀動了手術，歷時三個鐘頭。他在術後沒有服用止痛藥，只靠催眠自己來復原，這方法很管用，所有人聽了都很驚訝，但他自己心裡有數，因為他已經鑽研催眠四十五年了。

大家常把催眠誤認為類似睡眠的狀態，受催眠的人會睡去，別人要他做什麼，他就做什麼。但據大衛・史皮格爾博士的說法，催眠是集中注意力，且專心一志的狀態。受催眠的人對周圍的刺激大都置之不理，只注意眼前的事，別的事幾乎都沒想。催眠這種類似昏睡的狀態能夠抑制疼痛、減輕焦慮、紓解壓力。

不過並非所有人都容易催眠。照大衛・史皮格爾博士最近跟同事發表的研究看來，容易催眠的人往往很容易相信他人，有很高的直覺力，很可能看到精彩的電影就看得忘我。研究團隊比較容易催眠跟不易催眠的兩組人，利用功能性磁振造影來研究他們在幾個不同時候的狀態：休息、回想、兩次催眠。研究人員發現實驗對象受催眠時，腦部會出現一些有趣的變化，但這情形只有容易催眠的人才有。具體來說，人在煩惱時，大腦有個部位通常會活躍起來，但催眠時，這個部位的活動力會下降。

這有助於解釋何以催眠的效果可以這麼顯著，把壓力、焦慮、疼痛、自我意識都減小。大衛・史皮格爾博士希望催眠可以代替止痛藥。由他之前的研究可以看出，受疼痛折騰的人學會自我催眠，止痛藥的藥量就能少服一半，疼痛也比只服止痛藥的還少一半。然而，我們對催眠還是要多了解一些，才有辦法利用催眠的潛在效力。

(B) 40. 作者如何開始書寫本文？
(A) 藉由提供定義。
(B) 藉由提到一個事件。
(C) 藉由提供數據。
(D) 藉由比較人們的反應。

說明

作者在第一段以 Spiegel 醫師在 1972 年於手術過程中以自我催眠來取代止痛治療的事件開始本文對催眠的探討，因此答案應為(B)。

(C) 41. 根據本文，Spiegel 醫師的研究目標為何？
(A) 解釋疼痛的真正起因。
(B) 幫助人們專注於工作。
(C) 探討催眠如何能作為醫學治療。
(D) 強化大腦的功能以減少心理問題。

說明

第四段描述，Spiegel 醫師希望催眠的施行能取代鎮痛劑，也提及他之前的研究顯示遭受疼痛的人們在自我催眠下，只需要減半的鎮痛劑，並且遭受的疼痛程度也較服用鎮痛劑者少。由此可知，Spiegel 醫師主要研究催眠如何有助於醫學治療，答案選(C)。

(B) 42. 根據 Spiegel 醫師，當人們被催眠時，下列何者為真？
(A) 他們只回想到快樂回憶。
(B) 他們的心智只專注於正在做的事情上。
(C) 他們會做任何被要求要做的事情。
(D) 他們對身邊的事情更能察覺。

說明

(A)第三段末指出，受催眠者的腦部在擔心事情時受到激發的部分會減弱活動，但並未表示被催眠時只有快樂回憶，此選項為非。(B)第二段說明，被催眠時，人們會停止注意身邊的刺激，並只會強烈專注在手邊的事情，故為答案。(C)第二段提到催眠常被誤會為讓人進入睡眠狀態而聽從任何指令做事，此選項為非。(D)第四段說明催眠會減少人們的自我意識，此選項為非。

(C) 43. 何者為對高度易受催眠者的推論？

(A) 他們傾向於被社會隔離。
(B) 他們在白天更可能睡著。
(C) 他們可能更容易認同小說裡的角色。
(D) 他們比不易受催眠的人更值得信任。

說明

(A)本文未提及。(B)本文未提及。(C)第三段指出易受催眠的人更容易信任他人、更有直覺力、更容易沉浸在好的電影裡，故可推論此為答案。(D)根據第三段內容，易受催眠者容易相信他人，故此為錯誤選項。

44–47 為題組

很多語言跟英文一樣，並沒有直截了當的方法來表達氣味。由於英文缺乏氣味類的術語，說英文的人常常就只能迫於氣味的來源來表達氣味，好比「花香」、「香草」，以及隱喻如「甜甜的」、「東方的」。

但並非全世界的語言都難以描述氣味。泰國南部的馬尼人 (The Maniq) 靠狩獵還有採集維生，至少能夠使用十五個不同的詞語來描述氣味。這十五個字詞只用於氣味，並不適用其他感官。此外，還有一群同樣靠狩獵還有採集維生，且跟馬尼人住得很近的部族，研究員發現他們講的嘉海語 (Jahai) 裡，有十二個字是用來描述各種氣味的。

說來有趣，說英文的人覺得直接用文字來表達氣味很難，但這似乎跟他們的嗅覺沒有什麼關係。近來有篇研究發現說英文的人可以辨別一兆多種不同的氣味。那麼，何以他們辨識氣味的能力如此高，但跟氣味有關的字彙卻這麼少呢？研究員表示或許環境扮演了一個重大的角色。

尼人和說嘉海語的人住在熱帶雨林區，過著狩獵採集的日子。這兩個族群靠鼻子評估周圍環境，才得以在大自然裡生存。他們生活的環境還有一大部分都尚未有人類涉足，因此身邊總有很多氣味。他們需要運用嗅覺，找到獵物，並認出有危險的事物，像是壞掉的食物。不像馬尼人與嘉海族人，許多說英文的人都住在後工業化的西方國家，且不靠氣味來生存。這樣的差異或許就能解釋上面討論到的有趣語言現象。

(D) 44. 本文主旨為何？
(A) 為了評估不同民族所使用的語言。
(B) 為了證明文明化是如何減緩語言的發展。
(C) 為了描述跟氣味有關的詞語在不同語言中是如何被發現的。
(D) 為了指出語言運用和環境的關聯。

說明

本文提到馬尼人和嘉海人會使用不同的措辭來描述味道，第三段的末句點出是環境促成這樣的發展，第四段接著解釋原因，推知本文旨在說明語言使用和環境的關聯，故答案選(D)。

(A) 45. 第一段的「want」最有可能的意思為何？
(A) 缺乏。 (B) 成長。
(C) 失去。 (D) 尋找。

說明

第一段提到在許多語言中，如英文，沒有直接的方式來描述味道，說英語者被迫使用由味道來源所衍生的字或比喻來描述該氣味，可知是因為「缺乏」此類的措辭，故答案選(A)。

(D) 46. 下列關於馬尼人的敘述何者為真？
(A) 他們和嘉海族人居住在不同的氣候區。
(B) 他們的嗅覺比嘉海族人靈敏。
(C) 他們使用與氣味有關的詞語來描述食物的外觀及滋味。
(D) 他們的居住環境相似於人類歷史初期。

說明

(A)第二段的末句指出馬尼人的居住區鄰近嘉海族，第四段提及表示馬尼人與嘉海人均住在熱帶雨林區；(B)本文未提及；(C)由第二段可知，馬尼人用來描述氣味的措辭僅限於味道，無法使用在其他感官領域，所以此為錯誤選項；(D)第四段說明馬尼人與嘉海族居住的環境大部分人煙罕至，可推知尚未受人類活動影響，相似於人類早期的生活環境，故答案選(D)。

(B) 47. 為什麼說英語者難以直接描述氣味？
(A) 他們無法分辨身邊的氣味。
(B) 嗅覺不是他們生存的關鍵因素。
(C) 他們認為直接談論氣味是未開化的行為。
(D) 在他們的環境中，沒有很多氣味的來源。

說明

從第四段可知道說英語者大部分都住在後工業化的西方國家，並且在環境生存上不太需要依賴嗅覺，故答案選(B)。

48–51 為題組

獾㹢狓 (okapi) 這種哺乳類動物住在赤道的上方，生長環境是全中非生物種類數一數二多的地區。西方人要到了二十世紀初才知道有這種動物。牠常被形容成一半斑馬，一半長頸鹿的動物，好像牠是希臘神話中的混種生物一樣。不過剛果民主共和國 (the Democratic Republic of Congo) 裡盡是這種動物的圖像，因為唯有在這裡才看得到野生的獾㹢狓。獾㹢狓之於剛果，好比大貓熊之於中國或袋鼠之於澳洲。

雖然獾㹢狓身上有類似斑馬的條紋，但卻是長頸鹿的近親。獾㹢狓的脖子很長，耳朵又大又靈活，臉跟咽喉都是灰白色的，皮毛則是深褐色跟紅棕色，和腿上的白色橫條跟圓圈，以及白色腳踝形成強烈的對比。整體看來，要分辨獾㹢狓跟長頸鹿毫不困難。獾㹢狓的體型比長頸鹿小很多 (跟馬差不多大)，從外觀來看，比起長頸鹿，跟鹿倒還比較像。長頸鹿不分公母都有犄角，但是獾㹢㹢只有公的才有犄角。

1890 年，威爾斯記者亨利・莫頓・史丹利 (Henry Morton Stanley) 在他的書裡提到他對一種怪異的「非洲驢子」感到困惑，西方人這才對獾㹢㹢略知一二。其他在非洲的歐洲人也聽過，不過把這種動物叫做「非洲獨角獸」。探險家可能看過獾㹢㹢在灌木叢裡逃竄，但因速度太快，只能瞥見牠佈滿條紋的臀部。因此，才會有人推測獾㹢㹢是某種生長在雨林裡的斑馬。甚至還有人認為獾㹢㹢是新品種的斑馬。後來生物學家分析了獾㹢㹢的骨骼，才總算明白長頸鹿才是獾㹢㹢的近親。

1987 年，獾㹢㹢保護區在東剛果成立，以保護這種罕見的哺乳類動物。但剛果的政治幾十年來始終動盪不安，剛果政府也就無法再掌握住國內大部分的天然資源。從 1995 年至今，獾㹢㹢的數量已經減少了五成，時至今日，獾㹢㹢只剩下一萬頭。

(B) 48. 下列何者是獾㹢㹢的圖片？

說明

第二段第二、三句描述了獾㹢㹢的特徵：長脖子、寬大且可轉動的耳朵、臉與喉嚨為淺灰白色、毛皮介於巧克力與紅褐色間，腳部有橫條紋與圈形，足踝為白色，由此判斷正確圖片應為(B)。

(A) 49. 下列關於獾㹢㹢的敘述何者正確？
(A) 牠是剛果的重要象徵。
(B) 牠是來自希臘神話的神祕生物。
(C) 牠從 1987 年就受到很好的保護。
(D) 牠比較接近斑馬而非長頸鹿。

說明

(A)第一段末指出獾㹢㹢在剛果很普遍，這也是牠生存的唯一國家，所以答案選(A)；(B)第一段提到，獾㹢㹢既像斑馬又像長頸鹿的外型，彷彿是來自希臘神話的混種生物，此敘述僅表達獾㹢㹢像希臘神話的生物，並非真實情況，故此選項為非；(C)第四段提到剛果在 1987 年設立獾㹢㹢保護區，以維護這種罕見動物，但剛果政治的動盪讓政府難以致力維護自然資源，導致獾㹢㹢的數量從 1995 以降減少了 50%，故此選項為非；(D)根據第二段得知，獾㹢㹢最接近長頸鹿，故此選項為非。

(C) 50. 第三段的「whiff」最有可能是什麼意思？
(A) 堅定的信仰。
(B) 親切的意圖。
(C) 輕微的跡象。
(D) 強烈的厭惡。

說明

第三段指出記者 Henry Morton Stanley 於 1890 年首度在書裡提及奇怪的非洲驢子，可知西方國家當時第一次聽聞這種動物，故答案為(C)。

(C) 51. 下列何者為對於 Henry Morton Stanley 的推論？
(A) 他是第一個分析獾㹢㹢頭骨的歐洲人。
(B) 他在非洲發現許多新物種。
(C) 他不知道他書裡所稱的「非洲驢子」是獾㹢㹢。
(D) 他看過獾㹢㹢飛奔過草原的背影。

說明

(A)根據第三段，是生物學家分析獾㹢㹢的骨骼，而 Henry Morton Stanley 是記者，並非生物學家，此敘述錯誤；(B)文中只在第三段提到他發現獾㹢㹢，未提及他發現許多物種，此非正確選項；(C)第三段提到 Henry Morton Stanley 對「非洲驢子」感到很困惑 (puzzled)，可推測他並不知道這動物是獾㹢㹢，此敘述正確；(D)第三段指出有些探險家看過獾㹢㹢飛奔的身影，並非 Henry Morton Stanley 見過，故此非正確選項。

◆ 第貳部分：非選擇題

一、中譯英

1. Recently, creative banners have become effective advertising tools at night markets and stimulated consumption/boosted sales.

說明

❶ 參考句型：S + V + O + and + V + O
❷ 時態：談論最近的事實用現在完成式
❸ 創意布條 creative banners
❹ 廣告工具 advertising tool
❺ 刺激買氣 stimulate consumption/boost sales

2. Some of them (the banners) seem meaningless; however, they attract people's attention and can often bring people knowing smiles to their faces.
= Some of them seem meaningless; however, they are quite eye-catching and can often make people smile knowingly.

說明

❶ 參考句型：S + V + SC, but S + V + O + and + V + O
❷ 時態：談論事實用現在簡單式
❸ 看似 seem
❹ 引人注目 attract people's attention/ be eye-catching
❺ 帶給⋯會心的一笑 bring a knowing smile to one's face/ make someone smile knowingly

二、英文作文

作文範例

Recently, in response to teenagers' addiction to social media, there has been a trend toward encouraging teenagers to care about daily happenings around them.

This bar chart clearly illustrates the seven types of news that American teenagers pay attention to. As can be seen, news stories about environmental and natural disasters as well as social issues have attracted most American teenagers' attention, with the percentage being 69% and 64% respectively. In comparison, news about art and culture seems to draw the least attention from them, which accounts for 30% only.

As for myself, I am mostly concerned with environmental and natural disasters as well. According to scientists, our lives have been greatly affected, and even threatened, by severe pollutions and natural disasters; the former can deteriorate our living conditions, quality and life, and health, while the latter can claim hundreds to thousands of lives at a time. From numerous studies, we can learn that the causes of such disasters are human activities. Therefore, in my opinion, it is our duty to care about what is influencing us and how we can avoid harming our environment and improve our living conditions. As to the type of news that least interests me is entertainment and celebrity news. As a college-student -to-be, I need to equip myself with more knowledge and broaden my horizons so that I can find an ideal job and fit into society in the near future. Hence, it is important that I catch up on current big events that can help me grow mature rather than news stories about individual celebrities, which mainly serve as day-to-day conversation topics.

說明

今年的寫作主題為閱讀圖表與闡述見解，命題方式符合素養導向。第一段闡述圖表挑戰度高，學生必須先讀懂圖表，依照題目要求，描述最高與最低的類別，並在第二段具體描述自己的情形與說明理由。建議學生平日練習判讀各種圖表 (長條圖、圓餅圖等)，並嘗試有條理地說明圖表，也可練習依據圖表內容闡述自己的想法，才能面對不同的主題並增進自身寫作能力。

107 學年度　指考英文試題

◆ 第壹部分：單選題 (占 72 分)

一、詞彙題 (占 10 分)

說明：第 1 題至第 10 題，每題有 4 個選項，其中只有一個是正確或最適當的選項，請畫記在答案卡之「選擇題答案區」。各題答對者，得 1 分；答錯、未作答或畫記多於一個選項者，該題以零分計算。

1. Gorillas have often been portrayed as a fearful animal, but in truth these shy apes ________ fight over sex, food, or territory.
(A) constantly　(B) shortly　(C) nearly　(D) rarely

2. With her nine-to-five job, Sally sometimes has to run personal ________ during the lunch break, such as going to the bank or mailing letters.
(A) affairs　(B) errands　(C) belongings　(D) connections

3. After an argument with the parents of his students, the teacher finally admitted his mistake and ________ himself to ask for their forgiveness.
(A) resisted　(B) humbled　(C) detected　(D) handled

4. Instead of criticizing other people, we should focus on their strengths and give them ________.
(A) compliments　(B) compromises　(C) convictions　(D) confessions

5. Taking advantage of a special function of the search engine, users can ________ the Internet without leaving behind any history of the webpages they visit.
(A) browse　(B) stride　(C) rumble　(D) conceal

6. Due to extremely low rainfall and a dangerous reduction of reservoir water, the area is experiencing the worst ________ in 30 years.
(A) fluid　(B) scandal　(C) drought　(D) nuisance

7. On Teachers' Day we pay ________ to Confucius for his contribution to the philosophy of education.
(A) consent　(B) tribute　(C) devotion　(D) preference

8. When the fire fighter walked out of the burning house with the crying baby in his arms, he was ________ as a hero by the crowd.
(A) previewed　(B) cautioned　(C) doomed　(D) hailed

9. Due to the worldwide recession, the World Bank's forecast for next year's global economic growth is ________.
(A) keen　(B) mild　(C) grim　(D) foul

10. Jeffery has always been a ________ person, so it's not surprising he got into an argument with his colleagues.
(A) respective　(B) preventive　(C) contagious　(D) quarrelsome

二、綜合測驗 (占 10 分)

說明：第 11 題至第 20 題，每題一個空格，請依文意選出最適當的一個選項，請畫記在答案卡之「選擇題答案區」。各題答對者，得 1 分；答錯、未作答或畫記多於一個選項者，該題以零分計算。

第 11 至 15 題為題組

"Keeping up with the Joneses" is a catchphrase in many parts of the English-speaking world. Just like "keeping up appearances," it refers to the ___11___ to one's neighbors as a standard for social status or the accumulation of material goods. Generally speaking, the more luxuries people have, the higher their value or social status—or ___12___ they believe. To fail to "keep up with the Joneses" is thus perceived as revealing socio-economic inferiority or, as the Chinese would put it, a great loss of face.

The ___13___ was popularized when a comic strip of the same name was created by cartoonist Arthur R. "Pop" Momand. The strip was first published in 1916 in the *New York World*, and ran in American newspapers for 28 years before it was eventually ___14___ into books, films, and musical comedies. The "Joneses" of the title were rich neighbors of the strip's main characters and, interestingly, they were merely ___15___ but never actually seen in person in the comic strip.

11. (A) reaction (B) attachment (C) similarity (D) comparison
12. (A) still (B) so (C) yet (D) even
13. (A) phrase (B) signal (C) material (D) analysis
14. (A) adapted (B) admitted (C) advanced (D) advised
15. (A) checked out (B) watched over (C) spoken of (D) traded with

第 16 至 20 題為題組

Many people at some point in life have white spots on their fingernails. One of the most common causes for these little white spots is a condition called leukonychia. Although the name sounds pretty serious, the condition typically ___16___. And while many people think the white spots are caused by a calcium or zinc deficiency, that's generally not the case.

In reality, these spots most often develop ___17___ mild to moderate trauma to your nail. If you can't think of anything that would have injured your nail, consider the fact that nails grow very slowly, so the injury ___18___ weeks before the spots ever appeared. The spots could also be a sign of a mild infection or allergy, or a side effect of certain medications.

___19___ the source of the injury, these spots typically do not require any treatment and should go away as your nail grows out. And they should not return unless you suffer another injury to a nail. However, this generally ___20___ when only a single or a few nails are affected. If all of your nails are showing white spots, the leukonychia could be related to another more serious condition such as anemia, cardiac disease, diabetes, or kidney disease.

16. (A) isn't (B) doesn't (C) couldn't (D) wouldn't

17. (A) in spite of (B) as a result of (C) to the best of (D) for the sake of
18. (A) might occur (B) would occur (C) will have occurred (D) may have occurred
19. (A) Supposing (B) Including (C) Whatever (D) Whether
20. (A) indicates (B) defines (C) applies (D) confirms

三、文意選填 (占 10 分)

說明：第 21 題至第 30 題，每題一個空格，請依文意在文章後所提供的(A)到(L)選項中分別選出最適當者，並將其英文字母代號畫記在答案卡之「選擇題答案區」。各題答對者，得 1 分；答錯、未作答或畫記多於一個選項者，該題以零分計算。

第 21 至 30 題為題組

Aquaculture is the farming of any aquatic plant or animal. Aquaculture is of great importance because it reduces the possibility of over fishing wild fish, and also improves the quality and increases the __21__ of fish for human consumption.

Ancient civilizations throughout the world engaged in different types of fish farming. The indigenous people in Australia are believed to have raised eels as early as 6000 BC. Abundant __22__ indicates they developed volcanic floodplains near Lake Condah into channels and dams, then captured eels and preserved them to eat all year round. The earliest records of fish __23__, however, are from China, where the practice was in wide use around 2500 BC. When the waters subsided after river floods, some fish, mainly carp, were __24__ in lakes. Early fish farmers then fed their brood using nymphs and silkworm feces, and ate them afterwards.

In Europe, aquaculture first began in ancient Rome. The Romans, who __25__ sea fish and oysters, created oyster farms which were similar to swimming pools. Fish and crustaceans (such as shrimps and crabs) caught in lagoons were kept __26__ in these pools until it was time to eat them. The farms were often built inside __27__ homes, where well-to-do families could invite their guests over and choose the fish they wished to eat. This Roman tradition was later adopted by Christian monasteries in central Europe.

During the Middle Ages, aquaculture __28__ in Europe, since far away from the seacoasts and the big rivers, fish had to be salted so they did not rot. Throughout feudal Europe, monastic orders and the aristocracy were the main users of freshwater fish, for they had a __29__ over the land, forests, and water courses while the common people could seldom build ponds of their own. As with hunting, __30__ fishing was severely punished and the less well-off would have to wait a few centuries before fresh fish was served on their plates.

(A) spread (B) culture (C) trapped (D) adored
(E) alive (F) monopoly (G) delicious (H) illegal
(I) supply (J) wealthier (K) evidence (L) treated

四、篇章結構 (占 10 分)

說明：第 31 題至第 35 題，每題一個空格。請依文意在文章後所提供的(A)到(F)選項中分別選出最適當者，填入空格中，使篇章結構清晰有條理，並將其英文字母代號畫記在答案卡之「選擇題答案區」。各題答對者，得 2 分；答錯、未作答或畫記多於一個選項者，該題以零分計算。

第 31 至 35 題為題組

The causes of the French Revolution are complex and still widely debated among historians. However, many scholars agree that food played an important role in the socio-political upheaval. __31__

A main component in the French daily meal, bread was often tied up with the national identity. Studies show that the average 18th-century French worker spent half his daily wage on bread. In 1788 and 1789, however, when the grain crops failed two years in a row, the price of bread shot up to 88 percent of his earnings. __32__ The great majority of the French population was starving. Some even resorted to theft or prostitution to stay alive.

__33__ Started in the 15th century, this tax on salt consumption was applied particularly to the poor, while the nobility and the privileged were exempted. The high rate and unequal distribution of the tax provoked widespread illegal dealing in salt by smugglers, leading to skyrocketing salt prices.

However, the royal court at Versailles was isolated from and indifferent to the escalating crisis. The desperate population thus blamed the ruling class for the famine and economic disturbances. __34__ The results include the storming of the Bastille, a medieval fortress and prison in Paris, and the eventual beheading of King Louis XVI and his wife, Marie Antoinette.

__35__ Yet, the *gabelle* and the "bread question" remained among the most unsettling social and political issues throughout the Revolutionary and Napoleonic periods (1789–1815) and well beyond.

(A) External threats closely shaped the course of the Revolution.
(B) With the collapse of the royal family, calm was restored gradually.
(C) Meanwhile, peasants' resentment against the *gabelle* was spreading.
(D) The common household could not afford to buy enough food to meet their basic needs.
(E) The anger quickly built up, culminating in the massive riots of the French Revolution in 1789.
(F) Specifically, bread and salt, two most essential elements in the French cuisine, were at the heart of the conflict.

五、閱讀測驗 (占 32 分)

說明：第 36 題至第 51 題，每題請分別根據各篇文章之文意選出最適當的一個選項，請畫記在答案卡之「選擇題答案區」。各題答對者，得 2 分；答錯、未作答或畫記多於一個選項者，該題以零分計算。

第 36 至 39 題為題組

Born in 1785 in southwestern Germany, Baron Karl Drais was one of the most creative German inventors of the 19th century. The baron's numerous inventions include, among others, the earliest typewriter, the meat grinder, a device to record piano music on paper, and two four-wheeled human-powered vehicles. But it was the running machine, the modern ancestor of the bicycle, that made him famous.

The running machine, also called Draisine or hobby horse, was in effect a very primitive bicycle: it had no chains and was propelled by riders pushing off the ground with their feet. Though not a bike in the modern sense of the word, Drais' invention **marked the big bang** for the bicycle's development. It was the first vehicle with two wheels placed in line. The frame and wheels were made of wood; the steering already resembled a modern handlebar. Drais' big democratic idea behind his invention was to find a muscle-powered replacement for the horses, which were expensive and consumed lots of food even when not in use. The machine, he believed, would allow large numbers of people faster movement than walking or riding in a coach.

Drais undertook his first documented ride on June 12, 1817, covering a distance of 13 kilometers in one hour. A few months later, Drais created a huge sensation when he rode 60 kilometers in four hours. These were later followed by a marketing trip to Paris, where the hobby horse quickly caught on. The fad also quickly spread to Britain.

The success of the hobby horse was short-lived, though. They were heavy and difficult to ride. Safety was an issue, too: They lacked a brake, as well as cranks and pedals. There were frequent collisions with unsuspecting pedestrians, and after a few years Drais' invention was banned in many European and American cities. Drais' ideas, however, did not disappear entirely. Decades later, the machine was equipped by Frenchmen Pierre Lallement and Pierre Michaux with pedals to become the modern bicycle.

36. Why did Drais invent the running machine?
(A) To prove his creativity as an inventor.
(B) To protect the horses from being abused.
(C) To provide a new gadget for the royal class.
(D) To give the general public a better means of transportation.

37. What does "**marked the big bang**" mean in the second paragraph?
(A) Gave out huge noise.
(B) Created serious disturbance.
(C) Enjoyed wide popularity.
(D) Represented groundbreaking work.

38. Which of the following descriptions is true about the running machine?
(A) It was equipped with cranks and pedals.
(B) Its wheels and frame were made of iron.

(C) It had a brake to control the speed of its movement.

(D) Its steering was similar to the handlebar of a modern bike.

39. Why did the hobby horse fail to become a common vehicle in the 19th century?

(A) It was expensive and not durable enough.

(B) It did not go as fast as people had expected.

(C) It was hard to control and dangerous to ride on the road.

(D) It did not receive enough public attention in European cities.

第 40 至 43 題為題組

Flickering lamps can induce headaches. But if the flickering happens millions of times a second—far faster than the eye can see or the brain process—then it might be harnessed to do something useful, like transmitting data. **This** is the idea behind Li-Fi, or Light Fidelity. The term Li-Fi was coined by University of Edinburgh Professor Harald Haas in a 2011 TED Talk, where he introduced the idea of "wireless data from every light." Today, Li-Fi has developed into a wireless technology that allows data to be sent at high speeds, working with light-emitting diodes (LEDs), an increasingly popular way to illuminate public areas and homes.

Using LED lights as networking devices for data transmission, Li-Fi has several advantages over Wi-Fi (Wireless Fidelity). First, Li-Fi allows for greater security on local networks, as light cannot penetrate walls or doors, unlike radio waves used in Wi-Fi. As long as transparent materials like glass windows are covered, access to a Li-Fi channel is limited to devices inside the room, ensuring that signals cannot be hacked from remote locations. Also, Li-Fi can operate in electromagnetic sensitive areas such as aircraft cabins, hospitals, and nuclear power plants, for light does not interfere with radio signals. The most significant advantage of Li-Fi is speed. Researchers have achieved speeds of 224 gigabits per second in lab conditions, much faster than Wi-Fi broadband.

How could Li-Fi enrich daily life? Anywhere there is LED lighting, there is an opportunity for Li-Fi enabled applications. Li-Fi-enabled street lights could provide internet access to mobile phones, making walking at night safer. The LED bulbs in traffic lights could provide drivers with weather conditions and traffic updates. Li-Fi could help with tourism by providing an easier access to local information. At home, smart light could also provide parents with solutions to their children's Internet addiction: Just turn off the lights and you've turned off their access.

When 14 billion light bulbs mean 14 billion potential transmitters of wireless data, a cleaner, a greener, and even a brighter future is on the way.

40. What is this passage mainly about?

(A) A new design in lighting.

(B) Wireless transmission through illumination.

(C) Radio interference in public areas.

(D) Potential applications of Li-Fi for military use.

41. What does “**This**” in the first paragraph refer to?

(A) Flickering light is a nuisance.

(B) Light flashes can deliver messages.

(C) The brain can be affected by lighting.

(D) Human eyes can perceive changes in light.

42. According to the passage, which of the following statements is **NOT** true about Li-Fi?

(A) It passes through concrete walls. (B) It was first introduced in 2011.

(C) It transmits data at high speed. (D) It may help with parenting

43. According to the passage, which of the following is an advantage of Li-Fi over Wi-Fi?

(A) Li-Fi can be powered by radio and save more energy.

(B) Li-Fi guides pedestrians in areas where vehicles cannot travel.

(C) Li-Fi provides safer transmission of data during a power failure.

(D) Li-Fi can be used in areas where Wi-Fi may interfere with radar signals.

第 44 至 47 題為題組

Some of the world’s largest beetles are getting smaller because their habitats are warming up, according to new research from the University of British Columbia, Canada. The study, published in the *Journal of Animal Ecology* in January 2018, shows that climate change is having an impact on these “teeny tiny” organisms.

The study began with **a deep dive** into the scientific literature. Evolutionary ecologist Michelle Tseng and her students combed through all the articles they could find, looking for laboratory studies of temperature effects on insects. They found 19 that indicated at least 22 beetle species shrank when raised in warmer than normal temperatures.

To see whether this pattern held true in the wild, the team made use of the university’s 600,000-specimen insect collection, which included thousands of bugs collected locally since the late 1800s. The researchers took photographs of more than 6,500 beetles from the eight species with the most extensive records. They also looked at climate records to determine trends in rainfall and other factors besides temperature. Sorting the beetles into size categories, they found that five of the eight species have shrunk over the past century. The four largest species of beetles, including the snail-killer ground beetles, shrank 20% in the past 45 years. In contrast, smaller beetles were unaffected or even slightly increased in size.

Some ecologists are cautious about Tseng’s findings, saying that it hasn’t yet been proved whether the warming temperatures are the actual cause for the beetle shrinkage. UK biologist Alan Ronan

Baudron, however, is convinced. Baudron's studies have documented shrinkage of certain fish species due to climate warming. His account is that warmer temperatures lower the concentration of oxygen in the water, causing fish to burn energy faster and mature at a smaller size. But neither he nor Tseng is convinced that decreased oxygen can explain the shrinkage in the beetles.

44. What is the best title for the passage?

(A) Large Beetles Are Shrinking, Thanks to Climate Change

(B) Beetles vs. Fish: Are They Becoming Smaller?

(C) What We Know About Evolutionary Ecology

(D) Animal Ecology: Past and Present

45. What does "**a deep dive**" most likely mean in the second paragraph?

(A) A clear indication. (B) An important finding.

(C) A thorough examination. (D) An insightful comment.

46. Which of the following is true about the research method of Tseng's team?

(A) They conducted both laboratory and field studies.

(B) They took pictures of 600,000 specimens of insects.

(C) They divided the beetles into different size groups for examination.

(D) They recorded the degrees of oxygen concentration since the late 1800s.

47. Which of the following is a finding of Tseng's team?

(A) Eight species of beetles have shrunk over the past century.

(B) Some beetles were not affected by temperature change.

(C) Most beetles tend to live longer with climate warming.

(D) Beetles and fish may shrink down to the same size.

第 48 至 51 題為題組

In order to protect the diversity of crops from catastrophe, the Svalbard Global Seed Vault, a seed bank, was built beneath a mountain on an Arctic island halfway between Norway and the North Pole. The Vault is meant to help farmers and scientists find the genes they need to improve today's crops. It also aims to breed varieties that might better respond to emerging challenges, such as climate change and population growth. Currently, the Vault holds more than 860,000 samples, originating from almost every country in the world.

There is now, however, a growing body of opinion that the world's faith in Svalbard is misplaced. Those who have worked with farmers in the field say that diversity cannot be boxed up and saved in a single container—no matter how secure it may be. Crops are always changing, pests and diseases are always adapting, and global warming will bring additional challenges that remain unforeseen. In a perfect world, the solution would be as diverse and dynamic as plant life itself.

The dispute about how best to save crop diversity centers on whether we should work with communities in the fields or with institutions, since it will be extremely difficult to find enough funding to do both. Now the isolated Svalbard seed vault is sucking up available funding. Yet, **the highly centralized approach** may not be able to help farmers cope with climate change, fifty or a hundred years from now. According to new research findings, as much as 75 percent of global crop diversity exists outside the big institutional seed banks. Such diversity is held instead by some of the world's most marginal farmers. Moreover, it is argued with increasing force that seed banks can neither make up for the practical knowledge of farmers on the ground, nor compete with their ingenuity.

48. What is the main idea of this passage?
(A) Seed banks can help farmers improve their crops.
(B) The practice of seed banks requires global cooperation.
(C) The idea of saving crop diversity in seed banks is debatable.
(D) Seed banks are able to deal with challenges of climate change

49. According to this passage, which of the following statements is true about the Svalbard Global Seed Vault?
(A) It is using up a lot of the funding.
(B) It is located in the center of Norway.
(C) It aims to fight against gene modified crops.
(D) It holds 75 percent of global crop diversity.

50. Which of the following is true about the role of farmers in preserving crop variety?
(A) Competing with seed banks. (B) Providing practical knowledge.
(C) Packaging seeds for research. (D) Responding to population growth

51. What does "**the highly centralized approach**" in the third paragraph refer to?
(A) Working with institutions. (B) Working with farmers.
(C) Finding enough crop diversity. (D) Finding sufficient funds.

第貳部分：非選擇題 (占 28 分)

說明：本部分共有二題，請依各題指示作答，答案必須寫在「答案卷」上，並標明大題號 (一、二)。作答務必使用筆尖較粗之黑色墨水的筆書寫，且不得使用鉛筆。

一、中譯英 (占 8 分)

說明：1. 請將以下中文句子譯成正確、通順、達意的英文，並將答案寫在「答案卷」上。
2. 請依序作答，並標明子題號 (1、2)。每題 4 分，共 8 分。

1. 快速時尚以速度與低價為特色，讓人們可以用負擔得起的價格買到流行的服飾。
2. 然而，它所鼓勵的「快速消費」卻製造了大量的廢棄物，造成巨大的污染問題。

二、英文作文 (占 20 分)

說明：1. 依提示在「答案卷」上寫一篇英文作文。
　　　2. 文長至少 120 個單詞 (words)。

提示：如果你就讀的學校預計辦理一項社區活動，而目前師生初步討論出三個方案：(一) 提供社區老人服務 (如送餐、清掃、陪伴等)；(二) 舉辦特色市集 (如農產、文創、二手商品等)；(三) 舉辦藝文活動 (如展出、表演、比賽等)。這三個方案，你會選擇哪一個？請以此為題，寫一篇英文作文，文長至少 120 個單詞。文分兩段，第一段說明你的選擇及原因，第二段敘述你認為應該要有哪些活動內容，並說明設計理由。

107 學年度　指考英文試題詳解

◆ 第壹部分：單選題

一、詞彙題

(D) 1. 大猩猩常常被描繪成一種可怕的動物，但事實上這些害羞的猿類很少為交配、食物或地盤打架。

(A) 重複不斷地　(B) 不久
(C) 將近　(D) 很少

解析

由 but 得知前後句語意相反，前句指出大猩猩常被描繪成一種可怕的動物，後句則表示其為相反的事實，可知這些害羞的猩猩很少為交配、食物或地盤打架，故選(D) rarely。

補充

be portrayed as　被描繪成…

(B) 2. 由於她朝九晚五的工作，Sally 有時候得利用午休時間辦私人差事，像是去銀行或寄信。

(A) 公共事務　(B) 差事、跑腿
(C) 財物　(D) 聯繫

解析

❶ 本題可由片語 run errands (跑差事) 得知選(B) errands。
❷ 本題可由 such as 後的例子 going to the banks、mailing letters 回推答案為 errands。

(B) 3. 和學生家長們爭執過後，老師終於承認自己的過錯，並低聲下氣地請求他們的原諒。

(A) 抵抗　(B) 低聲下氣
(C) 發現　(D) 處理

解析

前句指出老師和家長有爭執，後句表示老師承認過錯，可由文意與 humble oneself (低聲下氣) 的意思推知答案為(B) humbled。

(A) 4. 我們應該注重他人的優點並給予讚美，而不是批評他們。

(A) 讚美　(B) 妥協
(C) 判罪　(D) 坦白

解析

由 instead of (反而…) 可知前後句文意相反。前句表示不批評他人，為否定句意，推知後句應為肯定意思，依據文意，我們應該注重他人優點並給予讚美，故選(A) compliments。

(A) 5. 電腦使用者可善用搜尋引擎的一項特殊功能，瀏覽網路時不留下造訪網頁的紀錄。

(A) 瀏覽　(B) 大步走
(C) 發出隆隆聲　(D) 隱藏

解析

❶ 本題可直接由搭配詞 browse the Internet 選出答案(A) browse。
❷ 本題也可由文意，電腦使用者可利用搜尋引擎的一項特殊功能，瀏覽網路時不留下造訪網頁的紀錄，選出答案(A) browse。

(C) 6. 由於極低的降雨量與水庫水位遽降，這個地區正面臨三十年來最嚴重的乾旱。

(A) 液體　(B) 醜聞
(C) 乾旱　(D) 麻煩

解析

由 due to (因為) 得知前後句為因果關係。前句「由於極低的降雨量與水庫水位遽降」，可推測此地區正面臨乾旱，故選(C) drought。

補充

due to = because of = owing to = on account of　因為

(B) 7. 我們在教師節對孔子表達敬意，因為他對教育哲學的貢獻。

(A) 同意　(B) 致敬
(C) 奉獻　(D) 偏好

解析

❶ 本題可由搭配詞 pay tribute to (向…表達敬意) 選出答案(B) tribute。
❷ 本題亦可從文意孔子對教育哲學的貢獻，回推我們應向他致敬，判斷答案為(B) tribute。

(D) 8. 當消防隊員抱著哭泣的嬰兒走出失火的房子，他被群眾譽為英雄。

(A) 預習　(B) 警告
(C) 注定失敗　(D) 讚揚

解析

❶ 本題可從 as 對應到 hail，由 hail A as B(將 A 擁立為 B) 的用法，答案應選(D) hailed。
❷ 本題也可由刪去法解答，四個選項中只有 hail 會搭配 as，故可選出答案(D)。

補充

將 A 視為 B 的用法：see/view/take/regard/think of/look upon/refer to + A + as + B
consider A (to be) B

(C) 9. 因為全球經濟衰退，世界銀行對明年的全球經濟成長極不樂觀。

(A) 渴望　(B) 溫和的
(C) 很不樂觀的　(D) 難聞的

解析

❶ 由 due to 得知前後句應為因果關係，前句提及因為

全球經濟衰退，後句可對應到世界銀行對明年的全球經濟成長極不樂觀，故選(C) grim。

❷ 本題亦可以 recession 當線索，推測整句為負面情形，可選出相關的 grim。

(D) 10. Jeffery 一直是個愛爭吵的人，所以他與同事們發生爭執的事並不令人意外。

(A) 分別的　(B) 預防性的
(C) 接觸傳染的　(D) 愛爭吵的

解析

本句中使用連接詞 so，可知前句為「因」，so 引導的句子為「果」，從文意「他與同事們發生爭執」回推他應是喜歡爭吵的人，答案選(D) quarrelsome。

二、綜合測驗

第 11 至 15 題為題組

「跟上瓊斯家」是許多英語系國家的一句流行語。就像「打腫臉充胖子」的意思，這個流行語指的是和鄰居家 11.比較，以他們做為社會地位或物質財富累積的標準。一般而言，擁有越多奢侈品的人，他們的重要性或社會地位越高──或者他們 12.這樣相信。因此，沒有「跟上瓊斯家」，就是透露出社經地位不如人，或是中國人說的很沒面子。

這個 13.慣用語在漫畫家 Arthur R. “Pop” Momand 創作同名漫畫時廣為流傳。1916 年，這部連環漫畫首次刊登在《紐約世界報》，在美國報紙連載了 28 年後，最終被 14.改編成書、電影和音樂喜劇。標題裡的「瓊斯家」就是連環漫畫主角的有錢鄰居，有趣的是，他們在漫畫中僅被 15.提及，但從未實際現身過。

(D) 11. (A) 反應　(B) 依戀
(C) 相似性　(D) 比較

解析

本題為定義題，四個選項都可接 to，必須由文意判斷。由空格後的句子得知應是以鄰居家的社會地位和物質生活為標準做比較，故選(D) comparison。本題亦可由片語 keep up with (跟上…) 推測出此片語指的是跟人比較。

(B) 12. (A) 依然　(B) 這樣
(C) 尚未　(D) 甚至

解析

本題的前句文意「擁有越多奢侈品的人，他們的重要性或社會地位越高」，後面以破折號提供進一步說明，得知答案選(B) so，意為「這樣」，指前面所提的事情，呼應前句。

(A) 13. (A) 慣用語　(B) 信號
(C) 材料　(D) 分析

解析

本文在第一行即指出 “keeping up with the Joneses” 是 catchphrase。由後面文意「同名漫畫」亦可回推指的是 “keeping up with the Joneses” 此慣用語，選(A) phrase。

(A) 14. (A) 改編　(B) 承認
(C) 進步　(D) 建議

解析

❶ 由文意得知此漫畫原在《紐約世界報》刊登，後成為書、電影和音樂喜劇，可知答案選(A) adapted。

❷ 本題亦可直接由介系詞 into 對應至動詞 adapt，adapt into 意為「改編成…」。

補充

change A into B 將 A 變成 B
transform A into B 將 A 轉變成 B
translate A into B 將 A 翻譯為 B

(C) 15. (A) 檢查　(B) 監督
(C) 提及　(D) 交易

解析

由後句文意「他們從未在漫畫裡實際現身過」，回推僅僅是被提及，所以選(C) spoken of。

第 16 至 20 題為題組

許多人在一生中某些時候會發現指甲上出現白色斑點。這些小白點最常見的成因之一被稱為白甲症。雖然名稱聽起來很嚴重，但狀況通常 16.不是這樣。而且雖然許多人認為這些白點是因為缺乏鈣或鋅所引起的，但通常並非如此。

實際上，這些斑點大多是指甲發生輕微至中度創傷的 17.結果。如果你不記得曾經傷到指甲，考量到指甲本來就長得很慢，所以，早在白點出現數周之前，創傷就 18.可能已經發生。這些白點也可能是輕度感染或過敏的徵兆，或是某些藥物的副作用。

19.不論受傷的原因為何，這些白點通常毋須任何治療，隨著指甲生長就會消失。而且應該不會再出現，除非你又讓指甲受傷。然而，這通常 20.適用於只有一片或數片指甲受影響的情況。如果所有指甲都出現白點，這種白甲症可能與其他較嚴重的疾病有關，如貧血、心臟病、糖尿病或腎臟病。

(A) 16. (A) 不是　(B) 不是
(C) 不能　(D) 不會

解析

前句指出，指甲出現白點稱為白甲症。本句接續表示，雖然病名聽起來很嚴重，但通常情況不是這樣。前句有 sounds serious，但本句是表達實際情形，並非「聽起來」的感覺，還原為 the condition typically isn’t serious，故答案選(A) isn’t。

(B) 17. (A) 儘管　(B) 結果
(C) 就能力所及　(D) 為了…緣故

解析

本句主詞為小白點，動詞為 develop，後句提到指甲的損傷，由文意推測，應是指這些小白點通常因為指甲受傷而造成，答案選(B) as a result of。

比較

for the sake of 意思是「為了…緣故」，表示目的。
= in order to + V = so as to + V (只置於句中) = with a view to + V-ing = for the purpose of + V-ing

例：Amber goes to the gym twice a week for the sake of losing weight.
為了減重，Amber 每周上兩次健身房。

(D) 18. (A) 可能發生　(B) 會發生
(C) 將已發生　(D) 可能已經發生

解析

前句提到指甲長得很慢，本格後有 before 與過去式 appeared，可回推本格應是比過去式更早的動作，應用過去完成式，候選答案為(C)與(D)，但表達過去不應有未來式的 will，故答案選(D) may have occurred，助動詞 may 表示可能性，意為可能已經發生。

(C) 19. (A) 推斷　(B) 包括
(C) 不論　(D) 是否

解析

上一段提到多種指甲白點產生的可能性，本段接續文意，「不論」受傷的原因為何，這些白點不需要治療，由此可知應選(C) Whatever。

(C) 20. (A) 顯示　(B) 定義
(C) 適用　(D) 確認

解析

前二句表示小白點不需要特別治療也不會再發生。本格前有 However 表示語氣轉折，由本句文意提到只有一片或數片指甲受影響的情況，後句文意則為所有指甲都出現白點，故答案選(C) applies。

三、文意選填

第 21 至 30 題為題組

水產養殖是飼養任何水生植物或動物。水產養殖很重要，因為能減少過度捕撈野生魚類的可能性，並且提高食用魚的品質和增加 21.供應量。

全球各地的古文明從事不同形態的魚類養殖。澳洲原住民據說早在西元前 6000 年就已經在養鰻魚。充足的 22.證據指出，他們將康達湖附近的火山氾濫平原開發成水渠和水壩，然後捕捉鰻魚，並蓄養牠們以供整年食用。然而，魚類 23.養殖最早的記錄來自中國，約西元前 2500 年，該地已廣泛利用這種養殖方法。當河水氾濫後積水消退時，有些魚類，主要是鯉魚，會 24.被困於湖裡。早期的養魚人用幼蟲和蠶糞來投餵魚，之後再把魚吃掉。

在歐洲，水產養殖最早始於古羅馬。25.喜愛海魚和牡蠣的羅馬人建了類似游泳池的牡蠣養殖場。在潟湖中捕獲的魚類和甲殼類動物 (例如蝦子和螃蟹) 被養 26.活在這些池裡，直到長大供食用。這些養殖場經常建在 27.較有錢的人家裡，在那裡富裕家庭可以邀請他們的賓客來家中，並挑選自己想吃的魚。中歐的基督教修道院後來承襲這個羅馬傳統。

在中世紀時期，水產養殖在歐洲 28.盛行開來，因為遠離海岸和大河，魚必須醃製以防腐壞。整個封建歐洲，修道院院士和貴族是淡水魚的主要食用者，因為他們 29.獨占土地、森林和水道，而平民百姓很少能建自己的魚池。跟狩獵一樣，30.非法捕魚會受到嚴懲，而財力較差的人得等上幾個世紀，餐盤裡才有新鮮的魚可吃。

(A) 普及，盛行 *vi.*	(B) 養殖，種植 *n.* [U]
(C) 使困於… *vt.*	(D) 喜愛 *vt.*
(E) 活著的 *adj.*	(F) 獨占 *n.* [C]
(G) 美味的 *adj.*	(H) 非法的 *adj.*
(I) 供應量 *n.* [C]	(J) 較有錢的 *adj.*
(K) 證據 *n.* [U]	(L) 招待 *vt.*

解析

(I) 21. . . . increases the ______ of fish for human consumption.，本空格在冠詞 the 之後，應填名詞，可能的選項有 spread (可當名詞或動詞)、culture、monopoly、supply、evidence。由文意得知水產養殖可減少過度捕撈野生魚類，後句亦提及此種方法的優點，推論應指可增加魚類的供應量讓人類食用，故空格應填(I) supply。

(K) 22. Abundant ______ indicates they developed volcanic floodplains near Lake Condah into channels and dams . . .，本空格在形容詞 abundant 之後，應填名詞當主詞，後有單數動詞 indicates，應選單數或不可數名詞，可能選項有 spread 或 evidence，且根據動詞的搭配慣用字，故選(K) evidence。

(B) 23. The earliest records of fish ______, however, are from China . . .，本空格前有介系詞 of，應與 fish 為名詞組當 of 的受詞，可能選項有 spread、culture、monopoly。由文意得知，最早的魚類養殖記錄來自中國，故答案為(B) culture。

(C) 24. . . . some fish, mainly carp, were ______ in lakes.，本空格在 be 動詞後，可填過去分詞 (表被動語態)。由後文「早期的養魚人用幼蟲和蠶糞來投餵魚」，可推知魚群被困在湖裡，故答案應選(C) trapped。

(D) 25. The Romans, who ______ sea fish and oysters, created oyster farms . . .，本句主詞為 The Romans，本空格前有關係代名詞 who，後有名詞 sea fish and oysters，判斷應填過去式動詞，可能選項有 spread、adored、treated。由文意羅馬人建造牡蠣養殖場，可推知他們喜愛魚和牡蠣，故選(D) adored。

(E) 26. Fish and crustaceans (such as shrimps and crabs) caught in lagoons were kept ______ in these pools . . .，根據 keep + O + OC (adj./N/p.p./prep. phrase) 的用法，與文意「直到長大供食用」，可推知選形容詞 alive，答案選(E) alive。

(J) 27. The farms were often built inside ______ homes, where well-to-do families could invite their guests over . . .，本空格在名詞 homes 前，應填形容詞，可能選項有 delicious、illegal、wealthier，由後面的關係副詞子句 well-to-do families 回推應是指富有人家才有養殖場，故選(J) wealthier。

(A) 28. During the Middle Ages, aquaculture ______ in Europe, since far away from the seacoasts and the big rivers, fish had to be salted . . .，本空格前有主詞 aquaculture，時間為 the Middle Ages，故應填過去式動詞，可能選項有 spread、treated，由文意因為遠離海岸與大河，推測因此水產養殖在歐洲盛行，故選(A) spread。

(F) 29. . . . the aristocracy were the main users of freshwater fish, for they had a ______ over the land, . . . while the common people . . .，本空格在冠詞 a 之後，應填名詞，後面有介系詞 over，可猜測應是表示控制的字，由文意「貴族獨占土地…而平民百姓很少能蓋自己的魚池」，故選(F) monopoly。

(H) 30. As with hunting, ______ fishing was severely punished . . .，本空格在名詞 fishing 之前，應填形容詞，由後面 was severely punished，可推論是非法捕魚，故選(H) illegal。

四、篇章結構

第 31 至 35 題為題組

法國大革命的起因很複雜，仍在歷史學家之間廣泛爭論。然而，許多學者同意，在這場社會政治動亂裡，食物扮演著重要角色。31.具體而言，麵包和鹽——法國菜裡最重要的兩種元素——是這場衝突的核心。

麵包是法國日常飲食的一種主要成分，往往與國家認同有密切關係。研究顯示，18 世紀的法國工人，會花每日工資的一半在買麵包上。但在 1788 和 1789 年，那時穀類作物連兩年歉收，麵包價格飆漲至工人收入的 88%。32.一般家庭買不起足夠的食物來滿足他們的基本需求。絕大多數的法國人都在挨餓。有些人甚至只能靠偷竊或賣淫來讓自己活下去。

33.在此同時，農民對鹽稅的憎惡正在蔓延。自 15 世紀起，特別針對窮人開徵鹽稅，貴族和特權階級卻得以豁免。高稅率和稅賦分配不均，使得到處都有走私者非法販鹽，進而導致鹽價高漲。

然而，凡爾賽宮廷對日益惡化的危機渾然不知、也漠不關心。因此，絕望的民眾將飢荒和經濟動盪歸咎於統治階級。34.民怨迅速累積，終致 1789 年法國大革命的大規模暴亂。後果包括攻占巴士底監獄，這是位於巴黎的一座中世紀堡壘和監獄，最後將法國國王路易十六和其妻瑪麗‧安托內特斬首。

35.隨著王室的瓦解，一切逐漸恢復平靜。但鹽稅以及「麵包問題」仍然是整個革命時期、拿破崙時代 (1789–1815) 以及在往後相當長的一段時間中造成最大動盪的社會政治議題。

解析

(F) 31. 本格前一句提到食物在這場革命動亂中扮演重要的角色，下段第一句說明法國人每日主食之一是麵包，由此可知空格應與食物、麵包相關，檢視(F)選項與後句的關聯後，除了 component 與 elements 相對應外，兩句也都有提及 bread，且由選項文意「麵包和鹽——法國菜裡最重要的兩種元素——是這場衝突的核心」可得知，確定答案為(F)。

(D) 32. 本格前句提到在 1788 與 1789 年農作物歉收，麵包的價錢飆漲，後句指出絕大多數的法國人民都在挨餓，可推論本格應與飢餓與買不起麵包有關。(D)選項中提到「一般家庭買不起足夠的食物來滿足他們的基本需求」，可確定文意連貫，因此答案為(D)。

(C) 33. 本格後句的主詞為 this tax on salt consumption，可知本格必與鹽稅相關。從只跟窮人課徵鹽稅，權貴則得以豁免等敘述，回推本格必與鹽稅、窮人有關。(C)選項中的 peasants 與 the poor 對應、*gabelle* (鹽稅) 與 this tax on salt consumption 對應，故答案為(C)。

(E) 34. 本格前句說明絕望的人民將飢荒與經濟動盪歸咎於統治階級，後句提及造成攻佔巴士底監獄的結果，回推本句應是人民的憤怒快速積聚，導致在 1789 年引發法國大革命。選項(E)的 anger、blame 與 desperate 相呼應，population 與 riots 對應，故此為答案。

(B) 35. 本格後句出現轉折詞 Yet，指出鹽稅與麵包不足的問題仍然持續，為否定意義的句子，回推前句應該為肯定句。並且在上一段句末指出法國國王路易十六與皇后被送上斷頭臺，呼應選項(B)「隨著王室的瓦解，一切逐漸恢復平靜」，此為正確解答。

五、閱讀測驗

第 36 至 39 題為題組

男爵卡爾杜萊斯 (Baron Karl Drais)1785 年在德國西南部出生，他是 19 世紀最具創造力的德國發明家之一。這位男爵的眾多發明包括最早期的打字機、絞肉機、將鋼琴琴音紀錄在紙上的裝置，還有兩輛四輪人力車。但讓他成名的是跑動機，也就是自行車的現代始祖。

這輛跑動機，又名杜萊斯車或玩具馬，其實是一部非常簡陋的腳踏車：沒有鏈條，由騎車的人用腳推地前進。雖然不符現代詞意的自行車，但杜萊斯 (Drais) 的發明代表自行車發展的開創性突破。這是第一輛兩個輪子排成一列的車。車身和輪子以木頭製成；車把已經很像現代的龍頭。杜萊斯 (Drais) 發明背後的大眾理念是想找到人力驅動的替代品來取代馬匹，馬匹很昂貴，且即使不使用時也要消耗很多飼料。他相信這臺機械裝置將會讓更多人比走路或坐馬車更快速地移動。

杜萊斯 (Drais) 在 1817 年 6 月 12 日進行首次記錄在案的試騎，一小時騎 13 公里。幾個月後，杜萊斯 (Drais) 在 4 小時內騎了 60 公里，引起了大轟動。稍後，他們到巴黎辦行銷活動，玩具馬在那裡很快流行起來。這股風潮也迅速傳到英國。

然而，玩具馬的成功很短暫。它們很笨重，而且很難騎。安全性也是另一個問題：它們缺少煞車、曲柄和踏板。常常撞上沒有防備的行人，幾年後，杜萊斯 (Drais) 的發明在許多歐美城市遭禁。然而，杜萊斯 (Drais) 的創意並未完全消失。數十年後，這臺機器由法國人皮爾・拉勒蒙 (Pierre Lallement) 和皮爾・米修 (Pierre Michaux) 裝上踏板，成為現代的自行車。

(D) 36. Drais 為什麼發明跑動機？
(A) 為了證明他身為發明家的創造力。
(B) 為了保護馬匹不受虐待。
(C) 為了提供新玩意給皇室。
(D) 為了給一般大眾更好的交通方式。

說明
第二段第五句提到 Drais 發明背後的想法是要以人力取代一般大眾負擔不起的昂貴又耗費食物的馬，答案應選(D)。

(D) 37. 在第二段中的「marked the big bang」指的是什麼？
(A) 發出巨大聲響。
(B) 製造嚴重的動亂。
(C) 享有廣大的受歡迎度。
(D) 代表開創性的產品。

說明
第二段第三句指出 Drais 的發明是第一輛兩輪的車輛，可回推第二句說 Drais 的發明雖然不是現代定義的腳踏車，但在腳踏車的發展上卻有開創性的突破，可知答案選(D)。

(D) 38. 下列關於這跑動機的敘述何者為真？
(A) 它配有曲柄和踏板。
(B) 它的輪子和骨架是鐵製的。
(C) 它有煞車可以控制移動的速度。
(D) 它的車把類似現代自行車的龍頭。

說明
(A) 第四段第三句表示它沒有曲柄和踏板，此為錯誤選項；(B) 第二段第四句指出骨架和輪子都是木頭製的，此為錯誤選項；(C) 第四段第三句提到它未具備煞車，此為錯誤選項；(D) 第二段第四句指出它的車把已經與現代的腳踏車龍頭類似，正確答案為(D)。

(C) 39. 為什麼玩具馬未能在十九世紀成為普及的車輛？
(A) 它既貴又不耐用。
(B) 它跑得不如人們預期地快。
(C) 它很難控制，在路上騎乘很危險。
(D) 它在歐洲城市未受到足夠的注意。

說明
第四段的第二句指出玩具馬既重又不好騎，第三句也提到安全問題，故答案選(C)。

第 40 至 43 題為題組

電燈閃爍會引起頭痛。但如果一秒鐘閃數百萬次——遠比眼睛看得到或大腦處理速度更快——那麼可以被用來做些有用的事，例如傳輸數據。這是 Li-Fi 或被稱為光照上網技術的背後原理。Li-Fi 是愛丁堡大學教授哈洛德・哈斯 (Harald Haas)2011 年上 TED 演講新創的詞彙，他於演講中介紹「來自每道光線的無線數據」構想。如今，Li-Fi 已發展成一種無線技術，與發光二極管 (LED) 配合，可以高速傳送數據。LED 是公共區域和家庭中越來越受歡迎的照明方式。

用 LED 燈做為數據傳輸的網路設備，Li-Fi 有幾點更勝於 Wi-Fi (無線上網)。首先，Li-Fi 可讓區域網絡擁有更好的安全性，因為不像 Wi-Fi 使用的無線電波，光線無法穿透牆或門。只要玻璃窗等透明材質被蓋住，就只有房內裝置可以進入 Li-Fi 頻道，確保信號不會從遠端被入侵。同時，Li-Fi 可在電磁敏感區域，如機艙、醫院和核電站運作，因為光線不會干擾無線電信號。Li-Fi 最顯著的優勢是速度。研究人員在實驗室條件下達到 224Gbps (十億位元 / 秒) 的速度，比 Wi-Fi 寬頻快上許多。

Li-Fi 能如何豐富日常生活？任何有 LED 照明的地方，就有機會應用 Li-Fi。有 Li-Fi 的路燈可提供手機連線上網，使夜間行路更安全。交通號誌的 LED 燈泡可以為駕駛提供天氣和交通資訊更新。Li-Fi 讓取得在地訊息更加方便，故有助觀光業。在家裡，智能燈具也可以為家長提供解決孩子網絡成癮問題的辦法：只需關掉燈，網路也就會斷線。

當 140 億個燈泡代表 140 億個潛在的無線數據傳輸器時，一個更潔淨、更環保、甚至更光明的未來即將到來。

(B) 40. 本文主旨為何？
(A) 照明的新設計。
(B) 透過照明的無線傳輸。
(C) 在公眾場所的無線電波干擾。
(D) 光照上網技術在軍事上的可能應用。

說明
本文整篇在描述如何利用無線光通訊傳輸資料與其特性，因此主旨應為(B)。

(B) 41. 第一段的「This」指的是什麼？
(A) 閃爍的燈光非常惱人。
(B) 閃光可以傳輸訊息。
(C) 大腦可能被光線影響。
(D) 人眼可以察覺光線中的改變。

說明
第一段的第二句指出閃爍的光線可被控制來做有用的事情，如傳輸資料，接著本句提到「這」是光照上網技術背後的概念。由此可知「This」指的是閃光可以傳遞訊息，答案選(B)。

(A) 42. 根據本文，下列哪個關於光照上網技術的敘述為非？
(A) 它能穿透水泥牆。
(B) 它在 2011 年首度被提出。
(C) 它可以高速傳輸數據。
(D) 它對教養子女有幫助。

說明
(A) 第二段的第二句提及光照上網技術無法穿透牆或門，由此可知它無法穿透水泥牆，此為錯誤選項，故選(A)；(B) 第一段的第四句指出，光照上網技術是在 2011 年由 Harald Haas 教授提出；(C) 第一段的末句表示光可高速傳送數據；(D) 第三段的末句提到光照上網技術的特性可幫助父母管控孩子網路成癮的問題。

(D) 43. 根據本文，下列何者是光照上網技術相較於無線網路的優勢？
(A) 光照上網技術可經由無線電供給電力，節省更多能源。
(B) 光照上網技術在車輛不能到達的地區引導行人。
(C) 光照上網技術在停電時提供更安全的資料傳輸。
(D) 光照上網技術可以被用在無線網路會干擾雷達訊號的地區。

說明
第二段第四句指出光照上網技術可用在電磁波敏感區域，因為光線不會干擾無線電波，故答案選(D)。

第 44 至 47 題為題組

根據加拿大英屬哥倫比亞大學的一項新研究，世上一些最大的甲蟲正在變小，因為牠們的棲息地越來越暖和。這份 2018 年 1 月刊在《動物生態學雜誌》的研究指出，氣候變遷正對這些「小小」生物造成影響。

這份研究先深入探討科學文獻。演化生態學家蜜雪兒・曾 (Michelle Tseng) 和她的學生仔細搜查他們能找到的所有文章，尋找溫度對昆蟲影響的實驗研究。他們發現 19 篇文章，指出至少有 22 種甲蟲培育在比常溫溫暖的環境下時體型會縮小。

為了觀察這種模式在野外能否成立，研究團隊利用大學校內收集的 60 萬個昆蟲標本，其中包括 19 世紀後期以來當地收集的成千上萬昆蟲。研究人員拍攝超過 6500 隻甲蟲，分屬記錄最完善的 8 個品種。他們也研究氣候記錄，找出溫度之外，降雨及其他因素的趨勢變化。將甲蟲依大小分類，他們發現，8 種甲蟲之中有 5 種在過去一個世紀裡變小了。在過去 45 年間，四種最大的甲蟲，包括蝸牛殺手步行蟲，都縮小了 20%。相反的，較小的甲蟲並未受到影響，尺寸甚至略微變大。

部分生態學家對曾的研究持保留態度，他們說尚未證實升溫是導致甲蟲變小的真正原因。然而，英國生物學家亞倫・羅南・波德隆 (Alan Ronan Baudron) 深信不疑。波德隆的研究記錄了一些品種的魚因為氣候暖化變小。他的說法是，較高的溫度會降低水中氧氣的含量，導致魚類更快消耗能量，而成年時體型也較小。但他和曾都不相信氧氣減少是甲蟲變小的原因。

(A) 44. 何者為本文的最佳標題？
(A) 由於氣候變遷，大甲蟲體型縮小
(B) 甲蟲對魚類：牠們的體型越來越小嗎？
(C) 我們所知道的演化生態學
(D) 動物生態：過去和現在

說明
本文整篇在探討大甲蟲體型越變越小的原因，得知標題應為(A)。

(C) 45. 第二段的「deep dive」最可能意思為何？
(A) 清楚的指示。

(B) 重要的發現。
(C) 完整的檢視。
(D) 有深入見解的評論。

說明

第二段第二句說明曾博士與學生徹底搜查所有能找到的文章，找尋針對氣候對昆蟲影響的實驗研究，故可知他們埋頭探究，答案選(C)。

(C) 46. 下列關於曾博士團隊的研究方式何者為真？
(A) 他們進行實驗室和實地研究。
(B) 他們拍了六十萬張昆蟲標本的照片。
(C) 他們將甲蟲分成不同的體型組別以進行研究。
(D) 他們記錄下自從 19 世紀後期以來的氧氣含量。

說明

由第三段第四句可知，曾博士的團隊將甲蟲依照體型分類，故答案應選(C)。

(B) 47. 下列何者是曾博士團隊的發現？
(A) 在上一世紀，有 8 種類的甲蟲體型縮小。
(B) 有些甲蟲不受溫度改變的影響。
(C) 大部分的甲蟲隨著氣候暖化活得更久。
(D) 甲蟲和魚可能縮小到同樣的尺寸。

說明

從第三段的末句可知道較小的甲蟲體型不受影響、甚至微幅變大，故答案應選(B)。

第 48 至 51 題為題組

為了保護農作物多樣性免於災害影響，在挪威和北極中間極地島嶼的一座山下，蓋了種子銀行「斯瓦爾巴全球種子庫」。種子庫是為了幫助農民和科學家找到要改善今日作物所需的基因。目的也在培育多元品種，更能因應新興挑戰，例如氣候變遷和人口增長。目前，種子庫擁有來自世界上幾乎所有國家的樣本，逾 86 萬個樣本。

然而，認為世界高估了斯瓦爾巴全球種子庫的輿論越來越多。那些與農民一起在田間工作的人說，多樣性無法裝箱保存在一個容器裡——無論有多安全。作物不斷改變，害蟲和疾病一直在適應環境，全球暖化將帶來無法預見的難題。在一個完美世界，解決方案會將像植物生命本身一樣的多樣化和不斷變化的。

如何能最佳保存作物多樣性的爭議，集中在我們是否應該與田間社區或機構合作，因為很難找到足夠的資金同時進行這兩項合作。現在，遺世獨立的斯瓦爾巴種子庫也正消耗著許多可用資金。然而，高度集中化的方法可能無法幫助農民因應 50 至 100 年後的氣候變遷。根據新的研究發現，全球多達 75% 的作物多樣性存在於大型機構的種子銀行之外。這樣的物種多樣性反而被掌握在某些全球最少數的農夫手中。此外，越來越多人主張，種子銀行既不能取代第一線農民的實務知識，也比不上他們的智慧。

(C) 48. 本文主旨為何？
(A) 種子銀行能幫助農夫改善作物。
(B) 種子銀行的做法需要全球合作。
(C) 在種子銀行中拯救作物多樣性的想法是有爭議的。
(D) 種子銀行能夠應付氣候變遷的挑戰。

說明

第二段第二句表示，與農夫實際共事過的人認為多樣性不能被保存在單一容器，因為物種、病毒與外在變化隨時都在演變，可知有些人不贊成種子銀行的做法，第三段亦表示有所爭議性，因此本文主旨應選(C)。

(A) 49. 根據本文，下列關於斯瓦爾巴全球種子庫的敘述何者正確？
(A) 它用光了許多資金。
(B) 它位於挪威的中心。
(C) 它的目標在對抗基因改造的作物。
(D) 它佔有全球作物多樣性的 75%。

說明

第三段第二句說明遺世獨立的斯瓦爾巴全球種子庫花費許多資金，由此推知答案為(A)。

(B) 50. 關於農夫在保存作物多樣性上的角色，下列何者為真？
(A) 和種子銀行競爭。
(B) 提供實務知識。
(C) 將種子包裝來做研究。
(D) 對人口成長做出應變。

說明

第三段的末句指出許多人認為種子銀行無法彌補農夫能提供的務農實際經驗，故答案為(B)。

(A) 51. 第三段的「highly centralized approach」指的是什麼？
(A) 和機構合作。
(B) 和農夫合作。
(C) 找尋足夠的作物多樣性。
(D) 找到足夠的資金。

說明

第三段的第二句指出獨立運作的種子銀行用了所有資金，第三句接續說明然而這種高度集中的方式無法幫助農民應付氣候變遷，第四句說明全球多達 75% 的作物多樣性存在於大型機構的種子銀行之外，可推測出「highly centralized approach」指的是和機構合作，答案應選(A)。

◆ **第貳部分：非選擇題**

一、中譯英

1. Fast fashion features speed and low cost, which makes/making it possible for people to buy/purchase fashionable clothes at affordable prices.

說明

❶ 參考句型：S + V + O, which V/V-ing + O + OC
❷ 時態：談論事實用現在簡單式
❸ feature 以…為特色
❹ low cost 低價
❺ affordable 負擔得起
❻ at a . . . price/at . . . prices 以…價格

2. However/Nevertheless/Nonetheless, the "fast consumption" (which/that) it encourages produces a considerable/large amount of waste, and results in/resulting in big/serious/grave pollution problems.

說明

❶ 參考句型：Adv., S + which-clause + V + O + and + V + O
❷ 時態：談論事實用現在簡單式
❸ a considerable/large amount of 大量的…
❹ waste 廢棄物
❺ result in 造成

二、英文作文

作文範例

As a member of the community, I definitely have strong willingness and the responsibility to perform community services. If offered the three options to host an event, I, together with my schoolmates, would choose to organize a fair where people can sell a variety of things, ranging from agricultural produce, cultural creative products, and second-hand items or unwanted clothing, books, or furniture, and so on. I opt to arrange such a fair, as the members of my community will gain the following benefits. First, sellers can have a good opportunity to demonstrate their fresh produce or products, while buyers can purchase quite a few things without having to run to different places. Second, sellers don't have to particularly rent a store or a stand in the market, which allows them to save money. As for buyers, it is likely that they can enjoy some discounts, as I suppose many people are acquaintances, so buyers would get good bargains. Last but not least, I firmly believe that through selling and buying, my community members will have more interactions and more chances to converse with one another.

To make the fair successful and enjoyable, I think it should consist of some activities. For example, we can invite the students from our school band or the dance club to give performances. In that way, more people would be attracted to watch the shows, thus making the atmosphere pleasant. We can also arrange a lucky-draw game. Those who participate in the fair will have a chance to receive prizes. People like to win awards; therefore, this special-designed activity should get more members involved. What's more, I would design a fund-raising or donation activity. The money, food, or items received will be dispatched to the needy or orphanages, which will improve our community and make this event more meaningful. In a word, by means of this "fun fair", I am sure it can get people out of their houses and we can better our community, in terms of both mutual profits and the improvement of relationships.

說明

第一段：先說明會選擇舉辦哪一項社區活動。
Topic sentence: As a member of the community, I definitely have strong willingness and the responsibility to perform community services. If offered the three options to host an event, I, together with my schoolmates, would choose to organize a fair.
接著闡述選擇的原因。
Supporting idea: I opt to arrange such a fair, as the members of my community will gain the following benefits.

第二段：敘述應該會有哪些活動內容。
Topic sentence: To make the fair successful and enjoyable, I think it should consist of some activities.
接著舉例說明活動設計理由。
Supporting idea: For example, we can invite the students from our school band or the dance club to give performances.
總結以上提到的特點，強調舉辦此活動有利社區成員，並讓社區變得更美好。
Conclusion: In a word, by means of this "fun fair", I am sure it can get people out of their houses and we can better our community, in terms of both mutual profits and the improvement of relationships.

英文騎士團長戴逸群與英文小說中毒團隊
打造英文小說專屬的「閱讀素養」課程

解開文本迷津、讀出深度思考力、
攻克閱讀英文長篇小說的完全攻略

- Wonder 解讀攻略

戴逸群 編著／ Joseph E. Schier 審閱
Lexile 藍思分級：790

☞ 議題：品德教育、生命教育
家庭教育、閱讀素養

- Harry Potter and the Sorcerer's Stone 解讀攻略

戴逸群 主編／簡嘉妤 編著／ Ian Fletcher 審閱
Lexile 藍思分級：880

☞ 議題：品德教育、家庭教育
閱讀素養、多元文化

1 + 1 = 小説解讀好容易！

- Love, Simon 解讀攻略

  戴逸群 主編／林冠瑋 編著／ Ian Fletcher 審閱

  Lexile 藍思分級：640

  ☞ 議題：性別平等、人權教育
  多元文化、閱讀素養

- Matilda 解讀攻略

  戴逸群 主編／林佳紋 編著／
  Joseph E. Schier 審閱

  Lexile 藍思分級：840

  ☞ 議題：性別平等、人權教育
  家庭教育、閱讀素養

解讀攻略有多種使用方式，含：

- 學習歷程檔案
- 輔導課教材
- 閱讀與寫作教材
- 自主學習課程素材
- 寒暑假作業指定教材
- 學測後英文教材
- 多元選修教材

全新改版

英文指考致勝：考前衝刺100天

王靖賢、曲成彬、蔡任翔、周彩蓉、蘇文賢　編著

★ **超詳盡應考策略：**
針對指考七大題型，從準備考試的複習方式，到實際應考時的答題技巧，極其詳盡，應有盡有！

★ **超精選單字片語：**
收錄指考必備單字1,000及片語200，並補充生字、介系詞及重點句型，讓您一書在手，完美複習！

★ **超豐富模擬試題：**
20回考前模擬試題，題題切中核心，打通英文任督二脈，保證讓您越寫越有自信，大考高分So Easy！

★ **超完美作文解析：**
含近十年歷屆指考試題的作文練習，附有優秀範文與詳實解析，讓您溫故知新，百戰百勝！

更多不同選擇盡在 三民網路書店 滿足各種教學需求

書種最齊全・服務最迅速 www.sanmin.com.tw

題本與附冊不分售

80468X4